A LADY WITHOUT PEER

TWO PREVIOUSLY PUBLISHED REGENCY NOVELLAS

GRACE BURROWES

GRACE BURROWES PUBLISHING

AUTHOR'S NOTE

I have been remiss toward some of my backlist—and thus toward my readers—in that many of my novellas have been de-published as various anthologies and duets have unbundled. The two stories in *A Lady Without Peer* both deal with women who are making their way in the world in professions about which they are passionate—and neither lady sees the need to encumber herself with a titled swain. The Earl of Ramsdale appears in both stories, and the heroines' shared perspective on swain-ly peers also seemed like a good reason to issue the novellas as a duet.

If you'd like to read the formerly co-published stories that go with these tales, **His Grace for the Win** appeared in a 2017 duet, *The Duke's Bridle Path*. Theresa Romain's tale, *Desperately Seeking Scandal*, is the story of the Duke of Lavelle's sister, Lady Ada.

The Will to Love first saw daylight as part of *How to Find a Duke in Ten Days*, a novella trio also published in 2017. Shana Galen's story is *How to Steal a Duke*, and Carolyn Jewel's is *The Viscount's First Kiss*.

Happy reading!
Grace Burrowes

HIS GRACE FOR THE WIN

HIS GRACE FOR THE WIN

His Grace for the Win

by Grace Burrowes

(Previously published in
The Duke's Bridle Path)

CHAPTER ONE

"Will I see you at the race meets, Your Grace?"

Lowered lashes and an arch smile suggested Lady Ambrosia Warminster wanted to see every naked inch of Philippe Albinus Bartholomew Coape Dodge Ellis, twelfth Duke of Lavelle. Many women sought the same objective—those inches were handsome, titled, and wealthy, after all. Alas for Lady Ambrosia, an equestrian gathering was the last place she'd find Philippe.

He took her proffered hand and fired off a melting smile.

"I've neglected my acres, my dear, and must forgo the pleasure of your company to make amends with my dear sister at Theale Hall. Might I ask where you'll spend the Yuletide holidays?"

He kept hold of her hand and looked hopeful, that being the protocol when declining an assignation, or when dodging the forcible trip to the altar such an encounter would likely engender where Lady Ambrosia was concerned.

"Papa hasn't decided about the winter holidays, or Mama hasn't," she said, retrieving her hand.

Philippe let her hand go, slowly. "I will live in hope of a waltz next season. Please give my felicitations to your family."

Add a touch of eyebrow, a slight flaring of the nostrils—Philippe's older brother, Jonas, had taught him that bit—allow the lady to be the first to turn away, and... With a curtsey and a smile, she was off, pretending to see a dear, dear friend on the other side of Lady Pembroke's music room.

"How do you do that?" Seton Avery, Earl of Ramsdale, had been born with an inability to whisper. He growled quietly or not so quietly. On rare occasions, he roared.

"How do I avoid capture?" Philippe asked. "I give the ladies a little of what they want—my attention—and they give me what I want."

"Their hearts?" Ramsdale wore the expression Philippe usually saw when he and the earl were sharing an interesting game of chess.

"My freedom. You are coming out to Theale Hall with me next week?"

Ramsdale lifted two glasses of champagne from a passing footman's tray and handed one to Philippe.

"If I allow you to abandon me in Town, the disconsolate widows and hopeful debutantes will swivel their gunsights in my direction. One shudders to contemplate the fate of a mere belted earl under such circumstances."

Ramsdale grew restless as autumn came on, while Philippe felt the pull of his family seat, despite the memories. Ada bided at Theale Hall, doing more than her share to manage the estate, and Philippe owed his sister companionship at this time of year above all others.

"Then have your belted self ready to depart no later than Wednesday," Philippe said. "The nights grow brisk, and harvest will soon begin in Berkshire."

Ramsdale lifted his glass a few inches. "Of course, Your Grace. My pleasure, Your Most Sublime Dukeship. We'll take that rolling pleasure dome you call a traveling coach?"

When did Philippe travel a significant distance by any other means? "If it's raining, you're welcome to make the journey in the saddle."

"And deprive you of my company? Don't be daft. Let's leave on Tuesday. I've grown bored with Town, and the debutantes circle ever closer."

"Monday," Philippe said. "We'll leave Monday at the crack of dawn."

~

"SUCH A BEAUTY," Lord Dudley cooed. "Such lovely quarters and elegant lines, such a kind eye. Makes a fellow itch to get her under saddle."

Titled men seldom rode mares, and thus his lordship's innuendo was about as subtle as the scent of a full muck cart. Harriet Talbot stroked the mare's shoulder, silently apologizing to the horse.

Utopia deserved better than a strutting clodpate.

"Shall I return her to her stall?" Harriet raised her voice to aim the question at her father, who was leaning heavily on his cane near the paddock gate.

"Your lordship?" Papa asked. "Have you seen enough? She's a superior lady's mount and enjoys working over fences. At the fashionable hour, she'll make an elegant impression, and she'll be eager to hack out of a fine morning."

Please don't buy her. Please, please do not buy this mare.

"She's very pretty," Dudley said, "very well put together. I like her eye."

Harriet did not like the covetous look in Dudley's eye. "While I commend your judgment, my lord, I hope you realize that she's not up to your weight. I was under the impression—we were, rather—that you sought a guest mount for a lady."

For one of his mistresses, in fact. Dudley's stable master had made that clear. "Utopia has some growing yet to do," Harriet went on, "some muscling up. With another year or two of work, she'll have more strength and stamina, but I'd advise against buying her for yourself."

His lordship stroked the mare's glossy backside. "Oh, but she's a chestnut. I cut quite a dash on a chestnut."

Besides, what lordling worth his port would make a decision based on a woman's opinion?

Utopia switched her tail, barely missing his lordship's face. This would not end well for the viscount or the mare.

"We can find you another handsome chestnut," Harriet said, before Papa could cut in with more praise for his lordship's discernment. "Utopia needs a chance to finish growing before she's competent to carry a man of your stature."

The mare had the misfortune to be beautiful. Four white socks evenly matched, excellent conformation, a white blaze down the center of her face, and great bloodlines. She was doomed to become some nobleman's plaything, though she truly wasn't large enough to handle Dudley.

Utopia was also not patient or forgiving enough. His lordship was tall and portly, and while many a large or stout rider sat lightly in the saddle, Dudley's horsemanship had all the grace of a beer wagon with a loose axle and a broken wheel.

"I do believe I shall take her," Dudley said. "I'll get her into condition and show her what's what."

The mare would be lame by the end of the year, possibly ruined. Why had Papa agreed to show her to Lord Dunderhead?

"Papa," Harriet called, raising her voice. "His lordship has declared himself smitten with Utopia. I'll leave the bargaining to you." And yet, Harriet had to give herself one glimmer of hope that the mare could yet enjoy a happy life. "Regardless of the terms you strike with my father, please recall that we stand behind every horse we sell. You may return her at any point in the next ninety days for a full refund, regardless of her condition."

That term was Harriet's invention, quietly tacked on to sales when she lacked confidence in the purchaser's ability to keep the horse sound and happy. Several times, Harriet's guarantee had spared a horse a sorry fate.

Papa took a different approach: Buying a horse was like speaking vows to a bride. The purchaser became responsible for the creature for life, to have and to hold, and to provide fodder, pasture, shelter, farriery, veterinary care, gear, grooming, and treats until such time as a subsequent sale, old age, or a merciful bullet terminated the obligation.

Papa was a romantic. Harriet hadn't had that luxury since her mama had died five years ago.

"Take the filly back to her stall," Papa said. "His lordship and I will enjoy a brandy in my study."

"Brilliant!" Dudley replied, slapping Papa on the back and falling in step beside him. "She'll be a prime goer in no time."

The mare would be back-sore before the first flight had pulled up to check for loose girths. Harriet was no great supporter of the hunt field, for it lamed many a fine horse while subjecting Reynard to needless suffering.

"Come along," Harriet said to the mare. "I can still spoil you for a short while, and you'd best enjoy the time you have left here." Dudley's stablemen would take as good care of Utopia as they could and argue for her to be bred when she became unsound under saddle. The situation could be worse.

And yet, Harriet's heart was heavy as she slipped off the mare's bridle and buckled on the headstall. Five years ago, Papa would have listened to her when she'd warned against the likes of his lordship as a buyer for the mare.

Five years ago, Mama would have been alive to make him listen.

"There's a gent waiting for you in the saddle room, miss," Baxter, the new lad said. "Doesn't look like the patient sort either."

Gentlemen in search of horseflesh were seldom patient. "Did he give you a name?" Harriet asked, unbuckling Utopia's girths.

"No, but he knew where he was going and knew not to intrude on your dealings with Milord Deadly."

"Dudley," Harriet muttered, though stable lads would assign barn names however they pleased.

A buyer who knew his way around the premises wasn't to be kept waiting. Harriet handed the mare over to Baxter with instructions to get her out to the mares' pasture for a few hours of grass before sunset.

Harriet peeled off her gloves, stuffed them into a pocket of her habit, and hoped whoever awaited her in the saddle room was a better rider than Lord Dead—Lord Dudley.

She tapped on the door, because wealthy gentlemen expected such courtesies even when on another's premises, then swept inside with the confident stride of a woman who'd been horse-trading with her betters for years.

"Good day," she said to the tall, broad-shouldered specimen standing by the window. "I'm Harriet Talbot. My father can join us shortly, but in his absence…"

The specimen turned, and Harriet's brain registered what her body had been trying to tell her. She'd come to a halt halfway into the room, assailed by an odd sensation in the pit of her belly—happiness and anxiety, both trying to occupy the same space.

"Philippe. You've come home."

He held out his arms, and Harriet rushed across the room, hugging him tightly. "Oh, you've come home, and you gave us no warning, and Papa will be so happy to see you."

Harriet was ecstatic to see him, though her joy was bounded with heartache old and new. Old, because this was a courtesy call on Papa, a gesture of affection toward the late Duke of Lavelle's retired horse master. New, because every time Harriet saw His Grace—His Current Grace, she must not think of him as Philippe—the gulf between them was a little wider, a little more impossible.

She was the first to step back, though he kept hold of her hand.

"Do you ever wear anything other than riding habits?" he asked.

"Yes. I often wear breeches, but you mustn't tell anybody."

He smiled, Harriet smiled back, and her heart broke. She hadn't seen the duke for nearly a year, and yet, this was how it was with them. Always easy, always as if they'd parted the day before with a smile and a wave.

Philippe slipped an arm across her shoulders. "I will keep your secrets, Harriet, because you have so graciously kept mine over the years. You won't tell anybody I'm hiding in here, for example. If that strutting excuse for bad tailoring, Lord Dimwit, should see me, I'll be required to invite him over to the Hall for a meal. He'll make a guest of himself—guest rhymes with pest—and my reunion with Lady Ada will be ruined."

"His lordship and Papa are secreted in the study bargaining over a mare. You're safe with me."

Philippe had always been safe with her, and she'd always been safe with him—damn and drat the luck. He folded himself onto the worn sofa Harriet had donated last year from her mother's parlor. When occupied by a duke, the sofa looked comfortable rather than at its last prayers.

When embraced by a duke—by this duke—Harriet felt special rather than eccentric.

He did that, made everyone and everything around him somehow *more*. Philippe was tall, dark, and athletic. In riding attire, he'd set hearts fluttering, though alas for Harriet, His Grace of Lavelle had no use for horses or anything approaching an equestrian pursuit.

For Harriet, by contrast, the horse was a passion and a livelihood —her only passion, besides a doomed attachment to a man to whom she'd never be more than an old, mostly overlooked friend.

ON SOME STONE tablet Moses had probably left up on Mount Sinai—stone tablets were deuced heavy—the hand of God had written, "Thou shalt not hug a duke, nor shall dukes indulge in any spontaneous hugging either."

The consequence for this trespass was so well understood that nobody—not Ada, not Ramsdale in his cups, not Philippe's

mistresses, back when he'd bothered to keep mistresses—dared trans-
gress on Philippe's person after the title had befallen him.

Harriet Talbot dared. She alone had failed to heed that stone
tablet, ever, and thus with her, Philippe was free to pretend the rules
didn't apply.

She was a fierce hugger, wrapping him in a long, tight embrace
that embodied welcome, reproach for his absence, protectiveness, and
—as a postscript noted by Philippe's unruly male nature—a discon-
certing abundance of curves. Harriet was unselfconscious about those
curves, which was to be expected when she and Philippe had known
each other for more than twenty years.

"You do not approve of Lord Dudley," Philippe said. "Did he
insult one of your horses?"

"He'll ruin one of my horses," Harriet replied, coming down
beside him on the sofa. "One of Papa's horses, rather."

Philippe didn't have to ask permission to sit in her company, she
didn't ring for tea in a frantic rush to offer hospitality—there being no
bell-pulls in horse barns, thank the heavenly intercessors—nor tug her
décolletage down with all the discretion of a fishmonger hawking a
load of haddock.

"Then why sell Dudley the beast?" Philippe cared only theoreti-
cally about the horse, while for Harriet the matter was clearly akin to
the fate of a dear friend.

"Because his lordship has coin and needs a mount for a lady, and
Papa has horses to sell and needs that coin. Papa has explained this to
me at regular intervals in recent months."

Never had the Creator fashioned a more average female than
Harriet Talbot. She was medium height, brown-haired, blue-eyed, a
touch on the sturdy side, and without significant airs or graces. She
did not, to Philippe's knowledge, sing beautifully, excel at the
pianoforte, paint lovely watercolors, or embroider wonderfully.

She smelled of horses, told the truth, and hugged him on sight,
and to perdition with beautiful, excellent, lovely, and wonderful.

"Do you have reason to believe the lady who will ride the horse is incompetent in the saddle?" Philippe asked.

"I have no idea, but his lordship is a terrible rider. All force and power, no thought for the horse, no sense of how to manage his own weight. He rides by shouting orders at the horse and demanding blind obedience."

Women criticized faithless lovers with less bitterness than Harriet expressed toward Dudley's riding.

"He might return the mare," Philippe said. "He might also pass her on to a lady after all."

"I live in hope," Harriet said, sounding anything but hopeful. "How are you?"

To anybody else, Philippe could have offered platitudes about the joys of the Berkshire countryside at harvest, the pleasure of rural quiet after London's madness.

This was Harriet. "Coming home at this time of year is both sad and difficult, but here is where I must be. At least I get to see you."

She fiddled with a loose thread along a seam of her habit. "Papa will invite you to dinner."

This was a warning of some sort. "And I will accept."

"You need not. Papa will understand."

Philippe hated that Harriet would understand. "I'll even bring along Lord Ramsdale, because you are one of few people who can coax him to smile."

"The earl is a very agreeable gentleman." Harriet affected a pious tone at odds with the laughter in her gaze.

"The earl is a trial to anybody with refined sensibilities. What is the news from the village?"

They chatted comfortably, until the wheels of Dudley's phaeton crunched on the gravel drive beyond the saddle room's windows and the snap of his whip punctuated the early afternoon quiet.

The sound caused Harriet to close her eyes and bunch her habit in her fists. "If his lordship isn't careful, some obliging horse will send him into a ditch headfirst."

"He's also prone to dueling and drinking," Philippe said. "Put him from your thoughts for the nonce and take me to see your papa."

"Of course," Harriet replied, popping to her feet. She never minced, swanned, or sashayed. She marched about, intent on goals and tasks, and had no time for a man's assistance.

And yet, somebody's assistance was apparently needed. The roses growing next to the porch were long overdue for pruning, the mirror above the sideboard in the manor's foyer was dusty, the carpets showed wear. Harriet's habit was at least four years out of fashion, but then, Harriet had never paid fashion any heed.

Philippe was shocked to see how much Jackson Talbot had aged in little over a year. Talbot still had the lean height of a steeplechase jockey. His grip was strong, and his voice boomed. Not until Harriet had withdrawn to see about the evening meal did Philippe notice the cane Talbot had hooked over the arm of his chair.

"You're good to look in on us," Talbot said. "Good to look in on me."

"I'm paying a call on a pair of people whose company I honestly enjoy," Philippe said. "Harriet looks to be thriving."

She looked... she looked like Harriet. Busy, healthy, indifferent to fashion, pretty if a man took the time to notice, and *dear*. That dearness was more precious than Philippe wanted to admit. He'd come home because duty required it, but seeing Harriet made the trial endurable.

"Harriet," Talbot sniffed. "She thinks because my eyesight is fading that I don't notice what's going on in my own stable. I notice, damn the girl, but she doesn't listen any better than her mother did."

That was another difference. Talbot's eyes, always startlingly blue against his weathered features, had faded, the left more than the right. He held his head at a slight angle, and his desk had been moved closer to the window.

And never before had Philippe heard Talbot disparage his daughter. Criticize her form over fences, of course, but not cast aspersion on her character.

"How much vision have you lost?"

Talbot shifted in his chair. "I can't read the racing forms. Harriet reads them to me. I still get around well enough."

With a cane, and instead of inviting Philippe to stroll the barn aisle and admire all the pretty horses, Talbot had barely stood to shake hands.

"Women are prone to worrying," Philippe said.

"Now that is the damned truth, sir. Harriet will fret over that mare, for example, though Lord Dudley's no more heavy-handed than many of his ilk. Will you have time to join us for dinner before you must away back to London?"

"Of course. I've brought Ramsdale along, lest he fall foul of the matchmakers while my back is turned."

"Man knows how to sit a horse, meaning no disrespect."

This birching to Philippe's conscience was as predictable as Harriet's outdated fashions, though far less endearing. "Talbot, don't start."

"Hah. You may play the duke on any other stage, but I know what it costs you to eschew the saddle. You are a natural, just like your brother. You'd pick it back up in no time."

"All my brother's natural talent didn't keep him from breaking his neck, did it?" The silence became awkward, then bitter, then guilty. "I'm sorry, Talbot. I know you mean well. I'll be going, and if you send an invitation over to the Hall, expect me to be on better behavior when I accept it. I can't vouch for Ramsdale's deportment, but Harriet seems to enjoy twitting him."

Perhaps Harriet was sweet on Ramsdale. She liked big, dumb beasts. Ramsdale might have agreed to this frolic in the countryside because he was interested in Talbot's daughter.

The earl was devious like that, very good at keeping his own counsel—and he rode like a demon.

"No need to get all in a lather," Talbot said. "Young people are idiots. My Dora always said so. Let's plan on having you and his lordship to dine on Tuesday."

Talbot braced his hands on the blotter as if to push to his feet, and that too was a change.

Not for the better. "Please don't get up," Philippe said. "Bargaining with Dudley was doubtless tiring. I'll see myself out."

"Until Tuesday." Talbot settled back into his chair. "Do bring the earl along with you. He's the only man I know who can make Harriet blush."

Talbot shuffled a stack of papers as if putting them in date order, while Philippe took himself to the front door. A sense of betrayal followed him, of having found a childhood haven collapsing in on itself. He'd always been happy in the Talbot household, had always felt like *himself*, not like the spare and then—heaven help him —the heir.

Harriet emerged from the corridor that led to the kitchen, a riding crop in her hand. "You're leaving already?"

Was she relieved, disappointed, or neither? "I have orders to return on Tuesday evening with Ramsdale in tow. Where are you off to?"

"I have another pair of two-year-olds to work in hand. I'll walk you out."

Philippe retrieved his hat from the sideboard and held the door for her. "You train them yourself?" When had this started?

"The lads have enough to do, and Lord Dudley's visit put us behind schedule. The horses like routine, and I like the horses."

She loved the horses. "So you're routinely doing the work of three men." The afternoon sunshine was lovely, and over in the stable yard, a leggy bay youngster stood in bridle and surcingle. Still, Philippe did not like the idea that Harriet had taken on so much of the actual training.

Perhaps all of the training?

"The work of three men is a light load for a woman," Harriet said. "I'll look forward to seeing you and his lordship on Tuesday."

She pulled gloves out of her pocket and eyed the horse as she and

Philippe walked down the drive. Already, she was doubtless assessing the beast's mood, taking in details of his grooming.

She paused with Philippe by the gate to the arena. "You walked over?"

"Of course. Most of the distance is along the duke's bridle path, and Berkshire has no prettier walk."

"Well, then, have a pleasant ramble home. I'll look forward to seeing you on Tuesday."

She was eager to get back to work, clearly. Eager to spend the next hour marching around in the sand, her side pressed to the sweaty flank of a pea-brained, flatulent horse.

Of whom Philippe was unreasonably jealous.

The least Philippe could do was give Harriet something to think about between now and Tuesday besides horses. He leaned close, pressed a kiss to her cheek, and lingered long enough to whisper.

"Until next we meet, don't work too hard." Up close, she smelled not of horse, but of roses and surprise.

Her gloved hand went to her cheek. "Until Tuesday, Your Grace."

Now here was a cheering bit of news: Ramsdale was not the only fellow who could make Harriet Talbot blush. Philippe offered her a bow and a tip of his hat and went jaunting on his way.

CHAPTER TWO

Dinner with the duke was a special kind of purgatory for Harriet.

Cook had outdone herself—two peers at the table, and one of them their own Lord Philippe!—and Papa tried to recapture the jovial spirit he'd exuded before Mama's death. Harriet attempted to play hostess, which was harder than it looked for a woman who got out the good china only at Christmas and on the king's birthday.

Philippe regaled them with tales of polite society's follies, while Ramsdale was mostly quiet. His lordship's dark eyes held a lurking pity that made Harriet want to upend the wine carafe into the earl's lap.

Sorely missing a friend was *not* the same as being infatuated with a man far above her touch. "If Ramsdale is insistent on being trounced at the chessboard," His Grace said when the clock struck ten, "then I'll see myself home. The moon is lovely tonight, and I certainly know the way."

Thank heavens, or thank Philippe's faultless manners. He was a considerate man, and Harriet would ever regard it as a pity that he eschewed equestrian activities. A little consideration went a long way toward success with most horses.

"Be off with you," Ramsdale said, waving a hand. "Lord knows, you need your beauty sleep, Lavelle, while I relish a challenge."

"And you shall have it," Papa rejoined, rising more energetically than he had in weeks. "It's your turn to be white, my lord, and if memory serves, you are down five games and very much in need of the opening advantage."

As Ramsdale politely bickered about the tally of victories, and Papa hobbled off with him to the study, Harriet's difficult night took a turn for the worse.

"He's lonely," she said.

Philippe paused by her chair. "Ramsdale? You are doubtless correct."

"Papa. He misses this. Misses the company of men, the jokes over the port, the slightly ungentlemanly talk that doubtless flows when he's at chess with Ramsdale. With the lads and grooms, Papa has to be the employer. With the buyers, he's the deferential horse master. With you and Ramsdale... he's happy."

Philippe bent closer, as he had when last they'd parted. "What of you, my dear? If your papa is lonesome for the company of men, whose company are you missing?"

Yours. "My mother, I suppose." And the father she'd once known, who'd been gruff but kindly, a hard worker, and a tireless advocate for the equine.

Philippe sighed, his breath fanning across Harriet's neck before he straightened to hold her chair. "Ada says you hardly ever call at the Hall."

Harriet *never* called at the Hall unless Papa insisted. "I am the daughter of a retired horse master, while your sister is a lady and always will be. I'll see you out."

"A horse master is a gentleman," Philippe said, "every bit as much of a gentleman as a steward or a vicar, and this might come as a revelation, but Ada is, like you, a woman living without benefit of female relations and in need of company."

Lady Ada was also a lovely person who adored her brother and took management of the ducal estate very much to heart. Harriet would endure Ramsdale's silent pity because she must. Pity from the duke's sister was unthinkable.

"If her ladyship needs company," Harriet said, "perhaps her brother should spend less time larking about London and more time where he belongs. It's a wonder women don't end every meal cursing," she muttered, disentangling her hem from beneath a chair leg. "These infernal skirts—"

"Are very becoming," Philippe said, offering his arm.

"I don't need an escort to my own front door, and I'll see you out on my way to the mares' barn."

Harriet wanted to elbow His Grace in the ribs, but he and she were no longer children; moreover, her elbow would get the worst of the encounter. Philippe was the duke. Over the past ten years, he'd transitioned from spare, to heir, to title holder. Generations of wealth, consequence, and yes—arrogance—regarded her patiently, until she took his arm simply to move the evening toward its conclusion.

I hate you. That pathetic taunt might have salvaged her pride in childhood, but now it was a sad echo of truer sentiments: *I miss you when you're gone for months. I worry about you. More often than you know, I wish I could talk to you or even write to you.*

I read the London papers for news of you. I dread the day I hear of your nuptials. For dukes married as surely as horses collected burrs in their tails.

"You're worried," Philippe said when they reached the foyer.

A single candle burned in a sconce on the wall, and when Harriet retired, she'd blow that one out.

"Papa will pay for this night's pleasures," Harriet said. "He forgets sore hips when he's in company or showing a horse to a prospective buyer, and I can't get him to touch the poppy or even white willow bark tea. I mentioned keeping a Bath chair on hand for the days when he's too stiff to walk out to the training paddock, and he nearly disowned me."

"I'm sorry. He's proud, and that makes it difficult to look after him." Philippe took Harriet's cloak from a hook near the sideboard, settled the garment around her shoulders, and fastened the frogs.

He knew exactly what he was doing, and not because he had a sister. Countless nights escorting ladies—titled ladies—to the opera, the theater, or this or that London entertainment had doubtless given him competence to go with his consideration.

Harriet treasured the consideration and resented the competence. "I can do up my own cloak, Your Grace."

Philippe shrugged into a shooting jacket and donned his top hat. "She's Your-Gracing me," he informed the night shadows. "I have transgressed. Perhaps my sin was complimenting my hostess's lovely attire. Maybe I mis-stepped when I commiserated about her father's waning health. Perhaps I've presumed unforgivably by performing small courtesies."

"You are being ridiculous." Harriet said. "So am I. I'm sorry." For so much, she was sorry.

"You are tired," Philippe replied, holding the door for her. "You work, you don't sit about stitching sanctimonious samplers while plotting adultery. You supervise men, instead of scheming how to get your hands on their coin or their titles. You want for respite, not a new diversion to go with the endless list you've already become bored with."

The moon was full, which meant Harriet had enough light to see Philippe's features.

The evening had apparently been trying for him too. All those stories about lordlings swimming in fountains, or young ladies whose arrows went astray, that was so much stable-yard talk. The reality was cold mornings and hard falls. Aching limbs and colic vigils. London had left Philippe tired and dispirited. He was bearing up and hiding it well.

"I'm glad you've come home," Harriet said, twining her arm through his. "I'll walk you to the bridle path."

"Unlike some people, I won't grouse at an offer of good company.

As a youth, I spent many a moonlit night wishing my true love would accost me under the oaks."

He referred to a ridiculous local legend: *The first person to kiss you under a full moon on the duke's bridle path is your true love.*

"The legend is very forgiving," Harriet said as they made their way between paddocks. "It doesn't specify that we're to have only one true love. I suspect many a stable lad has been relieved that subsequent interests aren't precluded by that first kiss."

And maybe many a duke? Tears threatened, and for no reason. What did it matter which squire's daughter, daring tavern maid, or merry widow had first kissed a young Lord Philippe on the bridle path?

"So who was your first true love?" Philippe asked.

Not a hint of jealousy colored his question. He was merely passing the time while tramping on Harriet's heart.

"He was tall," she said. "Quite muscular, a fellow in his prime. Splendid nose, moved like a dream, all grace and power."

"You noticed his nose?"

Was that disgruntlement in the duke's voice? "One does, when kissing."

"Not if one goes about it properly."

He spoke from blasted experience, while Harriet was spinning fancies. "I noticed his dark, dark hair, his beautiful eyes, his scent."

"You found a lad here in Berkshire who could afford French shaving soap?"

"He wasn't a lad, Your Grace. He was quite the young man, and all the ladies adored him." Which was why he'd been sold as a stud colt and was still standing at a farm in Surrey. "I kissed him good-bye under a full moon on the bridle path, and I will never, ever forget him."

Philippe slowed as they neared the trees. "You kissed him good-bye?"

"Years ago."

This part of the bridle path ran between two rows of stately oaks.

Nobody knew when the path had come into use, but the oaks were ancient. In places, the path wound beside a stream. At other points, it left the trees to cut along the edge of a pasture. Every square yard of the footing was safe. Every inch of the way was beautiful.

Especially by moonlight.

Philippe stopped at the gap in the oaks. The night was peaceful enough to carry the sound of horses munching grass in their paddocks. Harriet's slippers were damp—her only good pair. She'd neglected to change into boots, because shooing away His Grace had been the more pressing priority.

Shooing away His Grace, whom she missed desperately even when she was standing beside him.

"May I trust you with one more secret, Harriet?"

In the shadows of the trees, she couldn't make out his expression. "Of course. We are friends, and friends..."

He took off his hat and set it on a thick tree limb. "I waited in vain on this path. Nobody fell prey to my youthful charms, not on Beltane, not at harvest. Nobody would kiss the duke's younger son, though I witnessed several young ladies bestowing favors on Jonas."

That must have hurt. "Lord Chaddleworth was a rascal." A lovable rascal.

A foal whinnied, and the mama answered. A sense of expectation sprang up from nowhere, and two instants later, Harriet realized His Grace was through waiting for somebody to kiss him.

He touched his mouth to hers. Harriet stepped closer, and then his arms came around her.

The kiss resumed, and while Harriet noticed many things—how her body matched the duke's differently in the darkness, how the breeze blew her hair against her neck, how warm he was, and how his shaving soap smelled of sweet lavender—she did not notice his nose at all.

∾

PHILIPPE HAD GONE TO UNIVERSITY, and thanks to the Oxford tavern maids, he'd learned how to kiss. Those women instructed a fellow without regard to his title or wealth, demanding that he give pleasure where pleasure was offered. Thus Philippe had been introduced to the democracy of the bedroom where all—rich, poor, handsome, plain, young, and not so young—were reduced to common humanity in pursuit of common pleasures.

Then he'd kept discreet company with a young widow who ran a boarding house in Oxford. After university, he'd graduated to the wonders—and horrors—of London. Jonas had lectured Philippe at length about the French gout, fire ships, and other dangers, and a tour of Covent Garden after the theaters let out had underscored the need for caution.

Caution was expensive and tiresome, in the form of mistresses who expected regular visits and even more regular bank drafts. When Philippe realized that he'd not paid a call on his mistress for the duration of three bank drafts, he'd bid her a fond farewell—she pronounced him hopeless at debauchery—and resigned himself to the occasional frolic at a house party.

Two years later, he'd stopped accepting invitations to house parties. As Ada had pointed out, if he wanted to while away a few weeks in rural splendor, the peaceful, debutante-free luxury of his own Hall would suffice.

And all along, from university, to London, to the shires, and back, Philippe had wondered if something wasn't amiss with him. Intimate congress was pleasurable, but so was a ramble along the bridle path—and a good deal less complicated. Kissing had inspired sonnets and panegyrics in many languages, and yet, Philippe had regarded it as so much folderol to be got through while the lady made up her mind.

With Harriet, he never wanted the intimacies to end. Her kiss was everything—soft night sounds, breezes teasing the leaves that would soon fall to the lush grass, homecoming, joy, warmth of the heart and warmth—blazing warmth—where desire dwelled.

She wrapped her arms around him and shifted, so her breasts

rubbed against his chest. He suspected she had no intention other than to be closer, which was a fine, fine idea. He explored the contours of her back with one hand, not stopping until he cupped her derriere and pressed her closer.

She was luscious, eager, artless, and—some vestigial artifact of his gentlemanly scruples shouted—she was *Harriet*. Harriet, the pest who'd spied on him and Jonas; Harriet, who'd beat Jonas racing on her pony because she'd jump anything without checking her mount's speed; Harriet, who'd forget Philippe for another year because he hadn't a mane, tail, or hooves.

Philippe was a duke, a creature of discipline and duty.

His almighty discipline was barely sufficient to inspire a pause in the kissing.

"The full moon always makes the horses restless," Harriet panted.

What had horses—? Philippe eased his embrace and rested his cheek against Harriet's hair. The scent of roses was partly her, partly the night breeze.

"A mere kiss is not lunacy, Harriet. Not when we're on the bridle path. Kissing on the bridle path is what one does in this corner of Berkshire."

He felt the change in her, felt his attempt at levity fall flat and knock the wonder from the moment. Harriet doubtless had some equestrian analogy handy to better describe the unwelcome return of sanity.

"I thought bridle paths were for riding along," she said, resting her cheek against his chest. "I can feel your heart."

Philippe's attention was on another part of his anatomy, and yet, his heart was involved as well. He'd kissed Harriet Talbot, *his friend*, under a full moon on the bridle path. The kiss had been spectacular, but then, he was out of practice, and Harriet brought focus and energy to all she did.

He should turn loose of her.

He really should.

He stroked her hair, which was marvelously soft. "Are we still friends, Harriet?"

She stepped back and handed him his hat. "Of course, Your Grace. We will always be friends, and now when you are asked about our local legend, you can take your place among the village boys and stable lads who've at least kissed *somebody* on the duke's bridle path."

Her gaze wasn't on him, but rather, on the horses at grass under the full moon.

"You came out with me to check on a horse."

"A mare who has the audacity to be presenting us with an autumn foal. Such a thing shouldn't be possible, and if winter is early, it's surely not wise. She got loose, though, and was found the next morning disporting with Mr. Angelsey's stud. Heaven help the foal if it breeds true to the sire line, for that stud is cow-hocked and... I'm babbling."

Harriet wanted to see to her mare. Philippe wanted the last five minutes to never have happened, and he wanted to resume kissing her.

"Away with you," Philippe said, bowing over her hand. "I'll wait here until you're at the mares' barn. Thank you for a lovely meal and a lovely kiss."

He owed her that. He also probably owed her an apology, except he wasn't sorry. Confused, yes. Sorry, hell no.

"Good night, Your Grace." A quick curtsey, then Harriet stooped to remove her slippers, and off she went across the damp grass, her shoes in her hand.

Philippe remained by the oaks even after she'd disappeared into the mares' barn on the far side of the paddocks.

What had just happened? Harriet had kissed him as if she'd been longing for him to take that very liberty and needed to make up for lost time. Then she'd scampered off into the night—Cinderella taking both of her slippers with her—abandoning him yet again for the company of some smelly equine.

Philippe ducked into the shadows of the bridle path, and made his way back to the Hall, hat in hand.

"SOMEBODY MUST HAVE MOVED MY MARES' barn a mile or two down the bridle path," Jackson Talbot said.

Ramsdale's mind wasn't on the game, not on the chess game at any rate. Apparently, Talbot's wasn't either.

"Or perhaps," Ramsdale said, "like any self-respecting equestrienne, Miss Talbot saw a water bucket half empty and tarried to fill it. Or a mare who needed more hay, or a—"

Talbot waved his pipe. "The lads mope if Harriet steals all of their work. They take their responsibilities seriously."

"His Grace of Lavelle takes everything seriously." Though, because the duke also took his flirting seriously, and his gentlemanly bonhomie, and his cordial socializing, nobody seemed to notice—including the duke himself.

The front door closed, and a vague worry left Talbot's eyes. "All's well in the mares' barn. We're expecting a woods colt or filly."

The game had not yet progressed to the interesting phase. Ramsdale and his host were settling in, exchanging civilities, recalling each other's strategies.

"A maiden mare?" Ramsdale asked.

"No, but having chosen her swain for herself, I can't breed the damned horse to another until spring. Every foal counts, and this one, having a disgrace for a father, will be ewe-necked, over at the knee... It's your move, my lord."

Ramsdale moved his king's knight into position to threaten Talbot's queen. "An occasional outcross can strengthen a bloodline."

A duke's horse master had greater responsibilities in some regards than the land steward or house steward. He oversaw the coachmen and carriages, the breeding stock and farm stock, the stables and paddocks, the training and riding, the teams stabled at coaching inns all over the realm, and the money it took to keep that aspect of a dukedom functioning.

Anything associated with a ducal equine fell under the horse master's purview, and now Talbot was reduced to managing a few brood mares, some youngsters, a handful of riding stock in training...

And one smitten daughter.

"An occasional out-cross makes sense," Talbot said. "My darling mare chose the worst possible stud though. Damned colt should have been cut before he was weaned."

Talbot did not see the danger to his queen. "Lavelle is a gentleman." Which was half the problem. Somewhere along the way, His Grace had confused strawberry leaves for holy orders.

"His Grace is also a man without many close allies," Talbot said, moving his rook in a completely useless direction. "Harriet is ferociously loyal and unwise to the ways of men."

"To the ways of scoundrels, you mean." Ramsdale decided to draw the game out, for he had a delicate point to make, and he and delicacy were not well acquainted. "Lavelle hasn't a drop of scoundrel's blood in his veins."

"But every drop is male, and Harriet's future is dull enough to inspire her to rash acts. Her mother resorted to rash acts to gain my attention."

Ramsdale took a pawn with his bishop, a warning. "Her mother's strategy worked."

"I was a baronet's younger son. She was an earl's granddaughter. We knew what was expected of us, and times were different."

Talbot fell silent, and Ramsdale gave up on delicacy. "They would suit."

Talbot moved his *king*. Perhaps the horse master had begun a mental decline.

"Lavelle might make Harriet his mistress for a time," Talbot said, "and I'm sure he'd be generous and kind. Harriet was not raised to be anybody's fancy piece, though, not even a duke's fancy piece, not even a good duke's fancy piece."

Talbot wasn't angry, so much as he was bewildered. He'd never envisioned himself the father of a duke's fancy piece, or perhaps he worried about how to keep a stable afloat without Harriet to run it?

"I meant no insult to the lady," Ramsdale said. Then too, to be mistress to a duke was hardly the same as walking the London streets. "I meant that they're very nearly in love, and whom Lavelle falls in love with, he'll be inclined to marry."

Ramsdale wasn't sure what it meant to be in love, but whenever he accompanied Lavelle to the ancestral pile, the duke called first upon the Talbots, even before visiting the family graveyard. For a man who eschewed anything having to do with a horse, Lavelle was uncommonly fond of his papa's old horse master.

Also of the horse master's daughter.

"A duke must marry wisely," Talbot said. "Harriet is in no regard a suitable duchess. She knows that."

Ramsdale moved his queen again, though the king's shift by a single square was inconvenient to his intended strategy.

"Lavelle never wanted to be a duke, and every time somebody refers to him as such, he misses his older brother. In London, His Grace is endlessly popular, beloved by all, but known by virtually nobody. They were all too busy fawning over Lord Chaddleworth as the heir and didn't notice the younger brother. Now they notice him, and he can't be bothered."

His Grace was always polite, always charming, and always—to Ramsdale's discerning eye—bored with the life meant for his older brother. The boredom had become restlessness, and the restlessness was building toward some bad end.

Excessive drink, perhaps, or dueling, or—the worst fate imaginable—a Society match.

"My lord, your move has put us at a stalemate."

Ramsdale surveyed the board. "Bloody hell. My apologies. My mind is elsewhere."

"As is mine. Shall we call it a night, and shall I have a gig brought 'round to get you home?"

"I will enjoy a moonlit stroll and the peace and quiet of the Berkshire countryside. My thanks for a very pleasant evening, and I hope you'll join us for dinner at the Hall on Friday."

Talbot pushed to his feet. "His Grace left it to you to do the inviting, did he? Harriet would have conjured some excuse had he asked her directly—the mare, perhaps. No harm in a meal between neighbors, I suppose. Until Friday, my lord."

Talbot's grip was firm, though his gaze was troubled.

Best beat a retreat before Talbot also conjured excuses. "I'll see myself out. I promise you better play when next we meet."

Anything was better than playing to a stalemate, for God's sake. Ramsdale reserved the pleasure of reviewing the game move by move for the futile hours involved in falling asleep. As he made his way home down the legendary bridle path, a different challenge occupied him.

Harriet Talbot was from good family. Solidly gentry and entitled to a few upward pretensions. Had she been wealthy, a match with Lavelle would have been unusual, but not scandalous. Ramsdale was prepared to spread rumors of the young lady's magnificent dowry to still any wagging tongues.

A heart full of love, for those inclined to such nonsense, qualified as a magnificent dowry. Ramsdale had no doubt that Harriet would make a fine duchess, given some time and a few pointers from Lady Ada.

The problem was Lavelle. How could a peer who detested all things equine possibly become a suitable mate to a woman who—save for her interest in the duke—loved horses, only horses, and always horses?

CHAPTER THREE

Philippe had, as usual, not slept well.

London hours were backward. A man about Town sauntered forth with the setting sun to amuse himself with the social entertainments of his choice. When he'd waltzed to his heart's content—across some lady's sheets in many cases—he joined friends at the club for late-night cards and drinking.

By dawn's early light, the typical gentleman rode or drove in the park, and then he took himself off to bed, there to rest from his exertions in preparation for more of same.

In sheer defense of his sanity, Philippe had instead taken a serious interest in both his dukedom's commercial interests and in affairs of state. This was usually the province of men years his senior, and while Philippe liked taking a hand in politics, he didn't regard Parliament as the ultimate venue for blood sport.

In truth, he was glad to be back at the Hall for many reasons.

He was not, however, glad to regard Ramsdale over the breakfast table. His lordship wore a preoccupied expression that suggested blunt truths were about to issue forth from his unsmiling mouth.

"Have some ham," Philippe said. "Country air puts an appetite on a fellow."

"Country air must have addled your wits. I don't care for pork in any of its presentations, save for when it's on the hoof and downwind."

"Unpatriotic, Ramsdale, to turn up your nose at good English ham. Did Talbot trounce you last night?"

"Did Miss Talbot trounce you?"

Ramsdale was what some referred to as a worshipper of Aurora, goddess of the dawn. He began the day early and galloped at it head-long. By evening, he was a calmer, more settled creature.

"Now isn't that just like you, being adorably direct." Philippe caught the eye of the footman at the sideboard, who like any good house servant was impersonating a marble statue. "Thomas, you'll excuse us. Lord Ramsdale is about to deliver a proper dressing-down, and a peer of the realm wants privacy for his humiliations."

"I don't intend to humiliate you," Ramsdale said when the footman had bowed and withdrawn.

"I cannot say the same where you're concerned. You are a guest in my home, and I'll thank you to act like it. Your mention of Miss Talbot trouncing me bordered on ungentlemanly."

While stealing a kiss from Harriet by moonlight leaned in the direction of roguish.

Ramsdale rose, a slice of buttered toast in his hand. "The Talbots are not thriving." He wandered to the sideboard, added a dollop of scrambled eggs to his toast, and took a bite.

"I noticed as much last year, but told myself the evidence was simply a lack of the late Mrs. Talbot's guiding hand. She always ensured the roses were pruned, the fences whitewashed, and the carpets beaten. All the beating in the world does not make a worn carpet new, though."

The Talbots' manor house had been spotless, which made the creeping shabbiness more apparent.

Another portion of the toast met its fate. "What will you do about it?"

When Philippe hadn't been reliving his kiss with Harriet, regretting his kiss with Harriet, and longing for another kiss with Harriet, he'd asked himself the same question. His working theory was that Harriet had succumbed in a weak moment to his inappropriate overtures.

Like all theories, it wanted for supporting evidence. Her succumbing had been wonderfully enthusiastic, and a kiss was hardly a declaration of undying love. Nonetheless, Philippe had noticed the neglect on the Talbot property.

Weary, overwhelmed women were more prone to succumbing. So were weary, overwhelmed dukes.

"I have a few ideas for how to address the Talbots' situation," Philippe said. "I gather you do as well?"

Ramsdale's peregrinations next took him to the window, where mellow autumn sunshine illuminated dust motes and picked out the gold threads in his lordship's waistcoat.

"Talbot has his pride," Ramsdale said. "You'll have to tread lightly, but then, you've been treading lightly since your brother died."

"A man can choke to death on a slice of toast, Ramsdale." Though the earl was correct: Philippe had taken up his brother's responsibilities with equal parts resentment and reluctance. "Jonas was reared to become the duke, and he would have made a fine job of it."

Ramsdale turned, so the sunlight pouring over his shoulder lent him the air of a stern heavenly messenger. "You make a fine job of being a duke, but what about being a neighbor, a man, a brother?"

Or a lover? A husband even?

"I'm meeting with the vicar this morning, and I'll call on every one of my tenants over the next two weeks. For a duke, that's neighborly. I will lead my sister out at the blasted harvest ball and host the autumn open house the same as I usually do." The same as Jonas and Papa had done.

"And about the Talbots?"

"I have several options," Philippe said. "One is to ask Jackson Talbot to come out of retirement. My current horse master has been offered a post at a racing stable." In Berkshire, no mere ducal estate could compete with the joy and challenge of training racehorses.

Ramsdale finished his toast and circled back to the table to resume his seat. "Talbot is half blind and half lame. The horse master's post could well be the death of him."

"Or it might be the reason he lives another ten relatively happy years. If he took over for a few months and had reliable underlings, I'd be able to compensate him enough to tide him over."

This was a workable plan and afforded Philippe many opportunities to spend time with Talbot, which could result in opportunities to spend time with Harriet.

Maybe.

"You'd be gambling with his life, in other words," Ramsdale said. "How is Miss Talbot to manage without her father's presence on their property?"

Harriet would manage, but this was the fly in the horse lineament: Harriet would have to work harder than ever if her papa took a leave of absence to resume employment on the Lavelle estate.

"Another option is to buy the Talbot property and grant Talbot a life estate."

Ramsdale poured himself a cup of coffee. "Oh, right. Then when the old man dies, the young lady has some cash—assuming it wasn't frittered away putting the property to rights—but her pride and joy is in your hands, and you have not the slightest interest in adding a stable to your assets."

"I would never deprive Harriet of her stable."

Ramsdale stirred cream into his coffee. "She would never take charity from you. Has it occurred to you that the poor woman might be in want of a dowry?"

Philippe set his plate aside, and to hell with one's patriotic duty. "Why should she need a dowry?"

"So that she could marry a suitable successor to her dear papa. A man who could learn the business without displacing the woman who loves that business. A dashing horseman, a younger son who comes around pretending to be interested in buying a nag or two. Miss Talbot is comely, and she'll inherit a fine Berkshire stable. She could aspire to a title if she was ambitious."

Which Harriet was not.

Ramsdale took a sip of his coffee. His expression was thoughtful, and he was in *riding* attire. He'd tarried at the Talbots' last night, and he'd never turned down an invitation to join Philippe in Berkshire.

The earl was attractive, if a woman could overlook unruly dark hair, a lordly nose, and the shoulders of a blacksmith. Ramsdale and Harriet got on well. His title was ancient, and he needed heirs.

As did Philippe. "I'm considering another option. Considering it seriously."

"Do tell."

"The Talbots breed first-rate riding stock, they take excellent care of their horses, and their location is perfect for starting youngsters who won't have a career at the races. All they need is for polite society to take a little notice of them."

While Philippe needed for Harriet to take *more* than a little notice of him.

"You are polite society personified. If you were any more polite, you'd have to carry a harp and halo with you on occasions of state."

"Precisely the point. I am in a position to draw notice to the Talbots and increase their custom." Which was why this option, complicated though it was, had earned the majority of Philippe's consideration.

"You'll become a horse trader? Waste your coin on spavined, underfed, racing stock that will never be up to your weight? Shall you raise malodorous hounds and wear those execrable pinks for five months of the year?"

"Of course not. If I want to call attention to the fine stock in Jackson Talbot's stables, if I want to establish before all and sundry that I approve of the Talbots' operation, I have only to make one small gesture in the right direction, and all will come right."

Provided Philippe survived that small gesture.

"You'll dower Miss Talbot. Capital notion. She's a fine woman and deserves every happiness in this life. I'm sure once Talbot recovers from the apoplexy your insult serves to his pride, he'll remember to thank you."

"Ramsdale, have a little faith in your friends. I would happily dower Harriet—Miss Talbot—should the need arise. Until such time as it does, I'll do the one thing I promised myself I would never, ever do."

Ramsdale sat back and crossed his arms. "You'll marry her?"

Philippe nearly spluttered tea all over himself. "You consider marriage a small gesture?"

"Gentlemen do not discuss size."

While schoolboys discussed little else. "My plan was to ask for Talbot's assistance in regaining my skills in the saddle. I'll be home for the foreseeable future, Talbot was my first riding instructor, and I'm sure he'll have a mount that will suit me, once I recollect the basics."

The silence in the breakfast parlor was so profound, Philippe could hear his heartbeat pounding in his ears.

"You'll *get back on a horse* merely to help a former employee find a few more customers?"

"No, Ramsdale. I'll polish some neglected skills because it suits me to do so. I live in Berkshire, where every other farm aspires to produce the next champion stud. If in spring, I'm inclined to hack out in Hyde Park during the fashionable hour, or join a lady for a morning gallop, that is entirely my business."

"Please tell me you're not trying to impress that Warminster creature. All Mayfair will sigh in relief when she decamps for the Midlands."

Ramsdale hadn't laughed at Philippe's plan, which was encouraging. He also hadn't tried to talk Philippe into changing his mind, which was no damned help at all.

"You said it yourself, Ramsdale. Jonas has gone to his reward, and it's time I got on with being the duke." And if Philippe had to climb back onto a horse to impress his prospective duchess, then onto a horse he would climb.

HARRIET HANDED off the second two-year-old to a groom and headed for the house, intent on finding a midday meal, or a midafternoon meal. The hours in the stable flew, until she became famished. Only when famished progressed to thirsty, light-headed, and snappish did she force herself to do something about her hunger.

Snappish and young horses was a bad combination. Some bread and cheese, a mug of ale, and Harriet would return to the barn...

She had batted aside a skein of blown roses drooping over the front steps when raised voices from inside the house came to her notice. Papa had a grand bellow, such as anybody who'd taught horseback riding had to have. Harriet hadn't heard her father using his arena voice for some time though, and this was not a happy bellow.

The other voice was softer, but equally emphatic. Harriet let herself through the front door, and the words became clearer.

"You can't... damned... foolishness, Your Grace."

Your Grace? She stripped off her gloves and sat to unbuckle her spur.

"Damned stubbornness... simple request, Talbot."

Philippe, and he hadn't stopped by the paddocks to greet her. Harriet had hoped the duke would return to London, and when next they saw each other, they could make light of a kiss shared for the sake of legend.

Not a legendary kiss, not a kiss that had changed Harriet's view of herself and her future, merely a gesture between old friends.

She hurried down the corridor, tapped twice on the door to

Papa's study, and walked right in. The horses had taught her that: walk into the barn as if all was well, the day was beautiful, and great good fun awaited Harriet and her mounts.

Horses, unlike stable hands, customers, and fathers, *paid attention.*

"Pardon me," Harriet said. "Your Grace, good day. Papa, I was on my way to the kitchen. Would you gentlemen care to join me in a sandwich?"

"No, thank you," Papa growled.

The duke rose from the chair opposite the desk. "Miss Talbot, greetings. Sustenance would be welcome."

The two men Harriet cared about most in the world glowered at each other. Had they been a pair of yearling colts, she would have left them to their posturing and pawing.

"You're apparently having a difference of opinion," she said. "You could be heard halfway to the mares' barn."

His Grace snatched a pair of gloves from the desk. "Mr. Talbot is being unreasonable."

"The duke asks too much."

His Grace was not in the habit of asking anybody for anything. Even last night's kiss hadn't been the result of an overt request.

Harriet's gaze fell upon Philippe's mouth, which was set in a determined line. She knew the shape and taste of that mouth, knew its skill and the pleasure it could bestow.

"What has His Grace requested?"

"It's of no moment," the duke replied. "I'll just be going."

This was not good. Philippe had a temper—Harriet had seen it exactly twice. The first time, he had been thirteen and had come upon a bitch and her puppies in a shed at the back of the mayor's garden. The space had been filthy, the mama emaciated, the stench unbelievable. He'd bought the entire litter and their mama on the spot and sent Harriet for a dog cart to ferry them to the Hall.

The mayor had lost the next election.

The second time had been years later. Philippe had come down from university on holiday and stood up with the local young ladies at a tea dance at the parish hall. Harriet's mama had forced her to attend as well.

Bascomb Hardy had deliberately tromped on the vicar's daughter's hem.

Elspeth had been slow-witted, but sweet, an easy target for unkindness. Tearing the hem of her best dress should have meant that she missed out on the rest of the dance, the first that the ducal spare had attended.

Philippe had knelt at Elspeth's feet, used his cravat pin to hide the damage, and invited her to partner him for the next set. To the young lady, he'd been attentive, charming, and kind. To Harriet, his ire had been evident from the tension in his shoulders and the determined quality of his gaze. At services the next week, Bascomb had sported a noticeably swollen nose.

Harriet had learned to see her childhood friend with new and admiring eyes. Elspeth had married the blacksmith's son, who'd also stood up with her at that tea dance, and they now had five rambunctious children.

While Harriet had an argument to settle. "What is the issue?"

His Grace paused by the door. "Stubbornness."

Papa remained seated, which was rude, also an indication of how much his hip pained him. "Unreasonable expectations."

The duke strode back to the desk, his boot heels thumping on the thin carpets. "You were the one who suggested it! You all but dared me to try. Now I'm taking you up on your offer, and you spout inanities about suitable mounts and busy schedules."

Papa used the arms of his chair to push to his feet. "Autumn is always busy at a stable. Much of the training will cease when the weather turns nasty, and we must work while we can, especially with the youngsters."

His Grace picked up Papa's cane, the handle of which was carved into a horse head. "Talbot, you confound me." The duke studied the cane for a moment, then passed it across the desk. "Miss Talbot, you mentioned food."

The mood had shifted with the passing of the cane. Harriet had no idea what had caused this argument, but the duke had decided to retreat.

"Nothing fancy, Your Grace. A sandwich, a few biscuits, a peach or two."

The pair of peach trees had been a gift to Mama from the old duke, and the trees—unlike the rest of the facility—were having a good year.

"I adore a succulent peach," the duke said. "Talbot, good day. My apologies for any untoward remarks."

Papa subsided into his chair. "Likewise. Harriet, get the man something to eat."

With the horses, Papa was the soul of civility. He never commanded when he could invite, never insisted when he could suggest.

Harriet had given up expecting the same consideration. "Yes, Papa."

The duke looked like he was about to renew the altercation with Papa—perhaps scolding him for his peremptory tone—but Harriet was hungry, and arguing with Papa solved nothing.

"Your Grace, shall I serve you in the breakfast parlor?"

"Certainly not. I've taken the majority of my meals here in the kitchen, and we need not stand on ceremony now. Or perhaps we should make a picnic of our repast. One never knows when winter will come howling down from the north two and a half months early. We must enjoy the fine weather while it lasts."

With that parting shot, he held the door for Harriet, who paused long enough to kiss her father's cheek before joining the duke in the corridor.

"You have offended my father," she said. "We will sort that out once I've had something to eat. What did you ask of him?"

"He has offended me," the duke replied, accompanying Harriet down the steps. "Though I don't think he meant to. He teased me the other night, and I took his remarks to heart."

The kitchen was empty, the cook being in the habit of joining the housekeeper for a dish of tea at midafternoon. Long ago, the boy Philippe had downed many a mug of cider in this kitchen. The top of his head nearly brushed the dark beams now.

Philippe was not a boy. He was the man who'd kissed Harriet not twenty-four hours ago.

She'd kissed other men and then wondered why anybody would seek to repeat the experience. Mouths mashed together, teeth banging, hands landing in awkward locations then not knowing what to do. A very great bother, and for no reason.

"Are we drinking our ale from tea cups?" the duke asked.

Some hen-wit had begun assembling a tea tray. "We are not." Harriet set the tray aside. "I grow scatterbrained when I go too long without eating."

"Please do get off your feet," the duke said, leading Harriet by the hand to the hearth. "I recall well enough how to slice bread and cheese. I wonder if you recall how to sit for five minutes on anything other than a horse."

The hearth stones were cool, even through the fabric of Harriet's breeches and habit. Sitting down felt too good. Watching the duke impersonate a scullery maid felt even better.

Philippe was the duke—always would be—but part of him was still Harriet's friend. One kiss hadn't changed that. "The butter's in the—"

"Window box," he said, brandishing a small crock. "Same as always."

He unwrapped the morning's loaf of bread, unwrapped the cheese wheel, and put together sandwiches. The bread was sliced unevenly, the cheese was too thick, and he applied butter as if Papa had an entire herd of fresh heifers.

Moving around the kitchen, he also showed off a pair of riding breeches to spectacular advantage.

"What did you and Papa argue about?"

"I mistook a jest for a sincere offer," the duke said. "Where are the mugs?"

"Above the dry sink."

Harriet felt as if she'd fallen half asleep and was having one of those waking dreams that arose from sheer exhaustion in broad daylight. Dozing in the barn, she sometimes imagined the barn cats and horses could speak, or that the coronation coach awaited her in the drive.

A duke was preparing food for her, the same duke who'd kissed her last night.

And yet here, in the kitchen, he was also simply her Philippe.

Whom she'd like very much to kiss again.

A SKILLED ARTIST should be sketching Harriet seated by the hearth. She was like a setting sun, momentarily stilled above the western horizon.

Her coiffure, which had likely started the day as a sensible braid wrapped into a tidy bun, was now a frazzled rope down the middle of her back. She sat immobile—no part of her moved, not her hands, not her booted feet, not even her gaze. She leaned back against the hearth stones and simply watched Philippe bumble about in the kitchen.

This was why a man went to university—so he'd learn to make cheese toast, brew a pot of tea, and otherwise fend off starvation in the midst of plenty.

Or perhaps, so he might tend to a woman who was clearly in need of nourishment.

"Come sit," he said, patting the back of a chair. "Tell me about your day and lie to me about my skill at sandwich making."

Harriet crossed to the table and let Philippe hold her chair. "You got the cheese between the bread, which is the important part. Papa's hip must be paining him severely today."

Philippe took the place across from her, the better to enjoy looking at her. "I gathered as much. When I joined you for a meal yesterday, he was in high spirits."

"He'd been at the brandy, you mean." Harriet bowed her head to give thanks, and Philippe spent a pious little silence mentally undoing the rest of her braid.

He *was* thankful, not only for his pathetic attempt at sandwiches, but also for a chance to spend time with Harriet.

"As the weather cools, Papa's joints are affected," Harriet said, opening her sandwich and nibbling the buttered side. "Autumn also makes the horses frisky."

From Harriet, that was small talk—not flirtation.

"I had hoped to prevail on your father for some assistance at the Hall."

She set down her bread and butter. "Is something amiss?"

Such concern in her eyes, but nothing of longing, nothing of intimacies recalled. "I merely sought to consult with an experienced horse master. My current horse master will take a post at a racing yard at the first of the month."

"That started an argument?"

"The argument began before I could pass that news along to your dear papa. This is good ale."

"The last of the summer ale." Harriet swiped the tip of her tongue across her top lip, something she'd never have done in the dining room or breakfast parlor.

Philippe consumed better cheese and coarser bread than he was used to and rearranged chess pieces in his mind. His plan had been to have Talbot brush up his riding skills here, where nobody at the Hall would know what was afoot.

A duke could land on his arse in the dirt and usually walk away unscathed. His reputation before his employees was a more delicate article than his backside. Then too, a duke could change his mind more easily with a smaller audience.

Say, an audience of one.

He ate in silence while Harriet demolished her food. "You are a hungry woman. I should have made you more than one sandwich."

"You can slice the peaches. I'll make more sandwiches."

She rose and set a bowl of ripe fruit before him, as well as a cutting board and a knife. "Will you make peach jam?"

"Mama was the jam maker, though Cook assisted, of course. It's a messy, tedious job, and I haven't time."

The peaches were perfect—ripe and juicy but firm. By the time Philippe had pitted and cut up two of them, Harriet had another pair of sandwiches put together. Hers were tidy—evenly sliced bread, cheese a uniform thickness, not too much butter.

"Try a slice," Philippe said, holding a glistening portion of peach across the table.

Harriet reached for it, and he drew his hand back a few inches. "You'll get sticky."

She nibbled from his fingers delicately, her eyes closing as she swallowed. "That is luscious. Of all the generosity the old duke displayed toward us, Mama treasured those peach trees the most."

Philippe shared the rest of the peaches with her, until his fingers were covered with juice and sharing a peach topped his list of erotic ways to spend an autumn afternoon.

"I was hungry," Harriet said, rising. "I get so involved in what I'm doing with the horses, I forget to eat. Shall we take our ale out to the porch?"

"A fine notion." In view of the arena and the barns, Philippe had a prayer of behaving. He had not come here thinking to renew intimacies with Harriet, but in her company, little else wedged its way into his thoughts.

He washed his hands while Harriet wrapped up the bread and cheese, then they carried their mugs to the front porch.

"I love this time of year," Harriet said, taking a seat on a wrought-iron chair. "The harvest is a happy occasion, the animals are fat and healthy, and the light is beautiful."

Harriet was beautiful, with her hair coming undone and her habit dusty to the knees.

Across the stable yard, a groom was reviewing with a bay yearling filly the etiquette of work in hand. The groom walked a half-dozen steps and stopped. Walked a half-dozen more and stopped again, until the young horse recalled that she was to match her handler's behavior, not barge about on the end of the lead rope like a half-ton kite.

"She fancies him," Harriet said. "Trusts his patience and his calm. Jeremy is like you in that regard, seldom discommoded regardless of the circumstances."

Philippe was discommoded—by the interview with Talbot, by the breeze teasing at the curls lying against Harriet's neck. He'd come here for a reason, and Talbot had stymied him. Too late, Philippe had realized that Talbot's health was more precarious than anybody grasped.

Anybody save Harriet, perhaps.

To teach regular riding lessons required hours at the arena rail, in the cold, in the damp, in the hot sun, the flies, the relentless wind. The horse master of Philippe's youth had made those lessons the high point of Philippe's day, but that man was no more.

"I had best be going," Philippe said. "Perhaps you'll walk with me to the bridle path?"

Harriet set her mug on the porch railing. "Of course. I'm looking forward to dinner on Friday."

Philippe set his mug beside hers. "Because?"

"Because dinner at the Hall is always an enjoyable occasion," she said, starting down the steps. "Lord Ramsdale passed your invitation to Papa over the chess board."

Philippe would thank Ramsdale just as soon as he finished thrashing him for his presumption. "I'll look forward to it as well, but I've been anticipating something else more joyously than another shared meal. Something I've been meaning to ask you about."

Did you enjoy our kiss? Did you spend half the night recalling it?

Have you not brought it up because you hope I'll never presume to that degree again?

They ambled along the fence, to where the young horse was being put through her paces.

"Jeremy," Harriet said, "that's enough for today. She's being a good girl, and you want to stop before she's bored."

Jeremy, who looked to be about sixteen, petted the filly's neck. "Aye, Miss Talbot. Good day, Your Grace."

"Jeremy."

The groom led the horse away, praising her fine performance.

"He's one of the miller's boys, isn't he?" The entire family had height, white-blond hair, and prominent teeth.

"One of eight sons. Jeremy works hard and loves the horses, but the first time he has to sell a favorite or put a bullet in an old friend who's stepped in a badger hole, he'll be back at his papa's side, grinding corn."

For the rest of the distance to the tree-line, Philippe pondered how anybody—even a determined duke—could bring the conversation around to stolen kisses after an observation like that.

Harriet walked past the break in the trees, right onto the bridle path itself. "Will Ramsdale join us on Friday?"

"I assume so."

"I don't think he and Papa got very far with their last chess game. Both queens and kings were still on the chess board when I brought Papa the morning mail. What did you want to ask me about, Your Grace?"

She watched the retreat of the groom and filly, her question all but idle.

"Did you know your braid is coming undone?" The ribbon had nearly slipped off the end of her plait. Philippe moved behind her, tugged the ribbon free, and held it before her. "I'll do you up. Hold still."

Harriet gave him her back while Philippe undid and then rebraided her hair. He hadn't put his gloves back on after their meal, and so he was free to torment himself with thick, silky, lavender-scented skeins of cinnamon-brown curls.

"Do you do this sort of thing often?" Harriet asked, gaze on the hedgerow before her.

"What sort of thing?" Stare at the nape of a woman's neck until his tongue ached?

"Braid a lady's hair."

Philippe completed his task and tied the hair ribbon snugly about the end of the plait. "Like that kiss we shared, this is a first for me. I doubt my work will hold for long. Your hair is too... soft."

Harriet turned, and because Philippe wasn't about to step back, they stood quite close. Nobody would see them here, beneath the towering oaks, between the hedgerows. The moment was perfect for another kiss, if she *wanted* another kiss.

The moment was also perfect to tell a presuming duke to take his kisses and bugger off.

"You had a question for me," Harriet said, smoothing the fold of his lapel. She looked up, her gaze simply honest—no reproach, no flirtation.

He caught her hand in his. "Harriet... would you mind...?"

"Yes?"

"Would you mind...?" Her lips were parted. Philippe had touched peach slices to those lips. His dreams tonight would surely include ripe, succulent, sweet peaches.

She leaned nearer. "Your Grace?"

"Would you mind... teaching me to ride?"

CHAPTER FOUR

Harriet had been on many a horse who at the last instant refused a jump. She'd sink her weight into the stirrups—or stirrup, if she was riding aside—fix her eye on the next obstacle and anticipate the magnificent rise of more than a half ton of muscle and might beneath her—

And find herself clinging to a coarse mane and scrambling to regain her balance on a beast that had barely, barely managed to remain upright.

The duke's question left her similarly disconcerted. Her momentum had all been in the direction of a kiss, not... not... *What had he asked her?*

"I beg your pardon?"

Harriet stood so close to him that she could see how agate and slate came together to put the silver glint in his eyes, so close she could feel his breath fanning across her cheek. Her fingers had gripped his sleeve, and his hand rested on her shoulder.

"Will you teach me to ride again?" he asked. "I needn't qualify for the race meets. I simply want to acquit myself competently in the saddle of a morning in Hyde Park. I'd like to ride my acres as my father did. It's time, Harriet. Your father was right about that."

He brushed her hair back from her brow, and Harriet wanted to smack his hand. "Time for you to learn to ride again? You rode competently as a boy." More than competently, he'd ridden joyously.

His lashes swept down. "That was before Jonas's accident."

Before Lord Chaddleworth had died. His horse had either refused or slipped at a stile, and his lordship had come off, straight into the wall. He'd never regained consciousness and taken less than two hours to expire.

Harriet's ire slipped from her grasp, like wet reins in the hands of a beginner. "Oh, Philippe. Of course I'll help."

He rested his forehead against her shoulder, and Harriet wrapped her arms around him.

"Thank you, Harriet. Your father refused me, after he'd been the one to goad me into trying. I thought perhaps..."

This was a conversation to have heart-to-heart rather than face-to-face. Harriet rested her cheek against Philippe's chest and found the rhythm of his life's blood steady but pronounced.

"You thought Papa judged the task impossible," she said. "For him, it likely is. He can barely stand for ten minutes, and that's with the aid of his cane. Trudging through deep footing is hell for him, and his pride pains him as badly as his joints."

Philippe's hand cradled the back of Harriet's head, and thus they remained, embracing, for the time it took a golden leaf to twirl down through the afternoon sunshine. She willed him to understand that his request touched her—getting back on the horse was more than a metaphor for seizing one's courage after a setback.

Getting back on the horse could be the defining challenge of a lifetime.

"My pride pains me as well," Philippe said. "Might I further impose and request that our lessons take place here?"

"You will save me the time needed to hack over to the Hall," Harriet said, "and Papa will likely watch from the porch or a handy window and pass along pointers to me at supper. I'll swear the lads to secrecy, and nobody will be the wiser."

For a time. No power on earth could permanently still the tongues that wagged in a stable yard.

Philippe's embrace eased. "I should have asked you in the first place, but you have much to do already. You'll tell me if I'm imposing?"

Never. "I enjoy teaching, and you used to enjoy riding. This will be easier than you anticipate."

He brushed a kiss to her cheek. "I am in your debt. Shall we begin tomorrow afternoon?"

"Rain or shine, Your Grace. Two of the clock, and wear your oldest pair of boots."

"I have my orders." He bowed over her hand and then strode off down the path.

Harriet perched on a fallen log and sorted through her feelings as more leaves drifted to the golden carpet covering the grass.

She was proud of Philippe for taking this step.

She was proud of herself for being a good enough friend that he'd trust her to help.

She was happy that her stable would have the honor of reacquainting the Duke of Lavelle with his equestrian skills.

The next leaf smacked her in the mouth and refused to complete its descent. She brushed it aside and set it on the log.

Proud and happy weren't the entire list. Harriet was also confident that she could help Philippe—she'd coached other riders past a loss of courage and worked through the same problem herself more than once.

She was also determined. Very, very determined.

The duke would get back on his horse, and Harriet would have more kisses.

∾

"I AM A VERY, VERY BAD MAN," Philippe informed Saturn.

The dog panted happily at his heels as they strode along the bridle path.

"There I stood, thinking *untoward thoughts*, while Harriet offered me her moral support and compassion. I am the lowest scoundrel ever to steal a kiss." Though that's all he'd stolen—a kiss, a hug, a tender embrace that for Harriet had likely been between old friends, and for Philippe had been the sweetest torment.

"I'm not nervous," he went on. "Not about sitting on a horse again."

He was, though, looking forward to time with Harriet more or less alone, but for the presence of an equine.

He reached the boundary between the ducal estate and Talbot's property. Philippe hopped a stile rather than deal with the gate. Saturn wiggled under the gate, which was a bit of a squeeze for such a grand fellow.

"I should have made it apparent that Harriet will be compensated for her time."

Saturn stuck his nose into the carpet of leaves and began snuffling intently.

"I will insist on paying her in good English coin, and she'll have nothing to say to it. I'll be quite the—"

Philippe tripped over a tree root hidden by the fallen leaves and nearly went sprawling. The dog regarded him pityingly, then went back to his investigations.

"I'll be quite the duke," Philippe finished. "Though I'm not quite the duke." He was a spare pressed into service out of necessity, plain and simple. There were worse fates—bashing headfirst into a plank wall and expiring, for example.

He increased his stride. "Riding isn't difficult. The horse goes on the bottom, as Talbot used to say. The rest of it—the hands, seat, legs, and whatnot—are details."

Important details. Philippe had been on a runaway pony once.

Amazing, how an equine who'd barely moved when pointed away from the barn could cover ground in the opposite direction.

"But I stayed on. The little fiend was utterly winded by the time we trotted into the stable yard. Had to walk him for nearly an hour."

An hour of ignominy, for all the lads had known exactly what had happened. Talbot had pretended Philippe had meant to go tearing hell-bent across field and furrow, but the stable hands, Philippe, and the demon pony—Butterball—had known differently.

"I got back on then and learned to keep a firm hold of the reins. Not a complex concept."

The break in the trees that led to the Talbot paddocks came into view, and Philippe's belly did an odd leap. Saturn lifted his leg on an oak sapling, which gave Philippe an excuse to pause, reconnoiter, and say a prayer.

Let me not be put to shame.

"Watch over me, Jonas. If I follow your example and go early to my reward, the title ends up with dear cousin Oglethorpe, and the peerage will never recover from that abomination. Ada will kill us both all over again for abandoning her to his charming company."

Saturn finished watering the hedge and went trotting forth as if he well knew Philippe's destination, rotten beast. He'd been a puppy at the time of Jonas's death—Jonas's personal hound.

"I'm coming. We have plenty of time, and it's not as if Harriet has nothing else to do."

When Philippe emerged between the Talbot paddocks, Harriet was in fact striding along behind the two-year-old filly Jeremy had been working with the previous day. The filly was in long reins, Harriet marching smack up against the horse's hip.

This was a step in the direction of carrying a rider, allowing the horse to learn how to go along in a bridle without having to carry a rider's weight. Philippe had watched Talbot educate many a young horse in this manner. A surprising degree of fitness was required to guide the horse while striding about in deep footing, but Harriet managed it easily.

The horse turned, and Harriet came more fully into view.

"Gracious devils, have mercy upon me."

She was wearing breeches and tall boots, only an oversized riding jacket preserving a modicum of modesty. She spoke to the horse as they halted between two jumps, for this was also the phase of training at which voice commands could be taught.

"Walk on, Rosie, there's a girl."

The filly minced forward as daintily as a cat. Harriet steered her all about the arena, around jumps, past stable boys grinning on the rail, down the middle, and over to the mounting block, all the while guiding, chiding, and encouraging.

"And ho, Rosie. Ho."

The filly came to a smooth stop in the center of the arena, and after she'd stood quietly for half a minute, much patting and praising ensued. Jeremy left the rail to take the horse back to the stable, and Harriet waved at Philippe.

"Your Grace! Good day."

So she *had* noticed him. "Harriet. Very nicely done."

"She's a good girl. Is it two of the clock already? How time flies when the weather's fine. Come along, your mount should be ready."

Philippe joined Harriet at the arena gate. "Before you start lessons, don't you typically discuss compensation?"

Her coiffure was in good repair today, which ought to have helped Philippe keep his mind on the business to be discussed. Instead, he wanted to take down her braid and bury his hands in her hair.

While he was kissing her.

While she was kissing him back and clutching him in that lovely firm grip of hers.

I have lost my mind.

"We can discuss remuneration once I've done something to earn it," Harriet said as they reached the barn. "This is Matador."

A mountain of gray horsehair stood in the middle of the aisle. An equine nose tipped with pink protruded from the hair—a nose about a yard long. Two big brown eyes regarded Philippe from beneath two hairy ears.

"Hello, Mastodon."

The horse's lower lip drooped, giving him an air of permanently injured dignity.

"I'll need to use the ladies' mounting block to board him," Philippe said. "He does move without a hoisting sail? Stops, turns, backs up—the whole lot?"

"He'll do as you tell him," Harriet said, unfastening the crossties. "Let's see what you recall."

"*Now?*"

Harriet went about disentangling the reins from the throatlatch, then had to hop to loop the reins over the beast's great head.

"It's two of the clock, Your Grace, and I have much to do."

Whose ideas was this? "I'm a duke. I can't be seen riding a plough horse." Though dukes weren't supposed to dither, fuss, or prevaricate either.

Harriet stroked the horse's neck. "Matador is a retired drum horse. He's attended more funerals of state than you have, and you should be honored to have the use of him. He would still be in work, except his partner succumbed to colic and nobody could find another to match Matador's size and coloring."

Shamed by an orphaned mastodon. "Very well," Philippe said. "As I recall, one walks on the horse's left."

The equine cortege came along docilely, hooves the size of soup tureens clopping inches from Philippe's boots. Though the animal was apparently well trained, Philippe was abruptly aware that he was about to entrust his well-being to a creature who was ten times his size and who had no respect for the ducal succession.

And yet, the horse was a placid beast, handsome in its way, and Philippe was no longer a small boy with only a small boy's strength.

"Let's use the rail to get you into the saddle," Harriet said. "The first thing you should know about Matador is that he'll stand until Domesday. He's stood for hours in the line of duty, put up with crowds, barking dogs, disrespectful children, and drunken fools. There isn't much you can do to unnerve him."

"His job sounds rather like being a duke," Philippe said, swallowing back some inconvenient welter of emotion. Excitement to be taking on a challenge, impatience at the indignity of being a beginner, fear of mortal harm—might as well be honest—and also hope, that this adventure ended well for all concerned.

Then he was perched on the fence railing, making an awkward job of clambering into the saddle. The horse sighed as Philippe slipped his boots into the stirrups.

"Now what?"

Harriet led Matador a few feet from the rail. "Now we adjust your stirrups. You have longer legs than most stable boys."

The next few minutes were taken up with Harriet *handling* her pupil. Philippe lifted his legs, sat tall, had his boots turned to rest nearly parallel to the horse's sides, and generally endured fussing. When Harriet stepped back, Philippe's stirrups were at the correct length, and his insides were in a muddle.

He'd made the mistake of looking down, thinking to feast his eyes on the sight of Harriet's hands on his person. He'd instead seen the ground, miles and miles below where it should have been.

"Your stirrups are on the fourth hole," Harriet said. "Remember that, because when we're finished here in the arena, we'll review saddling and unsaddling."

"Right, fourth hole." Not that Phillippe could count to four in his present state. With no warning, his heart had decided to take off at a gallop, his mouth had gone dry, and his wits were probably somewhere in the muck heap.

"Now, you follow me," Harriet said. "Horses are herd animals. This shouldn't be difficult." She drew off her jacket—probably one of Talbot's castoffs, judging from the poor fit—and slung it over the railing. "Follow the leader, Your Grace, and I'm the leader."

She strode off. Matador swung his enormous head to sniff at the toe of Philippe's boot.

Get on with it, mate.

"Keeping you from your oats, am I?" Philippe gave a scoot with his seat.

Nothing happened.

He tapped his heels ever so gently at the horse's sides, and one hoof shuffled forward.

A firm tap produced a funereal toddle, which suited Philippe splendidly. The horse moved like an equine sea, rolling, rhythmic, and relentless, but also deliberate. One-two-three-four, one-two-three-four...

"Are your eyes up?" Harriet called without looking back. "Look where you're going. Don't stare at his mane."

Well, yes. Philippe tipped his chin up, and the rolling sea became a plodding horse. This was all in aid of the Talbots' future. A secure old age for a man who'd worked long, hard years. Harriet swung left around a jump, and Philippe guided his mount in the same direction.

She didn't even glance back, which Philippe suspected was her way of allowing him some privacy at an awkward moment. Two more turns, a halt, and onward... until Philippe realized that this game of follow the leader would be the undoing of him, for the leader, striding along in her breeches, had a very fetching derriere.

HARRIET GOT an education while teaching the duke.

By the second lesson, she realized that His Grace was an athlete. Being unwilling to ride meant that he walked far more than most of his peers. He mentioned that on holidays he'd go for a twenty-mile jaunt over the hills and consider that a pleasant day. He fenced, he rowed, he swam—the Duke of Lavelle was an intensely physical man.

And had the muscles to show for it. As Harriet moved his leg— here for the signal to move forward, there for the signal to move sideways—she grew distracted.

Ye gods, his calves. His *thighs*. As she adjusted his hands on the reins—black leather gloves notwithstanding—she grew muddled, for those hands had coaxed terrible longings from her.

As she watched his progress from behind—lest he be sitting subtly to one side or the other—she lost her train of thought entirely. Such broad shoulders, such excellent posture. Such...

"That's enough for today," Harriet said. "Posting the trot will leave you sore, regardless of your otherwise fine physical condition."

Posting the trot—rising in the stirrups to the rhythm of the horse's footfalls—made for a smoother ride than trying to match the horse's movement with the seat in the saddle. Matador had a nicely cadenced trot, but his gaits were enormously springy.

Philippe had caught Matador's rhythm easily, though this lesson would exact a toll in aching muscles tomorrow. Sunday would be uncomfortable in the extreme, if the duke's tutelage followed the usual course.

"I had hoped we might canter today," Philippe said, giving Matador a whacking great pat on the neck. "Two lessons and the whole business is already coming back to me."

"We'll canter soon enough. Today, you can take off his saddle and bridle and groom him yourself," Harriet said.

Philippe kicked his feet out of the stirrups and hopped off as nimbly as any cavalry officer. He ran the stirrups up their leathers, loosened the girth, and looped the reins over Matador's head.

"We have not discussed your compensation," Philippe said, leading the horse to the gate. "Come with me to the barn, and we can have that argument while I get horsehair all over my clothing."

"As you wish."

"You don't fool me, Harriet Talbot. You'll be agreeable until I put the HMS Mastodon into dry dock, and then you'll turn up contrary. If we had children, you'd reserve all your ire for when the little ones were tucked up into their beds and then open fire on your unsuspecting spouse."

If they had children... "Today you pick out Matador's feet, Your Grace."

Philippe was doing quite well in the saddle. Papa had said he had a natural seat, and Papa was—once again—right. On the ground, where a horse could rear, strike, bite, or knock a man flat, the duke wasn't as confident.

Matador had confidence enough for ten students and an abiding affection for his paddock. He'd endure fumbling and bumbling under saddle for the promise of an hour at grass. The duke couldn't know that. Matador had not earned His Grace's trust, and His Grace had not earned Matador's either.

Philippe was conscientious about removing the bridle and saddle, putting on the headstall, and fastening the crossties. He also went about the grooming—curry, coarse brush, then fine brush—without skimping anywhere. The bliss of a thorough brushing had Matador's eyelids drooping and his head hanging as low as the crossties would allow.

"You've groomed the baby to sleep," Harriet said. "Or tired him out. Soon, I might assign you a different mount."

"You dare not," Philippe replied, draping an arm across Matador's withers. "Mastiff will think he's fallen out of favor with me."

"Mast—Matador is accustomed to his pupils moving on to other mounts." Harriet had never quite got the knack. When her students went to other teachers—always to men, of course—she worried. Would this one learn to sit *straight*? Would that one ever keep her eyes *up*?

"About your compensation," Philippe said, giving Matador's shoulder a scratch.

The horse groaned like a heifer flopping into spring grass.

"You haven't cleaned out his feet." Harriet took a curved pick from a nail on the wall. "I'll do the first one. You'll do the other three."

Horses were trained to lift their feet for this process. The groom had simply to scrape the mud, stones, or manure from the concave area on the bottom of the hoof. Balancing on three legs was difficult for an animal weighing a ton, though, and thus a quick, competent touch was necessary.

Harriet reviewed the basics—run a hand down the horse's leg, tug at the hair on his fetlock, give him a moment to lift his foot, then cradle it like so in one hand...

"And use the pick with the other. *You* put his foot back on the ground. He doesn't get to snatch it away."

Philippe took the pick from her. "He outweighs me by a factor of ten. He gets to do as he jolly well pleases with his feet, and my primary concern is for my toes."

"Then don't bother trying," Harriet retorted. "Don't put your hand on this horse unless you are prepared to tell him exactly what he needs to do to earn your continued goodwill."

Matador was awake now, head up, listening to the conversation. He wouldn't grasp the words, but he'd grasp tone of voice. He'd note the posture of the humans on either side of him and probably even their expressions and subtle changes in their scents.

"I'm to be the duke even in this?" Philippe said. "Hurl orders and thunderbolts, demand proper address, brook no disrespect?"

Was that how he saw the title? "You are to be a person Matador can rely upon to see to his safety and well-being. That means he learns to obey you in small matters so that large matters never become an issue. Right now, you are his groom, Your Grace, nothing more."

Philippe bent to Matador's off foreleg, hoof-pick in his hand. "*Your Grace.*" He ran his hand down the horse's front leg, tugged on the hair in the general vicinity of the fetlock, and nothing happened. "Now what?"

"You have to mean it," Harriet said. "He has to know you're not mucking about for show."

A second attempt yielded the same result. This was Matador's version of a game, getting back a bit of his own. He'd been a good boy for well over an hour, doing exactly as he'd been told. In what passed for horsey thinking, he was owed a bit of sport.

Rotten timing, though.

"I have grooms," Philippe said, stepping back. "They will deal with the distasteful business of scraping manure from horse feet when the need arises."

"So if you're out on a hack, enjoying some solitude in the saddle, and your horse begins to go uneven in front, you'll make him walk all the way back to the barn with a stone lodged against his sole rather than dismount, get out your penknife, and solve the problem on the spot? A stone bruise can lead to an abscess and worse."

Matador shook all over, sending gray hair cascading in every direction. For him, the grooming session was done.

"Now you have me killing my horse before I've even cantered him," Philippe said.

Harriet remained silent.

She'd been waiting for Philippe in some corner of her heart for years. She could afford to wait a moment more. If he gave up now, that would be for the best, because the challenges only increased from this point forward. Philippe had made a good try, but he had reasons for stepping back, and if that was his choice...

Harriet would be eternally disappointed.

"You," Philippe said to the horse, "are a disrespectful back-bencher from the West Riding who doesn't know his place. Lift your damned foot, horse."

Matador obliged—for a moment coming within inches of putting his foot back atop the duke's boot.

Philippe passed Harriet the hoof-pick, and she nearly began to cry. *You cannot give up. Not on yourself, not so soon.*

Then he shrugged out of his jacket, slung it in the direction of a trunk, and caused Matador to shy.

"The hoof-pick, please."

Harriet passed it over.

"Now that I have the attention of yonder pleasure barge," Philippe said, "perhaps he'll condescend to allow me to scrape the manure from between his royal toes."

Matador hadn't bargained on his groom's strength or wiliness.

Philippe went through the routine—bend, run a hand down the leg, tug at the feathers around the fetlock—but at the last instant, Philippe shoved his shoulder against the horse's side.

The gelding lifted his foot as if to step to the side. Philippe caught it and curled the foreleg up to put the underside of the hoof skyward. In a few brisk swipes with the pick, he'd scraped out a pile of dirt.

"Two more to go, horse. I value this shirt more than your dignity, so plan accordingly."

The first back hoof went smoothly. On the second, Matador tried to wrestle his foot away, but he was merely playing, and Philippe was in earnest. The duke finished with the foot easily.

"Well done," Harriet said. "Now you can put him up."

Philippe led the horse to his loose box, which had the generous dimensions of a foaling stall. "If you'd bring me my coat?"

Harriet obliged, though seeing His Grace without benefit of his riding jacket was the best distraction of the day so far.

"The left pocket holds a carrot," Philippe said, unfastening Matador's headstall. "We're to end on a good note, despite our wrestling match."

Harriet had taught him that. End every lesson on a positive note, even if that positive note was merely a smooth halt or a quiet circuit of the arena on a loose rein.

Philippe broke the carrot in half, took a bite, and put the remaining portions on his flat palm. Matador whispered his lips over Philippe's hand. The carrot disappeared amid loud mutual crunching.

"I've done the same on many occasions," Harriet said. "They also like apples."

"I like a fellow who has some backbone," Philippe said, stroking Matador's neck. "I'm not sure I like an insubordinate horse."

"Did you follow every instruction from your tutors and professors? Did you never ask them a clever question to see if they were as learned as they pretended to be?"

Philippe stepped from the stall and closed the latch on the half door. "I challenged them all the time." He leaned near. "You are a good teacher, Harriet. A very good teacher. How do I repay you for your time, your patience, and your wisdom?"

Since undertaking these riding lessons, Philippe hadn't flirted with Harriet, not once. She'd touched him in the course of instruction, and he'd listened patiently to her lectures, as if he'd never kissed her, as if she were in truth the son Jackson Talbot should have had.

She was not that son, though lately she hadn't felt much like a daughter, either. She'd felt like an exhausted drudge, except for when Philippe had kissed her.

He was asking how to repay her for her time, her patience, and her wisdom. Harriet had a few ideas, and none of them involved pounds and pence.

CHAPTER FIVE

Riding lessons created a welter of conflicting emotions for Philippe.

He liked the scent and sounds of the horse barn. That hadn't changed. When he walked into the stable and caught a whiff of hay, manure, and equine, he relaxed, and his cares and worries temporarily roosted somewhere other than his too busy mind.

He did not like that horses, for all their size, could move at blinding speed. A jerk of the horse's head, a startle at a swooping barn swallow, a casual stomp of the hoof to dislodge a fly, and the nearest human could well be injured.

Though perhaps the need to remain ever alert was part of what made Harriet so vibrant.

She was a very competent instructor. Being around her was wonderful—and awful. Philippe did not enjoy his lessons, so much as he endured them. Harriet's tutelage was a barrage of admonitions worthy of Philippe's men of business:

Think ahead.

Eyes up; look where you're going.

For God's sake, the horse is a horse. You must plan ahead when moving that much muscle around the arena.

Riding a horse was too much like being a duke. All responsibility with very little recreation. The moments before and after the lesson were Philippe's reward for heroic sacrifice in the name of inchoate courtship.

He posed the question of compensation to Harriet and then propped a shoulder against a worn beam to await her answer. She was again in breeches and had again lost her jacket partway through the lesson.

"How do you pay me?"

"Coin of the realm, goods in kind, services rendered." Philippe draped his jacket over her shoulders. "Your time is valuable. What do I have that will compensate you for the thankless task of yelling at me for an hour?"

"Let's discuss this in the saddle room."

His spirits rose as he followed her down the barn aisle. If Harriet wanted privacy, then she was inclined to be honest with him, and honesty in private locations could lead to interesting destinations.

"Shouldn't you be returning to the Hall?" Harriet asked right outside the saddle room. "You're having guests for supper."

"Harriet, you needn't be embarrassed to discuss money with me. Contrary to popular perception, a titled man spends much of his time concerned with financial matters. If I'm not meeting with solicitors, I'm reviewing their reports, looking over ledgers, or writing bank drafts. Lady Ada is endlessly corresponding with me about this improvement or that expenditure at the Hall. I'll happily write a bank draft to your father."

Though he'd even more happily put coins directly into Harriet's hand. Talbot would use the money to paint fences, while Harriet might need the money for new fabric.

Or a bonnet. Every woman deserved the occasional new bonnet.

She let him hold the door for her. "I seek a different sort of remuneration from you, Your Grace. Coin is all well and good, but like you, I have requests I cannot make of just anybody."

Philippe stepped closer. "I fully intend to sing the praises of

Talbots' stables when you've repaired my equestrian capabilities. I'll buy my personal mounts from you, credit you with restoring my skills in the saddle, and otherwise recommend your services from here to Mayfair."

Harriet took down a sidesaddle from the rack protruding from the wall. "That is very... That is decent of you, but our reputation is already excellent among the discerning."

Not excellent enough, if the carpets in the house were any indication. Still, Harriet's dismissal was understandable. She didn't circulate among her clients socially and wouldn't grasp what a duke's cachet could do for her father's prospects.

She brought the saddle over to the windows, where afternoon sun fell on a worktable. Philippe had carved his initials on one of the table legs years ago.

"I insist on compensating you," Philippe said, getting the basket of rags and tin of leather balm down from the quarter shelves in the corner. "But I have no idea what a fair wage would be. You must tell me."

He brought the rags and balm to the table, took up a chair, and waited for Harriet to pass him the stirrup leathers and the girths. They'd spent many a rainy day as children cleaning the saddles and bridles. Bridles were the worst, for Philippe could never figure out how to get the dratted things back together.

"Thank you," Harriet said, dipping her rag into the tin. "You mentioned services in kind. I'd like that sort of payment."

"Shouldn't you take off the stirrup before you start on the saddle, Harriet?"

"Of course." She passed Philippe the rag, then the stirrup with its leather attached.

"What sort of service might I render you, my dear?"

Harriet took inordinate care selecting another rag from the basket. "Lessons."

"My Latin is serviceable, my Greek rusty, and my French in good repair. I'm proficient at adding and subtracting numbers in my head, and I know a fair amount of history. Other than that, the only subjects I know intimately are those relating to the dukedom. How many sheep per acre on the upland tenant farms, how many heifers on the home farm, that sort of thing."

Harriet's ears had turned pink. "I need you to teach me how to gain the notice of a gentleman." She chose a second rag and dipped it into the tin.

If she'd entered Philippe to ride at Ascot, he could not have been more unhappily surprised. "What need have you of such skills? Simply kiss the poor fool and he'll be your slave for life."

She swiped a dab of conditioner onto the flap of the saddle. The scent hinted of lanolin and beeswax, and it brought back pleasant memories.

This conversation had abruptly become unpleasant.

"There's more to courtship than kissing, Your Grace. A great deal more."

And how Philippe wanted to share that great deal more with her —though not if she pined for another.

"Harriet, have you been practicing on me?"

She folded the rag and began working the conditioner into the leather. "Not entirely. I know kisses mean little, and I also know yours were meant as only friendly flirtation. I have enjoyed your kisses, but you see how it is with Papa. He's failing, and being female, I cannot run this business on my own, at least not to appearances. My best hope for keeping Papa happy and a roof over my head is to find a man who thrives around horses and coax an offer from him."

She sounded as if she'd enjoy emptying the muck cart on Philippe's boots nearly as much as she'd enjoyed his kisses. Nonetheless, her logic made sense: Harriet loved horses, she loved her father, and she'd sacrifice even her happiness to see to the welfare of both.

Though Philippe was not, by any stretch, a man who thrived around horses. "I have enjoyed your kisses as well, Harriet."

"That's the problem, then, isn't it? If my kisses are merely sweet and friendly, I must be doing it wrong. I'm twenty-eight years old, and I've spent much of those twenty-eight years watching happy couples ride, walk, and flirt their way up and down the bridle path. You've kissed me more than anybody else has. What am I doing wrong?"

He'd kissed Harriet exactly once—well, one and a half times, if a kiss to the cheek counted. Philippe took heart from her admission, though she'd also apparently kissed that rascal with the beautiful eyes.

The one who, like an utter gudgeon, had left Harriet Talbot all alone on the bridle path.

"You shouldn't have to win a man's notice, Harriet. He should notice you out of his own perspicacity. You are a treasure as you are, and offering a fellow favors he hasn't earned won't lead in the direction you deserve."

Harriet dragged the saddle into her lap, flipped it over, and applied the rag to the panel. "How can anybody, no matter how perspicacious he is, notice me when I'm either marching around behind a horse, or wearing the plainest habits I could find the time to sew? I smell of horse, I haven't any fancy jewelry, and my only dowry is this property."

"I like the smell of horses." Philippe could shower her with jewels and had no need of her land, though clearly, the horses came first with her.

She shot him a sidewise glower. "Lavelle, you are not helping."

How he hated when she used his title. "Pretty frocks matter to some, jewelry to others. Are those the sort of men you want to attract?"

"Women are supposed to look like women, not like stable boys. I understand that."

She sounded so aggrieved, and Philippe wasn't much pleased with the conversation himself.

"Give me some time to think about this," he said. "I've never much considered how ladies go about... being ladies."

"I'll finish the saddle," Harriet said. "You'll want to get back to the Hall, so you can prepare for dinner tonight."

Being the duke meant Philippe had nothing to do in preparation for his guests. At the Hall, they only dressed for dinner on Sundays, a custom the late duke had started that Jonas had approved.

"Are you trying to get rid of me, Harriet?"

She ran the rag around the edge of the cantle. "You'll want a soaking bath. Riding can leave one sore."

Well, yes. A single hour in the saddle had been enough to remind Philippe of the peculiar affliction that was saddle soreness.

"I'll take my leave of you, then, though I'll need my jacket."

"Your—? Oh, sorry." She rose and shrugged out of his jacket, passing it to him without meeting his gaze. "You'll do it, though? Teach me about... flirtation? There's nobody else I can ask."

"You've mentioned that." Philippe wouldn't *want* her to ask anybody else. "I will certainly accede to your wishes, but the matter will take some thought. I'll see you at dinner."

He'd arrived to the property with every hope of stealing another kiss, most likely in parting. Now...

"You could kiss me good-bye, Philippe. For... for practice."

Which he apparently needed, if his initial efforts had struck Harriet as merely friendly. He picked up her hand, kissed her knuckles, and got a taste of sheep grease and beeswax for his efforts.

"A significant part of attaching the interest of most men," he said, "is acting as if they haven't attached yours. All quite silly if you ask me, but I'm told that's how the game is played."

He bowed and stalked off, taking minuscule comfort from the fact that Harriet looked disappointed.

❧

"YOUR MIND IS NOT on the game, my friend." Ramsdale moved his queen. "Check."

Talbot scowled at the board. "Checkmate, my lord, and my apologies. You are entirely correct that my thoughts are elsewhere this evening. Did His Grace seem distracted to you at dinner?"

Ramsdale began returning his pieces to their starting positions. "Entertaining does not appeal to Lavelle. He says he feels as if he's impersonating his father or older brother when there's company at the table." He'd said this once, shortly after Lord Chaddleworth's death, but Ramsdale saw the same subtle self-consciousness whenever Lavelle played a ducal role.

Talbot swirled his brandy. "His Grace is a damned fool, if your lordship will pardon some direct speech."

"A fool for seeing the ghost of his father and brother lurking in corners? My own departed sire sometimes plagues me similarly." Though mostly as a bad example. How much worse must it be when the ghosts had been beloved paragons?

"The late duke was a good sort," Talbot said. "He paid fair wages, appreciated a job well done, and was loyal to those who were loyal to him, but if His Grace hadn't ignored his own children, Chaddleworth might not have felt compelled to be the best at everything he turned his hand to."

The black pieces were sorted out, all in their rows. Ramsdale started on the white pieces. "You're saying Chaddleworth sought his father's approval?"

"He lived for his papa's approval. Poor lad detested dogs, but because his father adored those great slobbering Danish hounds, Chaddleworth had to adore them. Philippe, being the spare, did a better job of going his own way—then."

Philippe seemed to be treading a circle, from what Ramsdale could see. "Were you there when Chaddleworth died?"

Talbot cradled his brandy in a palm thick with calluses. "Half the shire was there. Everybody else had sense enough to just trot through the damned gate. Chaddleworth insisted on having a go at the stile, though it was damned foolishness on a green colt in boggy footing. His father had leaped that stile not a month past, but with a seasoned jumper on a dry day. One of the stupidest accidents I've witnessed in all my years as a horseman."

The details of the tragedy had never been bruited about. Even from Lavelle, Ramsdale had heard nothing more than *these things happen* and *such a shame.*

"Foolish young men with more pride than sense tend to have stupid accidents. Had Chaddleworth been drinking?"

"The weather was raw. Of course he'd been nipping from his flask."

Ramsdale knew huntsmen who'd stash full flasks in at least four pockets before shouldering a fowling piece. They would mostly tramp about the moors or quietly drink to the sunrise in grouse blinds. He expected equestrians to have more sense. "Was Lavelle there?"

"The present duke was merely a lad. He had sense enough to stay home when the weather was dirty, though I'm sure he's regretted that."

Ramsdale sipped his own brandy, while Talbot's logic sorted itself out. "Because, like every other person plagued with a conscience, Lavelle thinks if he'd been there, his brother would have been more prudent, more concerned with setting a sensible example."

"Chaddleworth loved his siblings. Of that I have no doubt." A concession, not a compliment.

"What happened to the horse?"

Talbot shifted on his chair. "The old duke wanted him shot, which would have solved nothing. Wasn't the horse's fault, and that colt was special to my Harriet. She'd started him under saddle, raised him from a foal. I bought him back for an exorbitant sum—His Grace did not want to sell me that damned horse—and passed the beast on to a farmer in Surrey who stands him at stud. A fine, handsome bit of horseflesh, overfaced by an ignorant, drunken fool."

Talbot remained a horseman, to his creaky, aching bones.

"Lord Chaddleworth's death is not what took your mind off the game tonight."

Another shift, as if the thickly cushioned seat were a hard plank. "I've been a bit foolish myself."

"Haven't we all?" Lavelle was being foolish as well, and not merely because he hadn't laid his brother's ghost to rest.

"His Grace—His Current Grace, Philippe—asked me to polish his riding skills."

"I did wonder if he'd make good on that threat. I gather that's where his afternoon rambles have taken him?"

Talbot held out his glass. "Perhaps a bit more of this excellent brandy, my lord?"

Ramsdale took the empty glass to the library's sideboard and poured a generous portion. "Does it help?" he asked, passing Talbot his drink.

"Nothing helps, but drink means the pain doesn't matter as much. I got to thinking about your remarks the other evening."

"I was loquacious, at least by my own standards. Which remarks?"

"About Harriet and His Grace."

"The same Harriet and His Grace who spent a long, convivial meal pretending to ignore each other?"

Half of Talbot's fresh serving disappeared. "You noticed that?"

"Lavelle usually has the cordial nobleman impersonation down to a fine art. Tonight, he was barely sociable, and I have occasion to know he esteems Miss Talbot greatly,"—Ramsdale lifted his glass a few inches—"as do I."

"To my dear Harriet." Talbot sipped this time. "She's a country-woman, not raised to split hairs when it comes to propriety. If Lavelle should offer her an arrangement, she'd be foolish to turn him down. The result for her would be a lifetime of security, even if His Grace set her aside after a few years. A father has to be practical, and nobody in this shire would think any the less of her for finding favor with the duke."

Well, no, they wouldn't. The average smallholder was no high stickler, and Lavelle would be discreet.

Then too, Talbot's chess skills might be in decline because the man could hardly see the chessboard. If Harriet had to look after a blind parent, she'd do well to supplement her resources with coin from the ducal coffers.

What a muddle.

"Have you conveyed your sentiments regarding Lavelle to your daughter?" And would Harriet be insulted by her father's opinion? Outraged? Hurt? Ramsdale accounted himself an adequate judge of men, but without the first insight regarding women.

"I did not. When Lavelle came around asking for my help with his riding, I refused him, knowing Harriet was His Grace's only other option, unless he wanted to admit defeat before he started. One can't teach a duke to ride without being in the same arena with him."

"I see." And in the same barn, the same saddle room. "Lavelle claimed he was brushing up his riding so that he might send you some business. He'll brag of your establishment to his London friends, once he's capable of hacking out with them."

Except, Lavelle didn't exactly *have* London friends. Ramsdale's association with the duke dated from public school, where they'd both been far ahead of their peers in Latin and French and thus had needed an advanced tutor in the person of Professor Phineas Peebles.

In London, Lavelle was plagued by sycophants, toadies, and matchmakers.

"Given how those two were acting at dinner," Talbot said, "I doubt His Grace will persist with the lessons, or that Harriet will be faced with an offer of ducal protection. I suppose that's for the best. She's a good girl, my Harry."

About whom Talbot should be worried, for that good girl had no husband to provide for her after Talbot's death.

"I have an idea," Ramsdale said. "I doubt either Lavelle or Harriet would be comfortable with a liaison, and their demeanor at dinner suggests their feelings are already engaged, do they but know it. I'll just give the situation a gentle nudge at the right moment, and all will come right."

Talbot peered at him. "Choose your moment carefully, my lord. I can't have you young fellows fighting any duels over my Harriet. She'd finish off whichever one of you was left standing."

"A sobering thought. Lavelle and I are good friends. We'll not be fighting any duels. Shall I have the carriage brought around for you?"

Talbot scooted to the edge of his seat, braced himself on the arms of the chair, and pushed to his feet. "Please. Do you know what troubles me most, your lordship?"

Ramsdale knew. "Your daughter."

"A father worries about his daughter, of course, but Harriet has taken over the whole job at the stable. It's as if she doesn't realize that one bad fall, one kick, one rambunctious two-year-old, and she could be more incapacitated than I am. She loves the horses, but I wish she had a choice. I took risks, and I'm paying the price for that, but they were risks I chose. I fear Harriet sees herself without options, and that's not right."

Ramsdale held the door for Talbot. "I will consider it my happy privilege to see to it that Miss Talbot has at least one very attractive option other than whatever offer Lavelle might eventually make."

RAIN COULD RUIN A HARVEST, and yet, Harriet prayed for rain.

Her daft challenge to Philippe had changed everything, and with each passing day, Philippe seemed less Harriet's friend and more her ducal neighbor. Rain would have meant the day's lesson was canceled and given Harriet twenty-four hours to ponder the muddle she'd created.

"You have made remarkable progress," she informed her pupil as the second week of lessons drew to a close. "Let's change the routine today and enjoy the bridle path."

Philippe—who had taken over grooming and saddling his mount at the beginning of the week—gave Matador's girth a tug.

"I am ever your obedient servant, madam. If you say that Masticate and I are ready for that adventure, then ready we shall be."

Perhaps in the relative privacy to be had under the oaks, Harriet might renegotiate the terms of her compensation—or collect her first payment.

Jeremy had saddled a youngster for her, a leggy bay gelding rising four. Orion was willing and athletic, but lacked confidence. Matador would be an excellent partner for him on an outing beyond the safety and predictability of the riding arena.

"Your riding has improved day by day," Harriet said as their horses ambled onto the bridle path. "I will understand if you regard your instruction as complete."

Philippe made an elegant picture, even on an unprepossessing fellow like Matador. The dignity of the drum horse shone forth when a duke was in the saddle, and Philippe was a meticulous groom. Matador's long mane lay smooth and shiny against his neck. His tail shone nearly white in the afternoon sunshine.

"My lessons complete?" Philippe replied. "When this is our first outing beyond the nursery? Come, Harriet. You can't be so eager to cast me aside as all that."

The words carried a flirtatious meaning, but Philippe wasn't smiling.

"Are you teasing me, Your Grace?"

He ducked beneath a branch at face-smacking height. "I'm by no means competent on horseback, Harriet. Cantering circles on a leash, trotting over poles... I was a better rider at age ten than I am now. Perhaps other interests demand your attention?"

Now he smiled, but not with his eyes.

"I am busy. You know that. I think we've walked long enough. Let's trot, shall we? Your job is to match Matador's pace to Orion's without either walking or cantering."

That was a fine exercise for taking up half a mile, and Philippe's ability to rate his horse's paces improved over even that short distance. They came to a bridge, and Harriet brought Orion down to the walk.

"They might want a drink," she said, steering her gelding to the bank of the stream. "And Orion needs a chance to regain his wind."

Philippe guided Matador to the stream bank as well. The larger horse slurped at the water, then pawed, making a great splashing mess. Orion danced around, while Matador, having come across a means of entertaining himself, took up pawing with the other hoof.

"Shall we cross?" Philippe asked, while Matador continued to churn the water.

"I suppose we'd better." Harriet sent Orion into the stream, and he obligingly waded across and leaped up the opposite bank.

Matador splashed away.

"Kick him, Philippe. Get his attention."

Philippe gave a stout nudge with his heels, and Matador whisked his tail. "He's like a university boy with his ale." Another, harder kick merited a double whisk of Matador's tail, but then Philippe added a tap to the quarters with his crop, and Matador deigned to toddle into the stream.

"That's better," Harriet said. "He's usually quite well behaved when reminded of his duties. I recall once—"

The churning resumed, and Matador snatched at the reins. Philippe snatched back and tried another kick.

Matador's right shoulder lowered as he braced himself on three legs and used his right leg to further stir up the water.

"Philippe, get off!"

"I'll not be unhorsed in the middle of a damned—"

"He's getting down to roll in the water. Get off!"

Had Harriet not seen the same scenario result in injury, she might have been amused. Philippe kept his head, though, and leaped out of the saddle just as Matador's forehand went down, followed with a heavy splash by his hindquarters.

The horse was under saddle, and this behavior was both dangerous and ill-mannered.

"Get up," Philippe growled, unlooping the reins from Matador's head. "Get up now, you wretched, rude, naughty excuse for a retired plough horse."

Matador's bulk was sufficient that the saddle hadn't yet got wet, but if the dratted beast rolled, he'd likely break the tree, ruin the leather, and—

Philippe delivered a side kick to Matador's shoulder, enough to get the horse's attention, not enough to hurt. "On your feet, or so help me, I'll see you made into dog collars and ladies' reticules."

The kick was unexpected, clearly, for Matador's head flew up.

Philippe glowered at the horse, eye to eye. "I said *now*."

Matador braced on his front legs, then stood, shook hard, and followed Philippe from the stream as docilely as a footman toting parcels for the lady of the house.

"Butterball used to attempt the same stunt," Philippe said. "And then, having thoroughly soaked his girth and ensured the damned thing was loosened by the wet, he'd kick out, buck, swerve, and otherwise get up to dirty tricks in an attempt to dislodge me."

Philippe took the girth up two holes.

Matador grunted.

"I have no sympathy for naughty boys," Philippe said. "My valet will have an apoplexy when he sees my boots, and that is entirely your fault."

A halfhearted swing of a sopping tail was Matador's reply, enough to send droplets directly into Orion's face.

"You handled that well," Harriet said as Philippe led Matador to a sizable rock several yards upstream.

"Thank you." He swung into the saddle. "Shall we be on our way?"

They trotted, they cantered, they observed the rule about always walking the last mile home. The entire time, Philippe's conversation was limited to civilities, and his riding was punctilious. Matador had sought to test his rider, and Matador had failed.

The weather, as if responding to the mood of the outing, shifted from sunny to overcast, and then the breeze picked up.

"Rain on the way," Philippe said as he assisted Harriet from Orion's back in the stable yard. "I'd best return to the Hall, lest I get another soaking."

She should make him look after his horse, she should make him kiss her. "If the rain continues until tomorrow, then your lesson will have to wait."

They stood as if prepared to share a dance, while Jeremy led Orion and Matador into the barn. Philippe's eyes gave nothing away, not relief, not irritation.

He was very much the duke, and while he was an impressive duke, this display of his titled self-possession also made her sad. Where was her friend, and why had he gone away? Had her honesty about the situation at the stables chased him off?

Papa *was* failing, and Harriet *was* without any means of keeping the stables going on her own. She either married someone who could manage the stables or she... the alternatives were too bleak to consider.

"If the weather is foul tomorrow," Philippe said, "then I will pay a call and take tea with you. We will flirt."

He made flirting sound as if it involved balancing ledger books or liming the jakes.

Harriet stepped back. "Will we?"

"I always pay my debts, Harriet, and you asked that in exchange for these riding lessons, I acquaint you with the means by which women attract the notice of men they fancy. My riding has progressed, and you are due payment in the coin of your choosing."

A raindrop landed on his cheek. Harriet expected to watch it freeze before her eyes. "Philippe, are you angry?"

"Vexed."

He was furious. "Over Matador's misbehavior?"

He propped his foot on the edge of a water trough and unbuckled a spur. "What possessed you to put me on a horse named *Killer?*"

If he'd leveled a curse at her, Harriet could not have been more horrified. "I never did."

"Matador, from the Spanish verb *matar*," he said, unfastening the second spur, "to kill, hence the term as used when playing ombre and related card games."

What had this to do with a naughty horse? "I was unaware of the meaning. The horse came to us already named, and the only card game I know is piquet, which I learned from my mother." Papa hadn't the patience for card games, or perhaps he could no longer see the pips.

"The horse," Philippe said, leaning close, "shall henceforth be known as Gawain."

Gawain, the chivalric ideal, defender of women, and a great healer. *Well.* "That is a fine name. I can hang up your spurs for you."

"I will decline that offer. Thanks to my untrustworthy steed, the leather needs conditioning. I bid you good day."

He bowed quite formally and tromped off, boots squeaking with each step.

The sight should have been comical. Harriet stifled the urge to run after him and instead went into the saddle room and cleaned every inch of gear hanging on the wall.

AS SOON AS Philippe gained the bridle path, he took off the boots that would soon give him blisters. Then he threw them, one at a time, at the nearest oak and muttered every English, Latin, and French curse he knew while searching the undergrowth for his wet boots.

Most un-ducal of him. Wet boots would cause his valet to have an apoplexy. Missing boots would likely result in giving notice.

When Philippe had retrieved his footwear, he took off his sodden stockings, stashed them in the boots, and marched in the direction of the Hall. By the time he reached home, he was soaked to the skin—for, of course, forty days' worth of rain had fallen in the space of an hour. He'd also cut his foot on some thorny weed growing where it had no business growing.

"I do believe you are bleeding on Lady Ada's carpets," Ramsdale remarked.

The earl stood on the third step of the main staircase, glasses perched on his nose, a book in his hand.

Philippe handed his boots, spurs, hat, and gloves to a silent butler. "They are my carpets, in point of fact."

Ramsdale came the rest of the way down. "So they are. Are we now bathing out of doors? You could not be more wet."

"Ramsdale, I'm in your debt for pointing out what I might never have noticed. I am indeed more than dampish. For that reason, I will now take myself upstairs and soak in a hot bath."

Philippe headed for the stairs, and Ramsdale fell in step beside him. "Don't suppose you took a fall? Landed on your head?"

"That is not humorous."

Except... it was. To anybody whose brother had not suffered a fatal fall, the comment was clumsily humorous.

"To see His Grace of Lavelle looking like a stray cat caught in a storm is hilarious," Ramsdale said, ascending the stairs with Philippe step for step. "You might have sent for the coach."

"Sent whom? The Talbot grooms are worked to exhaustion, and my lessons only put their schedule further behind. Besides, I was wet before Harriet and I even returned to the barn—or my boots were."

"Your boots are ruined."

"And our friendship might soon follow."

Ramsdale paused on the landing. "I can be packed and down the drive before noon, but if we're to have a grand row, let me say first that it's lovely to see you for once not acting like the damned duke."

Part of Philippe longed to toss Ramsdale down the drive, and his horse with him. That sentiment was so unworthy that Philippe sat on the steps, where he'd no doubt leave more wet on Lady Ada's carpets.

"I am being an ass. I apologize."

Ramsdale took the place beside him, as if peers of the realm routinely perched on stairways. "Your riding lesson put you in a temper. I almost forgot you had one."

So did I. "The perishing horse decided to roll in the stream." And what a ridiculous moment that had been. Philippe bellowing at a ton of mischievous equine, boots soaked, horse splashing merrily away.

"I hope you delivered a sound spanking. No animal under saddle should behave thus."

Philippe's breeches were chamois, and when wet, they clung and chafed in uncomfortable places. "I applied my boot sparingly to his shoulder, once, but Seton, I wanted to kill that horse."

"Ah."

"I wanted to end its life. On the instant, over and over. If I'd had a gun—a gun that hadn't got a soaking—the beast would be cantering across the clouds."

Ramsdale took off his glasses and polished them with the lace of his cravat. "You were angry, understandably so. When was the last time you used foul language and truly meant it?"

The day my brother died. "Not recently."

Ramsdale tucked his glasses away. "You were overdue. I daresay the horse isn't much the worse for the occasion. A few stripes from the crop on a hide thick with a winter coat probably didn't make much of an impression."

"One should never strike an animal in anger."

Ramsdale passed Philippe a silver flask. "Then one dropped his riding crop in the stream."

Well, no, actually. Philippe hadn't lost his grip on his crop. "I delivered a kick to the beast's shoulder, which seemed to offend his dignity more than anything else. What is this?"

"A medicinal tot. Drink up, Your Grace, lest you take a chill. Did the horse even notice that you'd kicked him?"

When a rider fell, he was typically offered a nip from the nearest flask. Philippe had not fallen—from the horse—but he'd lost his temper, which was worse in a way.

"Gawain was affronted. Not sporting, to kick a fellow when he's down."

"I daresay Gawain's grasp of Gentleman Jackson's rules of the ring is somewhat rusty, else he'd not have decided to indulge in an impromptu bath while under saddle. Leave some for me. The day has taken a turn toward winter."

The brandy helped. Sitting on the stairs to review the incident with Ramsdale helped too. "What would you have done in my place? Harriet had little to say once I was back in the saddle. Not a suggestion or a scold." Though she'd had a compliment, and she'd not made light of the potential danger.

"I'd likely have taken my crop to the ruddy beast, because what he did was dangerous and unmannerly. What if he'd tried that mischief on a less experienced rider? What if he'd got up to his tricks when Harriet wasn't on hand to ride for help if you'd been injured? You can't countenance dangerous behavior in an animal that large, or the beast will end up in the knacker's yard."

A valid point. "Jonas would have laughed and made a great joke of the whole thing."

"And the next time Jonas needed his mount's respect," Ramsdale said gently, "what do you suppose that horse's response would have been?"

Philippe lacked the fortitude at the moment to leap that hedge. "Ada will kick me for getting the wet on her carpets. I'm for my bath." He rose, and Ramsdale did likewise.

"The lessons must be progressing if you're hacking out on the bridle path."

"The lessons are progressing." While Philippe's attempt to woo Harriet had gone absolutely nowhere. Tomorrow, he'd advance that cause, and to blazes with hacking out on the bridle path.

CHAPTER SIX

Harriet was nervous, for she'd set out the good china for the second time in less than a month. His Grace of Lavelle had come for tea, and Papa had chosen today of all days to accompany the Earl of Ramsdale to watch some three-year-old filly run a match race in the rain.

That nobody thought Harriet required more than servants to chaperone her with the duke felt like more of an insult than a compliment. "More tea, Your Grace?"

"No, thank you. The biscuits were quite good."

"They were fresh." Harriet stuffed one in her mouth, because that comment was the farthest thing from flirtation. She dipped the remaining half biscuit in her tea and then realized what she'd done and set it uneaten on the saucer. "Excuse me."

Philippe took a biscuit from the tray, broke it in half, dipped a flaky corner into Harriet's tea, and popped the biscuit in his mouth.

"Scrumptious," he said, lowering his lashes. "Delectably sweet and very satisfying."

He chewed slowly, all the while treating Harriet to a coy half smile of the eyes. Her insides went melty, and her brain—well, she hadn't a brain when Philippe looked at her like that.

This was hopeless. The man she loved saw her as only a friend—present farce notwithstanding—and the man she needed to marry would sell their best stock to any strutting lordling with coin and always smell of the stable.

"You are being ridiculous, sir."

He finished his half biscuit. "I'm flirting, Harriet. You are not flirting back, and nothing I've tried today has inspired you to even make the attempt. That's a very pretty frock. Did you wear it for me? Wardrobe is one way a woman practices her wiles on a fellow."

The pretty frock was Harriet's best, the only new dress she'd had time to make last winter. On this chilly day, exposing so much of her décolletage had been an impractical choice.

She plucked a plain wool shawl from the back of her chair and wrapped herself in it. "I don't want to talk about my frock. I haven't any wiles, and I've asked you to address that lack, not strut your manly wares before me to no purpose."

Oh heavens, she was cross with herself and taking it out on him. This whole, doomed scheme had been her idea, and only a bad rider took her own mistakes out on a hapless mount.

Philippe dunked the second half of his biscuit and held it up to Harriet's mouth. "I'm trying, Harriet, to instruct by example, much like when you climb aboard Gawain and make him appear to be every sculptor's perfect equine model. You *show* me what my objective is. Have a nibble."

His tone was so reasonable. He coaxed rather than commanded, but Harriet had had quite enough of biscuits and tea. Time to end this interlude on a positive note, regardless of her blunders and wayward notions.

She appropriated the treat from him and held it up to his mouth. "Your turn."

The duke covered her hand with his own, bent his head, and took the sweet from her, his lips brushing over her fingers.

"You have wiles, Harriet Talbot. You have endless wiles."

Harriet had an endless ache that was equal parts longing, frustration, and despair. She rose, keeping the duke's hand in hers, and took the place beside him on the sofa.

"I do not have endless patience," she said. "My objective is to learn how to go on with a man I esteem. Show me what comes next."

Philippe kissed her knuckles, one by one, and she realized he'd chosen to come for tea precisely because nobody wore gloves when food was served. He'd thought that far ahead, or probably hadn't even had to think. He'd shared many a biscuit with many a woman, and thus he knew what he was about.

Harriet got him by the hair and shifted him, the better to kiss him.

"I thought you wanted to learn flirtation," Philippe said, pulling back two inches. "Flirtation requires patience."

"Training horses requires patience, drat it. Enough drooling on my hand. Kiss me."

Oh dear. Oh heavens. His expression went from surprised, to affronted, to something Harriet didn't recognize but found both fascinating and masculine.

"A gentleman never argues with a lady."

Philippe scooped her into his lap, and what happened after that was a muddle of kisses, caresses, rustling fabric, and lost wits.

This—this *passion*—was exactly what Harriet longed for, and Philippe was who she'd longed to share intimacies with, and yet, everything was all wrong too.

"Stop thinking," Philippe said. "Stop analyzing and labeling, Harriet, as if you're watching a new prospect go under saddle. Just be with me."

When would she have this opportunity again? When would she have privacy—true privacy, not simply a stolen moment in a saddle room—with the duke? When would she be free of the demands of stable boys, customers, horses in training, and riding students?

"You're thinking, Harriet," Philippe said, his hand gliding up her calf. "Your thoughts drum as loudly in your head as the rain beating on the windows, and that is no way to show that you fancy a fellow."

Not a fellow—Harriet fancied *him*. She'd worn her best pair of silk stockings for *him*, but they were only stockings. From the knee up, she was bare beneath her skirts.

"Be with me, Harriet," Philippe said, punctuating his words with a kiss. "Put all else aside and just be with me now."

His tongue danced across Harriet's lips, she gave chase, and then he opened his mouth and invited her to devour him. In the back of Harriet's mind, the voice of reason insisted that Philippe was *demonstrating* passion for her, manufacturing the actions and sensations in response to Harriet's demands rather than out of genuine attraction.

This was not what she wanted, and yet, it was as close as she was likely to get—ever.

Philippe's hand slid higher, above Harriet's knee, and abruptly, she faced a choice.

When approaching a jump on horseback, the likelihood of clearing a sizable obstacle increased when the horse had forward momentum. A trot was all very fine for popping over a low hedge or a small crossrail, but the canter and the gallop were better gaits for bigger challenges.

The problem with a headlong approach to a jump was that the rider had a much smaller window in which to adjust the horse's stride, assess the footing, or gauge the best moment to give the hands forward. The moment for the decision to attempt the jump or change course came and went in an instant.

That instant was embodied for Harriet in the moment when Philippe's hand glossed over her thigh, and he rested his forehead against hers.

"Say what you want of me, Harriet. I'm yours for the duration. You need only command me."

Was he hers, or was he saying what a man did when a woman was about to invite him to compromise her? Hers for the duration of a stolen interlude? For a few weeks?

"Don't stop," Harriet said. "I know only that I don't want you to stop."

~

PHILIPPE WASN'T sure he *could* stop. After years of trying not to notice Harriet *in that way*, years of telling himself that he'd ruin the friendship if he attempted a romance, years of forbidding himself from even improper speculation...

He had Harriet in his lap, demanding that he become her lover. She squirmed, her weight pressing on Philippe's arousal, which seemed to bother her not one wit.

"Harriet, we need to—"

"Don't you dare stop, Philippe. I've waited years, spent forever in that dusty arena going in circles..."

"We need to slow down." Rate their paces, conserve their passion for more than a short gallop. "Sit up, my dear."

She peered at him, blue eyes brilliant and determined, then she scooted higher in his lap. He set her aside and tried to find a coherent thought or two, because Harriet was depending on him to make this interlude go well.

Despite the clamorings of conscience, stopping was out of the question. Harriet would regard a refusal to leap into intimacies with her as a rejection.

"We have time," Philippe said. "We should make the best use of it." For when would he ever again find Harriet Talbot in skirts? If polite society were sensible, they'd dress ladies in nothing but riding habits, where both underskirts and breeches put all intimate decisions in her hands.

But no, fashion dictated that a properly dressed woman have not even clothing to protect her.

"I'd prefer a bed," he said. "Your bed."

Harriet took the pin from his cravat and set it aside. "My bed is little more than a cot. I've slept on it since early childhood. We'll use the guest room."

Why was she sleeping on a damned cot? "Lead on, my lady." Philippe assisted Harriet to her feet, and she allowed it, which was encouraging. They traversed the corridor hand in hand, Harriet leading, and came to a room Philippe hadn't seen before.

A lovely bedchamber, all flowers and light, not a speck of dust to be seen. The quilt, curtains, carpet, and upholstery were spotless and united by a theme of irises—purple, yellow, cream, and green—that was even echoed on the pitcher and basin on the bureau.

"For London guests," Harriet said, "who prefer not to stay at an inn, though we haven't had any of those for several years."

The nicest room in the house went empty. "Move your things in here, Harriet. This should be your room now."

"But the guests—"

He took her in his arms. "Can stay at the Hall. Hospitality is only one of a duke's duties, and heaven knows we have the room."

"Thank you."

She rested her cheek against his chest and went still in his embrace. The headlong impulsivity over the tea tray was replaced for Philippe by a sense of protectiveness that eclipsed anything he'd known in his ducal role. He managed his family's assets, oversaw the estates, waved his title about among polite society, and appeared for state functions.

All of which was mere duty.

With Harriet in his arms and the bed two yards away, duty paled compared to his determination to be what she needed, even if she wanted him to go duking on his way after he'd appeased her curiosity.

"You must help me," he said, kissing her ear. "We've a lot of clothes to deal with, and I'm all thumbs."

She peeked at him. "You want my clothes off?"

"Mine too."

Harriet considered this and apparently found it a fair bargain. "I would like to see you in your glory. You're very fit."

He was also still a trifle sore, but it was the familiar soreness of the regular equestrian, not the beginner's agony.

"Then I will go first. If you'd help with my sleeve buttons?"

He held out his wrists, and she unfastened his cuffs. "Now what?"

"Now you unbutton what's buttoned, untie what's tied, and then I'll do the same for you."

This wasn't necessary. Lovers intent on sharing intimacies often merely pushed clothing aside or undressed as quickly as the situation allowed.

But for Harriet, haste would not do—not yet. Philippe stood quietly while she undid his cravat, peeled his coat from his shoulders, then relieved him of his waistcoat.

"My turn," he said, turning her by the shoulders. By twisting and arching, Harriet doubtless could have unbuttoned her own dress—the buttons weren't that close together—but Philippe enjoyed being her lady's maid.

He learned more about her with each piece of clothing that came off. She preferred buttons to hooks, though buttons were more expensive. Buttons were easier when a lady had to dress herself. Her chemise was so thin with age as to be nearly translucent, but the embroidered hem of delicate violets was in perfect repair. She wore jumps—country stays—that laced in front, which meant Philippe could watch her face when he untied the bow and worked the panels loose.

"This is not a steeplechase, Harriet, where you must clear every obstacle once the starting gun has sounded. We can turn back any time you choose."

"Said the man still wearing his shirt, boots, and breeches."

Harriet had a marvelous figure. This had for the most part escaped Philippe's notice over the years. He'd been too busy appreciating her humor, her affection, her warmth and friendship. But then, clearly, Harriet herself took no notice of her feminine attributes, which was likely why flirtation hadn't come her way in any quantity.

Philippe sat on the bed to pull off his boots and stockings. "My offer stands, Harriet. Don't do this because you've dared yourself to leap the hedge. Do this with me because it's what you want."

He'd dodged the obvious challenge: Do this with me because I am *who* you want. Maybe soon, maybe after today. Not now. When he made her an offer, he'd do so as a man confident in the saddle, however long that took.

She started on the buttons of his shirt. "Are you nervous, Philippe?"

Dukes were never nervous. "A little. I don't want to disappoint you."

Harriet smiled, a familiar, mischievous, Harriet smile. "We are of the same mind, for I have a similar concern. I'm the beginner here, and—"

Philippe had risen and pulled his shirt over his head. "This is part of being lovers, Harriet. The newness and adventure of it. Courage and trust come into it, or they should."

Perhaps this was why Philippe had given up on mistresses, affairs, and flings. Without the courage and trust, the encounter was no more interesting than what went on in the breeding shed of any stable.

"Is this how you go on with London ladies?" Harriet asked, unfastening the first button of his falls.

She'd tried for a flippant tone, but Philippe heard the uncertainty. "There haven't been any London ladies for years, Harriet. Nor Berkshire ladies, Kent ladies, or Paris ladies. They all wanted to bed the duke, and he's a tiresome fellow whose company I would like—at least in this—to escape."

He hadn't put that logic together previously, hadn't worked it out.

Harriet wrapped her arms around him. "I was right to worry about you. I'm sorry, Philippe."

He was aroused—he was all but skin to skin with Harriet, and he'd been honest: no ladies for years.

And he was also touched. Harriet had *worried* about him. She'd known that being the duke was a burden for him, when everybody else—probably even Ramsdale—envied him the title and felt free to turn that envy into jokes and innuendo.

Philippe let himself be held, let himself bask in the pleasure of an intimate embrace with a lady—perhaps the only woman on earth—who would rather he wasn't the Duke of Lavelle, but merely her dear companion, Philippe Ellis.

"Let's to bed, before you take a chill," he said, smoothing a hand over a derriere that had sashayed through his dreams for the past two weeks.

"Your breeches," Harriet said, stepping back.

"Are about to come off." He finished unbuttoning his falls and stepped free of his clothing. Nature had been kind to him, giving him proportions that went well with a delight in physical activity. He was muscular and well built—enough women had said as much—and he was grateful for his good health.

Harriet wasn't looking at his brawn or his build. "You desire me," she said with a small frown. "We've barely kissed, and there you are, as randy as any three-year-old colt."

"And now," Philippe said, tossing the covers aside, "my challenge and delight is to ensure that your desire for me is equally evident." He bowed and swept a hand toward the bed, a ridiculous gesture when a man hadn't any clothes on, but he made Harriet smile.

"I can assure you, that challenge is easily met," Harriet said, bouncing onto the bed. "This is a lovely mattress."

Any mattress Harriet Talbot graced would be lovely. Philippe climbed onto the bed and positioned himself on all fours over her.

"You are lovely," Philippe said. "You are scrumptious, delectable, fascinating..." He punctuated his description—this was not flattery—with kisses, and Harriet retaliated by running her hands all over his back. Her fingers and palms were callused, her touch sure.

No wonder the horses adored her, because that touch was confident and lovely.

Philippe waited for some awkwardness to creep into the bed with them, some sense of incredulity to be sharing intimacies with his friend Harriet, but no such convenient hesitation obliged him.

She switched to caressing his chest, investigating his muscles and bones, brushing a thumb over the hair of his armpits, then over his nipples.

"You are thorough in your investigations, madam."

Her hands went still. "I'm not supposed to be? Am I to lie here with my hands at my sides, sighing at regular intervals?"

This was bravado, and Philippe loved her for it. "You are to make a banquet of me. You are to indulge your every fantasy, your wildest curiosity, and not allow me to leave the bed until your dreams have come true."

What twaddle, though he meant every word. His dreams were certainly coming true—almost.

Harriet did sigh at regular intervals, and her hands ventured lower to caress Philippe's backside, his hips, and then to more intimate territory.

"So soft," Harriet muttered, running her fingers around the head of his cock. "Like a horse's nose."

Philippe laughed, and Harriet smacked his chest. "How will I look Gawain in the face now?" he asked. "The damned horse has a nose the size of Hyde Park."

He kissed Harriet, for making him laugh, for driving him daft. She arched up, her breasts to his chest, and Philippe went on a mission to pleasure those breasts. Harriet's sighs became moans, pants, and muttered orders, until her chemise was lost among the covers, and Philippe was confident she did, indeed, desire him as much as he desired her.

"Now comes the fascinating part," he said, spooning himself around her. "This is where you trust me, Harriet."

She twisted about to send him a rumpled glower. "What was all this other? I thought you were rather enthusiastic about—"

He wrestled her back into his arms. "I was and am interested, as are you. Interested is a fine beginning, but we're about to move on to fascinated." If not obsessed.

Because surely, after an encounter like this, he'd be more than her friend? More than just the man she could trust with her intimate education?

She fit him wonderfully, though Philippe could feel some caution in her, some worry. He shifted back enough—a few inches seemed like half the width of the bed—to rub her shoulders.

"Do you ever get sore from the riding?" he asked.

"Sometimes, if I'm on a horse that's too narrow or too broad, if I work too many youngsters in hand. That feels good."

She made no mention of Philippe's obvious arousal tucked between her legs. He moved on to caressing her back, then to her hips and her backside.

"That should not feel so good," she said as he gave a firm squeeze to rounded muscle. "But it does. Nobody touches me, you know? Papa has to keep his cane on hand at all times, and it's hard to hug somebody when you're afraid of him toppling at any moment."

What a metaphor. Philippe kissed her nape. "I can imagine."

She prattled on, about the challenge of being a woman in a man's role, riding the hedges between eccentric, quaint, and scandalous, about wishing she'd been the son her father wanted and needed and always feeling as if she was falling short.

He gathered her close. "Harriet, you do not fall short. You could never, ever fall short. I respect you above all others and always have."

She shuddered in his arms, though when Philippe kissed her cheek, he tasted no tears. The rain had slackened, and Harriet too became more relaxed. Some burden she'd been carrying, some tension, had finally left the bed.

Philippe drifted his hand lower, over a flat, smooth belly to soft curls, and then to intimate flesh. Harriet lifted her knee, and he touched heaven.

He went slowly at first, listening for bodily hesitation Harriet might be unwilling to speak aloud. He explored, he teased, he soothed and teased again.

And then, when Harriet had settled into a relaxed rhythm, he grew serious. A few minutes later, she was thrashing against his hand, clutching at his hip, and breathing hard, and then she became wonderfully frantic, a woman in the throes of both satisfaction and surprise.

When the storm passed, she rolled over and wrapped herself around him. "Hold me."

Philippe *was* holding her, every inch of him plastered to every inch of her. He held her more tightly. Desire was a demon galloping in his blood, and yet, tenderness soothed that savage beast. Harriet, his Harriet, was warm and naked in his arms, and she'd found her pleasure, well and truly.

"Harriet?"

She kissed his chest.

He waited for the words of affection and wonder, words that confirmed they were not merely friends and would never again be merely friends. Her breathing became even, a soft breeze against his chest. She nuzzled his throat and tucked her leg over his hips.

Then she was asleep.

IN THE WEEK after taking tea with Philippe, Harriet started him over low jumps and on the basic lateral movements. He wasn't a beginner, but rather, an experienced rider regaining his skills. If she'd had to judge, she would have said Philippe had more natural equestrian talent than his brother, Jonas, had had, though Philippe lacked Lord Chaddleworth's outgoing nature.

Philippe was quietly confident, in the saddle and elsewhere.

Not so, Harriet. She was all at sea, waiting for Philippe to invite himself to tea again, or waiting for him to declare that the lessons had achieved their purpose. Lord Ramsdale had started coming along, perching himself on the rail and calling encouragement or making jests as the mood took him.

And even that, Philippe bore with equanimity.

"The harvest ball is tomorrow," Philippe said as he swung down from Gawain's back. "You will save your supper waltz for me, please."

Harriet had used Philippe's cravat pin to secure her stock tie every day for the past week. Today was no different, and still, he hadn't noticed. If a man could misplace a gold pin so cavalierly, perhaps he could *take tea* with just as little thought.

"Half of polite society is in Berkshire this time of year," Harriet said. "Surely a more eligible lady will claim your supper waltz?"

"That's the beauty of the ballroom," Philippe said. "In that one preserve, the gentleman gets to choose. He needn't wait for the lady to show him her favor."

That comment had hidden meaning Harriet was too exhausted and bewildered to parse out. She'd spent her free time moving into the spare bedroom, dodging her father's pointed questions about where they'd house guests and what was wrong with the bedroom she'd slept in since leaving the nursery.

Harriet had held her peace, though Papa had deserved at least a scolding.

"Well, some other lady will have to waltz with you, sir. You'll want to walk Gawain up and down the lane before you put him up. Winter coats take longer to dry, and that was a fine session you put in over the jumps."

The compliment had no visible effect. Philippe ran his stirrups up their leathers and loosened Gawain's girth. "As you wish, but if I don't waltz with you, I won't waltz with anybody, save my sister, with whom I must open the dancing."

He led Gawain away, and Harriet remained in the arena, feeling as if she'd lost some gladiatorial match.

"He rides as if born in the saddle," Lord Ramsdale said, striding up from the rail. "Truly, you have worked a miracle."

"Phil—His Grace has worked the miracle. He has faced his demons and ridden them down. He's more than prepared to hack out in Hyde Park if he chooses to add that to his social schedule."

And Hyde Park was doubtless full of earls' daughters who had more than one nice dress to their names.

"So why don't you look like a riding instructor who's proud of her pupil?"

Why didn't Ramsdale look like a lord? He wasn't blond and slim and polished. He was dark and muscular—as was Philippe—and those characteristics did not entirely ruin his pretentions to grace. What rendered his lordship something of an impostor in fine tailoring was his voice.

Ramsdale's voice was as dark as his countenance, all rumble and growl. His was an eloquence suited to pronouncing dire judgments on hopeless miscreants, for issuing challenges on the field of honor, or reading tragic poetry.

Harriet had the sense he liked his voice, liked being able to open his mouth and speak darkness into any conversation, and yet, she also liked him. Ramsdale was kind to Papa without being condescending, and he was, in a backward, subtle way, tolerant.

"I am very proud of His Grace," Harriet said as that good fellow led Gawain down the lane. "I wish he were more proud of himself."

"Dukes are supposed to be arrogant, not proud. I think that duke is smitten and knows not what to do about it."

"Phil—His Grace would never be arrogant." Though he could be exceedingly hard to understand.

Ramsdale glanced around and leaned nearer. "Miss Talbot, did I, or did I not, hear him announce that he'd waltz with you or no one?"

"Look down your nose at me all you wish, your lordship. You should not have been eavesdropping."

He straightened. "That's a handsome pin you're using to secure your stock tie. I recall giving Lavelle one exactly like it on the occasion of his investiture."

Men. "If you have something to say, my lord, please be about it. Your missishness is keeping me from my responsibilities."

"Good God, no wonder he's in love. In all the world, the word missish has never been used to describe the Earl of Ramsdale. You may account me impressed."

In love? Philippe? Harriet was torn between a desire to swat his perishing lordship with her crop—which he'd probably find amusing —or to take off hellbent down the bridle path at a tearing gallop.

Which would not do. "Be as impressed as you please. I have work to do."

Ramsdale stepped close and put a hand on her arm. "I am trying, in my bumbling way, to matchmake, you daft woman. Lavelle stares off into space for half the evening and barely touches his breakfast. He bolts luncheon so he might be punctual for his lessons, and one must repeat pleasantries to him twice before he realizes he's being spoken to."

Oh, Philippe. "Because his brother died at this time of year, my lord. The duke and Lady Ada are haunted by tragedy in autumn, and when the leaves fall, they recall their brother falling as well."

Ramsdale's gaze narrowed, and still he did not move away. "By damn... by damn you have the right of it, but not the whole of it. Lavelle goes quiet and mopish every autumn, but he's not moping this year. He's brooding. Why won't you waltz with him?"

Philippe was coming back up the lane, and in the stable yard, Jeremy held a new horse, a mare who'd been taken out of training by an injury and who was now ready to complete her education.

"Why are my decisions any of your lordship's business?"

"Because your father and that lonely duke are my friends," Ramsdale said gently. "Because I esteem you greatly, Miss Talbot, and think you'd make a very fine duchess. You come from an old, respected family, your father is a gentleman, you're not without an inheritance, and your land marches with the ducal estate. Why shouldn't you waltz with Lavelle?"

Harriet could have stood against scolding, lectures, high-handedness, or even rudeness. Ramsdale's kindness made her throat tight and her eyes sting.

"When I was attending tea dances, the waltz was not yet popular, my lord. I'll make His Grace look a fool if he tries to waltz with me, for I don't know how."

Didn't know how to flirt, didn't know how to sew the fancier riding habits, didn't know the latest dances. Didn't know how to keep her miseries to herself.

Ramsdale kissed her cheek and winked. "As it happens, I am very proficient at the waltz. I will await you on the side terrace as the ball gets under way. While His Grace is opening the dancing, I will instruct you on the very simple exercise known as the waltz. Name your firstborn son after me, and I'll consider our accounts squared."

He was making a jest, and being generous. "One lesson won't be enough."

"Bollocks, Miss Talbot—if I might be excused for departing from missish vocabulary. The waltz is based on three simple movements, and I could show them to you right here and now, except this footing would be the devil to dance in and Lavelle would skewer me with his ducal glower. You find me tomorrow as soon as you arrive, and I'll have you dancing like a duchess in ten minutes flat."

Harriet should say no. She should laugh and offer a witty riposte, except she knew less about witty ripostes than she did about waltzing.

"His Grace is looking splendidly thunderous," Ramsdale said, patting Harriet's arm. "Promise you'll meet me on the terrace."

"I'll meet you, just to be free of your meddling, my lord." And to learn how to waltz.

Ramsdale kissed her cheek *again* and lingered over her hand, and generally comported himself like an ass, and yet, he'd given Harriet hope.

While Philippe put his horse up, bowed his farewell to her, and gave her not even a backward glance.

CHAPTER SEVEN

Philippe had not wanted to believe his eyes. He'd been behaving like a good student, walking his horse as Harriet had told him to, while Ramsdale had literally hung on her arm, taken liberties with her person, and kissed her in public.

Twice.

Harriet—who suffered no foolishness from anybody—had smiled up at the earl as if he'd promised to grant her every maidenly wish.

And now, as the line of guests outside the ballroom doors stretched down the steps and out into the receiving hall, Philippe must again behave like a biddable gentleman when he wanted instead to kick fragile heirlooms.

Or a certain earl's backside.

Philippe longed to believe something besides mutual attraction explained the affection Ramsdale had shown Harriet the previous day. And yet, Ramsdale's overtures made a bleak kind of sense.

Harriet had been *practicing* on Philippe. She'd never represented anything to the contrary. In the long week since that wonderful interlude in her guest bedroom, she'd not so much as patted Philippe's cravat. She had nattered on about his riding position, gradually raised the crossrails to the dizzying height of two and a half feet, and congratulated him effusively on being able to ride as well as a ten-year-old boy.

Did she even realize that was his cravat pin mocking him from beneath her chin every day?

Like a gentleman, Philippe had not presumed that one liberty granted meant others were welcome.

Because they weren't.

"Your Grace, good evening!" Lady Ambrosia Warminster offered her gloved hand, sank into a slow curtsey, and came up, eyelashes batting away.

"My lady, a pleasure," Philippe said, the same as he'd said a hundred times in the past hour. "I'm so glad you could join us this evening." Though she must have traveled half the day to accept what Ada had doubtless intended as a courtesy invitation.

"I anticipate nothing but joy this evening, particularly if you'll join me on the dance floor, Your Grace. A lady mustn't be forward, of course, but I do so love to waltz."

Other guests in line were smirking at this boldness, and a month ago, Philippe would have yielded his waltz. Give the woman a bit of what she wanted and then disappear among the wallflowers, bachelorhood intact.

Philippe dropped her hand. "You dare me to deprive an entire shire's worth of eager bachelors of the opportunity to turn down the room with you, my lady? I could never hold my head up in society if I should be so selfish. Ah, Mr. Stolzfuss and Mrs. Stolzfuss. I hear your filly did quite well in the rain last week."

Lady Ambrosia went smiling on her way—she had dozens of titles to chase after if that was her game of choice—while Philippe greeted more neighbors and willed the line to end.

The Talbots were among the last to arrive.

"My friends," Philippe said, shaking Jackson Talbot's hand. "A pleasure to see you both."

He bowed to Harriet and maintained his composure by a slim

thread. She wore a new dress, a soft brown velvet trimmed in red piping that revealed to the entire world the lush perfection of her figure.

"Harriet looks a treat, don't she?" Talbot said. "Resembles her dear mother more each day. Come along, Harry. A man needs fortification for socializing in a crowd this big."

When had Talbot become so oblivious to manners where his daughter was concerned?

Philippe possessed himself of Harriet's hand when she was half-turned to follow her father.

"Miss Talbot," Philippe said. "You're looking very well." Delectable, radiant, *beautiful*. "I don't believe I've seen that frock before."

Oh, that was original.

"I restitched one of Mama's dresses."

"Harriet," Talbot barked, leaning heavily on his cane. "I need to get off my damned feet."

Harriet snatched her hand away.

"Mr. Talbot," Philippe said, "surely you don't begrudge me a moment to appreciate the beauty before me?" A moment to work up the nerve to ask Harriet what exactly Ramsdale meant to her?

For Philippe could not believe that the woman who'd admitted him to her bed a week ago felt nothing but friendship for him. She could have easily shared that experience with the earl if he was her choice, and Harriet—Philippe's Harriet—wasn't a woman who proceeded by indirection or intrigue.

"You flatter me, Your Grace," Harriet said, smiling graciously. "I'll wish you a pleasant evening and see you in the ballroom."

She curtseyed, he bowed, and away she went, Talbot leaning on her arm.

The line eventually dwindled, and Philippe vowed that next year, the harvest ball would instead be a picnic. Papa and Jonas had loved all the folderol and pageantry, but Philippe's dancing slippers were already pinching, and the evening had barely begun.

"Has Lord Ramsdale come down?" Philippe asked the first footman when the final guest had been greeted. Thomas had been with the family for ages, and counted as an ally.

Unlike a certain earl.

"Indeed, he has, Your Grace. He's taking the air on the side terrace, where the other guests have yet to intrude."

"I'll fetch him inside," Philippe said. Lady Ambrosia required at least a consolation earl for the opening set, and the dancing would not start until Philippe signaled the musicians.

He slipped down the footmen's stairs to the corridor that led to the side terrace, which was dimly lit to encourage guests to tarry in the better-illuminated back gardens. Philippe at first didn't see Ramsdale, though he should have been hard to miss.

The earl stood in the shadow of an overhanging balcony, a woman before him.

"Had I known what treasures those riding habits kept hidden," Ramsdale said, "I'd have forbidden you to wear them years ago."

"My lord, no man tells me what I might or might not wear."

That was Harriet, and she was being playful—flirtatious even.

"Somebody ought to provide you some guidance," Ramsdale said, standing much too close to her. "Your papa is preoccupied with working you to death, but I daresay some changes are in the offing that will redound to your everlasting joy. Are you feeling more prepared to face the crowd inside? I, for one, would rather tarry out here under the stars."

What manner of discussion was this, and why would Ramsdale anticipate taking a hand in Talbot's business?

Harriet went up on her toes and kissed Ramsdale's cheek. "I am much fortified by your company, my lord, and while I too would prefer the quiet of a pleasant autumn night, we've been away from the festivities too long."

She hugged him—purely, openly hugged him, and Ramsdale sneaked a kiss to the top of her head.

"Then let's away to the ballroom, my dear. Before you know it, the evening will be over and all our tribulations behind us."

Ramsdale offered his arm with a gallantry Philippe hadn't seen from him in London and escorted a beaming, beautiful Harriet down the path that led to the back gardens.

Philippe took a solitary bench at the edge of the terrace and watched Harriet and her swain as they joined other couples strolling beneath the torches.

In the past five minutes, nothing had changed. Philippe was still the Duke of Lavelle.

Ramsdale was still his best friend.

Harriet was still Philippe's... more than his best friend. His dearest friend, his almost lover on one very special occasion. The woman for whom he'd climbed back onto a horse. She had given him something important over these past few weeks, made him take stock of his life and his priorities.

She was truly his friend, and if Ramsdale was her choice, so be it.

Philippe rose, affixed a gracious smile to his features, and returned to the house. Papa had likely never faced such a conundrum, and Jonas would have laughed, or taken charge of the situation with a combination of charm and influence Philippe would never claim and no longer wanted.

The way forward was clear, and a duke might hesitate to take it, but as Harriet's friend, as the man who loved her dearly and wanted only her happiness, Philippe knew exactly what he must do.

"YOUR GRACE IS HAVING A BAD RIDE," Harriet said, trying to keep the consternation from her voice. "They happen. Sometimes we're tired and don't realize it. Sometimes the horse is out of sorts. You must not take it personally."

Gawain was being contrary, which made no sense, though often a horse grasped emotions a rider was trying to ignore. Philippe had been courteous and pleasant through the grooming and saddling, but from the first moment he'd set a boot in the stirrup, he and Gawain had been having a difference of opinion.

While Harriet had... not even a difference of opinion. Ever since the ball last week, her friend Philippe, her lover Philippe had disappeared. The Duke of Lavelle had taken his place, and the loss cut her to the heart.

"Let's try a few jumps, shall we?" Philippe suggested. "Perhaps Gawain needs to work some fidgets out?"

Gawain wouldn't know a fidget if it had been braided into his tail.

"You want to jump?" Harriet asked. "I was under the impression you dreaded work over fences."

Philippe patted Gawain's neck. The horse switched his tail and stomped at imaginary flies. "Gawain is a trusty fellow. We've managed adequately thus far. Perhaps he's bored and seeks a greater challenge."

At the ball, Philippe had partnered a different woman at every dance. That was polite behavior for a host, of course, but why did all his partners have to be beautiful, fashionable, and from the best families? Was that Philippe's idea of a greater challenge?

"Gawain is no longer young," Harriet said, dropping a rail from the nearest jump. "He can start out with a modest effort and work his way up, the same as he always does."

Harriet was no longer young, no longer a girl. She ought to have the backbone to simply ask Philippe why, when the supper waltz had come around, he'd merely suggested that Ramsdale stand up with Harriet, while Philippe had partnered some Amazonian creature who appeared to use shoeblack on her hair.

"Trot this rail a few times," Harriet said, stepping out of Gawain's path.

Philippe and Gawain bickered their way over the low rail three times, though Gawain never quite refused. Philippe's timing was off, though, and that was unusual.

"Raise the damned bar," Philippe said. "Gawain isn't paying attention."

This, in fact, might have been true. The lesson horse's greatest woe was boredom, and trotting crossrails was tedious in the extreme. Harriet added a second jump, raised the bar on it a few inches and silently willed the horse to settle to his work.

Gawain seemed to have forgotten where his feet were. He took off too close to the first jump, then too far away. He ignored the second jump until the last minute and then charged through the line as if the horses of hell were trying to steal his dinner.

"Philippe, I really think that's enough for today. Sometimes, the best you can do is put the horse away and hope for a better ride tomorrow."

"He's being contrary," Philippe said, trotting Gawain in a circle that included a small, ponderous buck. "Raise the damned bar, and we'll end on a good note if I have to toss him over the jump myself."

On the next circle, Gawain kicked out, but he was such a large, well-padded animal that even this misbehavior posed no danger to the rider.

"You haven't jumped more than two and a half feet," Harriet said. "Are you sure?"

"For heaven's sake, Harriet. How many times have you told me that it's easier to jump three feet than two?"

There came a time to raise the bar, and no instructor knew for sure when the pupil was ready. Philippe wasn't riding well today, but then, perhaps *he* was bored—ready to be through with his instruction, even.

"That's three feet and three inches," Harriet said, moving the rail upward. "Gawain can handle that height easily. Try it at a forward trot."

Philippe adjusted his reins and guided the horse in a circle, but as Gawain came out of the circle, he broke into the canter. Harriet kept her peace, rather than hollering adjustments when Philippe might already be coping at the limit of his abilities.

"Drat you," Philippe yelled as Gawain sped up.

Oh, no. Oh, dear angels. "Ride around!" Harriet called, heart sinking. "Pull him in a circle!"

Philippe ignored her, though he wasn't in position. Gawain took off in a mighty leap half a stride too soon. He also chose to jump a good foot too high, and in the middle of his airborne arc, he twisted his back, sending Philippe flying into the dirt.

The duke landed in a heap, a puff of dust rising around him. Jeremy, who'd been wheeling a load of muck to the manure pit, came clambering over the rail, and Harriet ran the breadth of the arena to kneel in the dust beside her duke, and still, Philippe did not move.

"YOU'RE AN IDIOT," Ramsdale said, pacing before the breakfast parlor's fire. "A very great idiot, and if you don't soon show some sense, I will decamp for London and let all and sundry know that the Ellis family has fallen prey to a strain of lunacy."

Philippe was not an idiot, unless being in love qualified. "You must do as you see fit, Ramsdale, though I'm sure the Talbots will miss you. I'm for a walk."

"What you call a walk these days would cover half of Spain. Why not ride with me? Everybody falls off from time to time—everybody—and we get back on, Lavelle."

Being angry with Ramsdale was difficult when he was determined to be so loyal, and in truth, Ramsdale had done nothing wrong.

"I've had that discussion with Miss Talbot," Philippe said. "She was desperate for me to get back on the horse, but my mind is made up. Horses are dangerous and smelly. They attract flies and drain a man's exchequer. I'm done with horses."

In truth, Philippe missed his rides with Gawain, and if anything plagued his conscience, it was the look of reproach in the beast's eyes as the stable lad had led him away from Philippe's last lesson.

"For reasons beyond my humble ken," Ramsdale retorted, "I'm

sure Miss Talbot has missed you, but you haven't so much as paid a call on the Talbots since your fall."

"Miss Talbot is quite busy. Perhaps you hadn't noticed how hard she works to keep her father's stables in business, but I won't bother Miss Talbot when she has other tasks to see to."

Leaving the lady to her horses had been rather the point. A clean break, cede the field, stand aside so that two people in love might find their happily ever after—or whatever version of love one of Ramsdale's nature ascribed to. Harriet would *pity* Lavelle if he explained that he'd had aspirations in her direction, and her pity would have unhorsed his pride more thoroughly than Gawain had tossed him bodily in the dirt.

No need for messy explanations or awkward scenes.

Like this one.

Philippe patted his lips with the serviette. "We have few beautiful days left before winter arrives. If you should take the bridle path in the Talbots' direction, please give them my fondest regards, but don't expect to see me on horseback ever again."

Philippe had hiked the bridle path in both directions for miles. His steps always took him past the Talbot property, and most of the time, he tarried behind the hedges as Harriet rode one horse after another, coached the grooms, or stood by while her father and a client watched sale stock put through their paces.

Ramsdale visited Jackson Talbot frequently—or Jackson and Harriet, both.

Soon there wouldn't be enough leaves left to conceal Philippe's spying, and that was for the best. Regardless of how a rejected swain behaved, a duke did not lurk in hedgerows.

"If you're determined to tramp over half of Berkshire, I'll tramp with you," Ramsdale said. "We should pack some comestibles, for the pace you set leaves a man peckish."

"I'm paying a call on my nephews," Philippe said. "By this time next year, they'll be at public school. I'm their guardian, and a consultation with their tutor is in order. You'd be bored witless."

A local widow had presented Jonas with twins before Jonas had completed his university studies, and they, along with two girls—one each in Kent and Sussex—were Philippe's responsibility. He'd looked in on the boys within two days of returning to Berkshire, but not since.

They were lively, dear, and he missed their high spirits.

"I forget how many little darlings Chaddleworth left you. Three? Six? It's a wonder he didn't work his wiles on Miss Talbot, though I suppose he knew you'd hold him accountable for that folly."

Philippe set aside half a plate of hot, fluffy eggs. "Ramsdale, are you trying to get yourself evicted? One mustn't speak ill of the dead."

"Admitting the truth is not speaking ill, and your sainted brother was a hound. Thank God, you never sought to emulate him in that particular."

Just the opposite. Philippe considered that insight as he finished a lukewarm cup of tea. "Perhaps I did learn from my brother's bad example. If you're intent on burdening me with your company when I visit the boys, then meet me at the front door in fifteen minutes."

Ramsdale took the place at Philippe's right and appropriated the unfinished plate of eggs. "You are daft, hiking all about the shire at a time of year when the weather changes by the minute. We could ride the distance in a quarter of the time."

Well, yes, they could, and a pleasant hack it would be. "I tried getting back on the horse, and despite Miss Talbot's best efforts, I failed. A fool persists at a doomed endeavor, a wise man gives up and accepts what cannot be changed."

Ramsdale gestured with his fork. "Very profound. Perhaps you should make that the family motto. These are superb eggs. You will please not hold supper for me. I'll be dining with the Talbots this evening, for Mr. Talbot and I have much to discuss, and I'll wish you the joy of your perambulations."

This casual announcement, made between bites of egg—bites of Philippe's eggs—was a death blow to Philippe's faint, ridiculous hopes where Harriet was concerned. Ramsdale planned to closet himself with Jackson Talbot. Given what Philippe had witnessed the night of the ball, the agenda for their conversation was all too easy to imagine.

"I'll wish you a pleasant day and let Lady Ada know you won't be joining us this evening."

At least Ramsdale had spared Philippe the necessity of asking an old friend what his intentions were toward a dear friend.

A dear, much-missed friend. Who'd almost become Philippe's lover... and his duchess.

Breakfast with Ramsdale was sufficiently unsettling that even walking five miles to call upon the widow and her offspring wasn't enough to raise Philippe's spirits. He went two miles out of his way to pick up the bridle path on the return journey, and there he found a measure of peace.

Jonas might well have seduced Harriet.

Jonas might have been up to eight by-blows by now, had he lived.

Jonas should have known better than to attempt that damned stile, but at Philippe's last riding lesson, he'd finally gained some insight into his brother's life and death. Riding was a risk, but the greater risk was in living a life without challenge, a life that refused to grapple with the difficult questions.

Besides, the first thing Jackson Talbot had taught Philippe long ago was how to take a fall safely, and Philippe had learned that lesson well.

If Philippe loved Harriet—and he did—then her happiness mattered more than his own. If Philippe loved Ramsdale—and he more or less did—then honor demanded that Philippe not question his friend's claim on the lady's affections.

That conclusion wasn't ducal, wasn't even particularly gallant, but simply where common sense and honor led.

Philippe had traveled a mile down the bridle path when he spied a riderless horse cropping grass beneath a stand of oaks. The bay gelding's reins were drooping over its neck, which was bad news all around. A hoof could get caught in those reins, a leg tangled.

"Halloo, horse," Philippe said as he approached the animal. The last thing a loose horse wanted was an excuse to spook. "Having a light snack, are we?"

The horse's head came up abruptly, and it dodged off a few paces.

"You're a fine, big specimen," Philippe said, "and you look familiar, but you're not too bright a fellow if you intend to jaunt off across the countryside with your reins dangling."

The horse took another mouthful of grass, keeping an eye on Philippe all the while.

This could go on for the rest of the day, until the horse either galloped off down the bridle path or stepped on a rein and fell in a heap. A day that had begun sunny and mild was turning overcast, and Philippe was still several miles from home.

Several miles from anywhere, given that this little corner of Berkshire was more woods than cultivated land.

"You've had your snack," Philippe said, walking right up to the horse. "Time to be a good boy and tell me what you've done with your rider."

In the face of confident handling, the horse stood docilely. Philippe got the reins sorted out and took stock of the surrounding terrain. No coat of sweat suggested the gelding had galloped any distance, but a relaxed trot with time for the occasional graze could still cover five miles in an hour.

Philippe examined the saddle, lifting the flaps and peering behind the cantle. A stylized coat of arms had been burned into the leather beneath the offside flap—a ram's head, caboshed.

Unease wafted on the freshening breeze. Philippe got a firm grip of the reins, because he was about to shout at the top of his lungs and the horse would doubtless startle.

"Ramsdale! Ramsdale! Where the bloody hell are you?"

CHAPTER EIGHT

The Talbot conveyances were humble but well maintained. Harriet had finished the last ride of the morning when the ancient coach rumbled around from the carriage house, Jeremy at the ribbons.

"Is Papa going somewhere?" Harriet asked, shading her eyes to peer up at the groom.

"Aye, miss. Got a note from the Hall, and said to have the carriage ready at noon."

The coach mostly collected dust. If Harriet had errands to run, or the housekeeper or cook needed to attend the market, they took the dog cart. But then, clouds were gathering and the wind had picked up half an hour ago.

"Have you any idea where Papa's off to?"

Papa himself came thumping down the steps from the front porch. He'd troubled over his appearance, combing his hair, donning his top hat, and scaring up a pair of clean gloves. He dressed thus for services and for calling on his banker or his solicitor.

"Has Ramsdale bothered to come by yet?" Papa asked. "His lordship assured me he'd be here well before noon."

"I haven't see him. Are you and his lordship paying calls this afternoon?"

Papa pretended to inspect the coach, though at this distance, he was unlikely to see details. "Aye, we're off on a business appointment."

Harriet had been preoccupied lately—missing Philippe, wondering what she might have done differently at his last lesson, wondering what in blazes had gone amiss between them—but her father's sheepish expression got her attention.

"Where are you going, Papa?"

"To see a man about a horse."

When Harriet's mother had been alive, that phrase had been a euphemism for everything from a trip to the jakes, to a ramble down to the village tavern, to an actual transaction involving an equine.

"With Lord Ramsdale?"

"Aye, if he'd deign to keep his appointments. He should be here by now."

"Let's sit on the porch while you wait for him," Harriet said. "Jeremy, you may walk the lane a time or two while my father and I await his lordship."

Papa's ascent of the steps was uneven. He used his right foot to gain a stair, then brought the left even. Up with the right, even with the left.

"Your hip hurts," Harriet said. "You will take some willow bark tea tonight if I have to pour it down your throat myself. Am I to know the nature of your business appointment?" For the past year or so, she'd lived with a gnawing fear that Papa would sell the stable. She wouldn't miss the endless work, but she'd miss the horses.

She'd miss knowing she had a livelihood very much, and in a hopeless way, she'd miss knowing she had an inheritance to bring to any union.

Not that she'd be marrying anybody. Philippe had obliterated any schemes in that direction. He'd given her some lovely memories, along with an inability to consider making similar memories with any other man. Ever.

Ramsdale was a keen horseman, had means, and had visited the area often. He might well be accompanying Papa to a call on the banker in Reading.

"Where exactly are you off to, Papa?"

"Please do not think to intrude into the financial aspects of running this property, Harriet," Papa said. "I can't stop you from taking the horses in hand, and I mean no criticism of your domestic skills, but I am the owner, and you are my daughter. I'll manage this stable as I please."

Harriet had ridden many—many—a fractious horse. When a beast many times her size decided to turn up sullen and contrary, she knew better than to allow its bad behavior to upset her. She corrected the horse's errors firmly but without rancor and offered it a chance to do better next time.

She ought to have reminded Papa of his manners long, long ago. "When I inquire as to your destination, I am hardly wresting the ledgers from your grip. If you're making decisions that affect me, then I have a right to know of them."

Though as to that, Papa's entries in the ledgers had become all but unreadable. Harriet had taken to reconstructing the monthly figures by virtue of studying the tradesmen's bills, the wage book, and the receipts herself.

And those figures were sometimes discouraging.

"I provide for you more than adequately," Papa replied, "and no daughter of mine will presume to insert herself into a domain wherein for nearly forty years I have—"

Harriet rose, because her own hips ached, because her heart ached, and because *Papa was wrong.*

"I am your daughter," she said. "Also your barn manager, trainer, chief groom, breeding consultant, groundskeeper, hostess, nurse, veterinarian, foaling expert, assistant farrier, equine dentist, harness repairer, and—because you are too stubborn to purchase a pair of dratted spectacles—also your eyeglasses. I have long since intruded into the male sphere, and you were the first to boost me into that saddle. You own this stable, you do not own me."

"Harriet Margaret Talbot, you will not take that tone with me."

The coach had lumbered down the drive and with it went the last of Harriet's self-control.

"I am tired, Papa. I stink of horse all the time. I no longer have a nice pair of boots because the sand in that arena has ruined them all. I spent so much time repairing bridles, saddles, and harnesses last winter that I have barely anything decent to wear to services. I haven't embroidered a pretty handkerchief since Mama died, and now you are about to sell the stable that I have all but married myself to. The least you can do is warn me."

The jingle and creak of the wagon faded, and a cloud of dust slowly dissipated over the drive.

Harriet made unruly horses, cheeky grooms, and presuming customers mind their manners with her. Why hadn't she demanded the same respect from her own father? Like Gawain with an inconsiderate rider, she should have tossed Papa's high-handedness to the dirt long ago.

Papa rose shakily, balancing both hands on the head of his cane. "I am taking on a partner, Harriet. Lord Ramsdale has funds to invest, a sharp eye for young stock, and a fine appreciation for a well-run operation. You have nothing to say to it. We're meeting with the solicitor this afternoon, if his lordship hasn't cried off."

A partner.

Harriet did most of the work and much of the worrying that kept the stable from failing, and Papa was *taking on a partner,* everything but the handshake already in place.

"I see."

He brushed a glance over her. "What do you see?"

"I see that I am through being helpful, biddable, good-natured, meek, and dutiful. I see that this operation has been well run for the past five years because I've run it, despite your insistence on selling good horses to bad riders. Despite your unwillingness to expand our breeding program. I wish you and his sharp-eyed lordship the joy of your partnership. I'm off to see about finding a partner of my own."

She passed him her riding crop, sat long enough to remove her spur, and tossed her gloves at his chest for good measure.

"Harriet, where are you going?"

"To the Hall. I've tried being patient. I've tried being a *good friend*, being understanding, and tolerant, and saintly, but it won't wash, Papa. Philippe owes me—and Gawain—an explanation, at the very least, and I intend to have it, even if that means I never set foot in the Hall again."

Papa thumped his cane against the porch planks. "The damned man took a fall, Harriet. Leave him his pride and let good enough be good enough."

"Good enough is *not* good enough," Harriet said, marching down the steps. "A cot that grew too small fifteen years ago isn't good enough. Waltzing with the earl isn't good enough. Selling a gorgeous mare to that bumbling toad Dudley isn't good enough. And kisses and pleasure aren't good enough either."

Papa shook the crop at her like an admonitory finger. "Young lady, you will control your words lest I—"

"I'm not a young lady, Papa. At my age, Mama had a ten-year-old daughter. Philippe will listen to what I have to say if I have to kick, buck, snort, strike, bite, paw, clear the arena, and—who on earth is that?"

The bridle path curved around the Talbot pastures and paddocks, and for much of the year, the way was shrouded in greenery. As autumn advanced and the leaves fell, riders traversing the path became visible, mostly for the simple fact that they were moving objects against a backdrop of fixed trees and fences.

Somebody was coming around the curve at a dead gallop.

"He's going to take the stile," Papa said. "Going to aim that beast straight for our lane."

The rider's form was excellent. He stood in the stirrups, balanced over the horse's withers to free its back from his weight, hands moving to follow the rhythm of the horse's head. He wore neither coat nor hat, which made his horsemanship more evident.

"They make a handsome pair," Harriet said, then an odd shiver traveled over her arms. "That's Philippe, Papa. That's Philippe, and that gate is nearly four feet—"

For a silent eternity, Harriet's heart went airborne as fear, hope, and admiration soared with Philippe's horse.

"Well done!" Papa exclaimed when the horse landed as nimbly as a cat and cantered on around the far end of the arena. "Foot perfect and right in rhythm."

"But, Papa, *that's Lavelle*. His Grace promised me he'd never sit a horse again, and he just cleared a four-foot gate at a gallop and made it look easy."

Papa sat back down, using his cane and the table to brace himself. "Well, then, the duke must want to talk to somebody rather badly. Do you suppose it could be you?"

"I certainly want to talk to him," Harriet said, taking off at run for the stable yard.

When she got there, and Philippe had leaped from his heaving horse, Harriet didn't say a word. She simply hugged him, and hugged him and hugged him, until he put his arms around her and hugged her back.

"WHAT WERE YOU THINKING," Harriet shouted, once the stable lad had led Ramsdale's horse down the drive. "Jumping an obstacle like that on a horse you're not familiar with? You fell not two weeks ago, before my very eyes and over a much smaller jump in good footing. You could have been hurt. You could have been killed! Philippe, you c-could have been k-killed."

She went from shaking him—or trying to—to squeezing Philippe so tightly he could barely breathe.

"That gelding is nothing if not athletic," he said, speaking as calmly as he could when his lungs were ready to burst. "We hopped a few stiles in the last mile, and I knew he was up to the challenge, but, Harriet, it's Ramsdale who's taken a fall. He said he was merely winded, but I know he took a knock on the head, and I fear a worse injury."

"Hang Ramsdale," Harriet retorted, pulling back but keeping a good grip on his arms. "You rode like a demon, Philippe. Like a winning steeplechase jockey when you swore to me..." Her eyes, which had been filled with concern, narrowed. "You swore to me you were done with horses forever. You had tried and failed, and nothing I could say, threaten, or promise would change your mind. You *gave up.*"

Jackson Talbot thumped down the porch steps. "What's all this about? Good form, Your Grace. Harriet, let the man go."

"Send the lads to assist Lord Ramsdale, Papa. He's taken a fall, and I will not turn loose of His Grace until I've had an explanation."

Talbot's eyebrows climbed nearly to his hat brim. "Ramsdale's taken a tumble?"

"I left him sitting beneath an oak where the bridle path, the woods, and the stream all meet east of here," Philippe said. "He seemed right enough, if a bit dazed, but the clouds are gathering, and he's miles from shelter."

"And you left him your coat," Harriet said. "What if it had started to rain, and you on a strange horse, in bad footing, no coat... I taught you better than this, Philippe."

She was scolding him, also stroking the lace of his cravat and calling him Philippe.

"You are concerned for me," Philippe said.

"Of course she's concerned," Talbot said. "Else she'd not be so ill-mannered as to use your Christian—"

Harriet left off petting Philippe's chest and faced her father, hands on hips. "Hush, Papa. I can speak for myself. Your business partner is sitting beneath a tree nearly three miles away, possibly addled and injured and storm on the way. Hadn't you best concern yourself with *him?*"

Philippe slipped an arm around Harriet's waist. "I'd be obliged if you'd send Ramsdale some aid, Talbot. I can continue on to the Hall, but your property was closest to his mishap, and I'd hoped to count on my friends for assistance."

Harriet stiffened beneath his arm.

"Of course," Talbot said. "Cooper! Hitch up the dog cart. Tell Jeremy to put up the coach and get word to the solicitor that I'll have to reschedule my appointment. Lerner, you go down the bridle path on horseback. Earls can't be left out in the wet or they grow contrary."

A raindrop landed on Philippe's cheek in the midst of Talbot's stream of orders.

"You come with me," Harriet said, wrapping an arm around Philippe's waist and urging him in the direction of the barn. "I have a few things to say to you, and I want to say them in private."

Philippe had things to say to Harriet as well—a question to ask, rather. They left Talbot barking more instructions to the grooms as the raindrops organized into a cold drizzle. Some considerate soul had lit the stove in the saddle room, though, so it was warm, which—now that Philippe was no longer riding at a gallop—felt good.

Harriet's hug, when he'd dismounted had felt wonderful.

"What did you want to say to me?" Philippe asked when Harriet had closed and locked the door. The look of her—hems wrinkled, the toes of her boots dusty, braid coming a bit undone—warmed his heart.

"I've missed you." They spoke the same words at the same time.

"Ladies first," Philippe said, gesturing to the worn sofa.

Harriet took a seat, very much on her dignity. "Can you, or can you not, acquit yourself adequately on horseback?"

"*That's* what you wanted to ask me?"

She nodded, gaze solemn.

Philippe took the wing chair—he did not dare sit beside her—and now, when his arse was planted on a flowered cushion, he felt as if he faced an obstacle too high and wide to negotiate confidently. He could continue to dissemble, to stand aside for true love, or he could trust Harriet with the truth.

"I can acquit myself adequately on well-trained mounts," he said. "I have had the benefit of good, patient instruction, and my skills rest on a solid foundation."

Harriet bent to unlace her boots. "You rode like Lord Dunderhead's incompetent older brother at your last lesson. What was that about?"

The sight of her removing her footwear—her old dusty boots—was distracting. "I saw you with Ramsdale, Harriet, at the ball. He's clearly smitten, and I'm happy for you. I hope he offers for you and spares me the burden of calling him out."

She set her boots aside. The soles and the uppers were coming apart near the toes, a common injury to riding boots.

"Ramsdale is smitten, and you are happy. What about me, Philippe?"

She was not happy, but beyond that, Philippe dared not venture. "You are Harriet, my dearest Harriet, and if the earl is your choice, then I owe you both my best wishes."

But if Ramsdale was *not* her choice? A chat on a secluded terrace wasn't the same as an afternoon spent without clothing on a wide and comfortable bed, was it?

"Did it not occur to you, Your Grace, that I might have required some practice at the waltz? London ways are slow to catch on in the country, and I've been too busy waltzing with equines. Ramsdale was instructing me, or humoring me. I wanted to do you credit when I stood up with you, and then you couldn't be bothered to ask for my supper waltz."

This was... this was very bad, and possibly wonderful.

"You never granted me your supper waltz. I assumed Ramsdale—"

Harriet smacked his arm. "Why must you assume anything when I'm right here, where I've always been? If I'm your dearest Harriet, you can ask me. You can simply put a question to me—not to Ramsdale, or Papa, or Gawain, for pity's sake." She jabbed her thumb at her chest. "Ask *me*."

Do you and Ramsdale have an understanding? But that wasn't what Philippe wanted to know. Understandings were private and not exactly binding.

Do you love me? She'd say yes. That question was almost cowardly, because he knew she'd say yes.

So Philippe aimed his courage and his heart at the most important challenge he'd ever faced. "Will you marry me?"

Harriet sat very tall, and very still, like a skilled whip at the start of a carriage race. "I beg your pardon?"

"I love you. I have always loved you, and when I finally set aside the notion that I must martyr myself to my brother's sainted memory, or to the title, or to polite society's inanities, I see that you have always been in my heart. You have never treated me as anything less than your honored friend. You have had faith in me and been patient and kind, and then I kissed you, and... God, Harriet. I do know what it's like to take a bad fall."

She put a cool hand to his temple. "Does your head pain you?"

"Not in the least. Twenty years ago, your dear papa made sure I knew how to take a mere tumble into the sand. My heart pains me. I saw you with Ramsdale, overheard your conversation with him, and realized you would be better off with a man who could ease your burden here, not take you away from who and what you love."

She was frowning at the worn carpet, and frowning was bad.

"You appeared to return his affections," Philippe went on, "and it's as if the breath left my body and hasn't returned. I can't think, I can't sleep. I am nobody's Philippe. Nobody's friend. Nobody's dearest anything. I ceased in some vital way to function, as if I left the best of me in the sand of your riding arena."

Harriet drew her feet up and wrapped her arms around her knees.

So much for the efficacy of an impassioned proposal, and yet, affection for her—bottomless, admiring, desiring affection—welled in

Philippe's heart. He would always love her, and that would always give him joy and cause him an awful ache.

"Say something, Harriet. You told me to put my question to you, and that means you owe me an answer."

She turned her face, resting a cheek on her knee, her expression cross. "I'm making up my mind, choosing my words, trying to train myself out of a bad habit. If I'm to answer with anything other than 'Yes, Papa,' or 'Of course, Philippe,' this will require some effort on my part."

Philippe wanted desperately to kiss her, but she'd probably whack him, and then he'd want to kiss her even more.

"Tell me if you'll be my duchess," Philippe said. "We can sort the rest out from there."

Her glower became ferocious. "No, I will not be your duchess."

HARRIET WAS ANGRY, and not with herself. Papa's decision to take a partner—meaning to bring a titled lord with money into the business, because what mattered hard work and loyalty—and the notion that Philippe had fallen on purpose at his last lesson left her upset in ways too numerous to list.

She and Philippe had much to sort out, but as with any spirited mount, she would begin as she intended to go on.

"A duchess is not a prime filly," Harriet said, "to be owned by this or that lordling, raced by this or that stable. She's a person married to a man who has a title. If I marry you, we will be husband and wife, but I hope I don't consider you *my duke.*"

Philippe stared across the room, at the rack of saddles and bridles neatly arranged on the wall. "Is that a yes, Harriet, or a no?"

She dropped her feet to the floor and smoothed her skirts. She'd told Philippe to ask her, but the habit of answering for herself would take some time to develop.

"I love you," she said, taking him by the hand, and drawing him to sit beside her. "You have been in my heart forever too, and when you took me to bed... I will never be the same, Philippe. I like that. I like that I chose to share that with you, despite propriety, despite common sense. I want to marry that man, the one who can inspire me to reach for my heart's desire, to step off the bridle path and gallop the fields and forests."

Philippe slipped an arm around her shoulders. "I want to be with the woman who gave me the confidence to get back in the saddle and to pitch myself from it. The woman who made me think about whether I'm living my life or trying to live my brother's. I'll never be an avid horseman, Harriet."

"I'll never be an avid duchess."

He took her hand. "Fair enough. I'm not an avid duke, and with you, I'll never need to pretend otherwise."

The rain began to beat against the windows in earnest, and Harriet tucked closer to Philippe's warmth. "You needn't be an avid horseman either, Philippe. I'll be an avid wife, though."

"I will be a passionately avid husband."

He kissed her, and what happened next had to qualify as the fastest disrobing of a woman in a riding habit in the history of equitation. Philippe made a bed of wool coolers before the parlor stove, and amid the good smells of leather, horse, and hay, Harriet made the decision to anticipate her vows.

Two hours later, a sopping, irascible Earl of Ramsdale had been retrieved by the grooms, and Philippe was passing out toddies in the Talbot family parlor.

"A toast," Ramsdale said, "to new ventures succeeding beyond our wildest dreams."

"To new ventures," Philippe said, lifting his glass and smiling at Harriet over the rim.

She'd asked that they not announce their engagement until Philippe had told his sister. Philippe had asked if Harriet wanted him to observe the protocol of asking her papa for permission to court her.

"You can ask Papa for permission to court me," Harriet

murmured as Papa and the earl began bickering about a filly they both—apparently—had agreed to purchase for the stable.

"And if he says no?" Philippe asked.

"He won't. He wants to be asked, though, included in the discussion. I know this, because I'd stopped including him in matters relating to the stable. I didn't want to bother him, he probably didn't want to bother me. I see that now."

She also saw that Ramsdale was equal to Papa in stubbornness, and that was a fine thing in a prospective partner.

"I'll bother you frequently, Harriet," Philippe said, "and I'd rather not have a long engagement."

"What are you two whispering about?" Ramsdale groused.

"Breeding stock," Harriet replied, which retort had the earl and her papa looking perplexed, and Philippe grinning.

As it happened, the firstborn child of the Duke and Duchess of Lavelle arrived a scant eight months after the wedding and, true to Harriet's promise, was named after the Earl of Ramsdale.

Lady Seton Avery Ellis rode like a demon and waltzed like a dream, but that's a tale for another time.

As for the earl himself... his happily ever after lay in the direction of a long-lost Italian manuscript that scholars claimed held the arcane secrets of capturing the affections of another. Ramsdale certainly didn't believe in Cupid's arrows or Aphrodite's potions... and yet, he fell in love anyway.

And fell very hard, indeed, which is also a tale for another time!

THE WILL TO LOVE

THE WILL TO LOVE

The Will to Love

by Grace Burrowes

Originally published in
How to Find a Duke in Ten Days

CHAPTER ONE

If you can read Magna Carta, association with the undersigned could be lucrative. Inquire at the Albion.

"How is a lady to inquire at the Albion," Philomena Peebles muttered, "when that blighted bastion of male bloviations refuses to permit a female foot to cross its threshold? Have you seen my cutwork scissors?"

Jane Dobbs peered into the workbasket on Philomena's lap. "How can you find anything in there? Use mine." She passed over a tiny pair of scissors on a silver chain. "Why would you want to go to the Albion Club, other than for the obvious pleasure of shocking the dandiprats?"

Jane was twenty years Philomena's senior, part companion, part poor relation on Mama's side, and all friend. She'd joined the household shortly after Mama's death, though nobody had explained exactly how she and Mama were related.

Philomena hadn't cared then and didn't care now.

She trimmed out the newspaper notice and passed it to Jane. "I can read Magna Carta and am in want of funds to finance my search."

"You always turn up alliterative when you're restless. Are you off to hunt for the Duke again?"

"Of course. All the evidence points to at least parts of the manuscript being right here in London, and Papa's retirement banquet is a mere ten days away."

As Papa's amanuensis, Philomena had memorized every scrap of information known about *The Duke's Book of Knowledge,* or the *Liber Ducis de Scientia.* Papa was considered the international expert on the manuscript, though being an expert on a book nobody had seen for two hundred years was a vexing contradiction. Some claimed that the *Liber Ducis* didn't exist, and that the good professor had been hoaxing his academic associates for years.

"If the Duke is here in London, what do you need funds for?" Jane asked, giving the notice back to Philomena.

"Research is costly. Everything from cab fare to bribes to the occasional male escort takes a toll on a lady's exchequer."

In Paris, a woman could walk the streets without fear of being either judged for her independence or attacked for her coin. London, self-proclaimed pinnacle of human civilization, was generally considered unsafe for a genteel lady on her own.

Some civilization.

"It really is too bad that nice Tolerman fellow went off to Peru," Jane said, threading her embroidery needle with gold silk. "He let you drag him all over creation and nary a word of protest. The poor man was quite devoted."

"He's off to Egypt, and he wanted to entice me away from Papa because I can transcribe notes in all the classical languages." Beauford Tolerman had been a handy escort, until he'd confessed a violent passion for Philomena's nose.

Not even her eyes—her nose, or in Beauford's words, her pulchritudinous proboscis. She might have forgiven him his outburst, but then he'd tried to kiss the object of his ardor. Philomena had suggested to Professor Arbuthwhistle that Mr. Tolerman would make an excellent addition to the very next expedition to the pyramids.

Beyond the parlor door, a maid welcomed a caller. Visitors were frequent because Papa knew absolutely everybody who took an interest in ancient literature or philosophy, and many were paying calls to wish the professor a happy retirement.

For Papa, *happy retirement* was a contradiction in terms, hence Philomena's determination to find the Duke, or at least the portion of the manuscript that dealt with secrets of the human heart.

The Duke knew all the answers, if Papa's research had any validity. Page by page, the manuscript documented the most sophisticated thinking from all over the Renaissance world, grouped into four subjects: natural science, arcane medicine, fabled lands, and sentiments of the heart.

Philomena wished the entire manuscript would be found, but her personal objective was the treatise on human emotion, *De Motibus Humanis.* That tome was said to include recipes for tisanes for everything from grief, to jealousy, to melancholia. Perhaps she might find a potion that could help Papa attract a companion for his autumn years.

"Ladies, good day." Seton Zoraster Avery, Earl of Ramsdale, bowed to the room at large.

Philomena slipped the little notice into her pocket. Ramsdale was skilled with modern languages and particularly skilled at using the English language to talk about himself. No need for his overly active mind to light upon a lowly newspaper advertisement.

Philomena rang for tea, schooled her expression to patience, and sent Jane a look: *Please be gracious, for in the face of such unrelenting tedium when I have a Duke to catch, that sacrifice is beyond me.*

At least Ramsdale was interesting to behold—dark where the usual lord was fair, muscular rather than slim, and possessed of a voice Jane referred to as a *bello basso*—a beautiful bass. Philomena liked that about him.

And not much else.

HAVING DISPENSED with the tedium of a social call upon Professor Peebles's household—the professor had literally stuck his head through the doorway, and that head had still worn a sleeping cap at midafternoon—Ramsdale sought out that haven of rational conversation and fine fellowship, the Albion Club. Its appearance was unprepossessing, the location just off St. James's Street ideal.

And the quiet in the reading room was blessedly reliable.

This was a club for grown men, not raucous youths looking to make extravagant wagers or debate politics far into the night. The food was good, not merely expensive, and the service attentive rather than haughty. Ramsdale occasionally took rooms here rather than bide at his own town house, and thus nobody looked askance as he proceeded to the second floor and let himself into a familiar parlor.

"Good day, my lord," said Pinckney, his valet and general factotum at this location. "Three more responses came while you were out. The first of the gentlemen is scheduled to arrive within the hour."

Ramsdale turned so Pinckney could take his greatcoat. "That's five altogether. Only five people in all of London, Oxford, and Cambridge can read medieval law Latin?"

For Ramsdale had advertised at the universities as well.

"Perhaps it's the case that only five people who need coin can fulfill your request, my lord. But surely, from among a field of five, you'll find one who's acceptable."

The Duke's Book of Knowledge was reportedly written in plain, straightforward Latin, which owing to a lack of marching centurions or strutting gladiators, hadn't changed much over recent centuries. The problem was not the long-sought Duke, but rather, Uncle Hephaestus's will. Uncle had believed that medieval monks invented the crabbed, complicated law Latin to save on ink and parchment and that saving on ink and vellum remained a worthy goal.

Hence, he'd written his damned will in law Latin, and in the abbreviated version of the abomination still practiced by elderly clerks and particularly mean judges. Such was the incomprehensibility of that hand that, in the last century, it had been outlawed for court documents.

"Shall I ring for tea?" Pinckney asked.

Ramsdale had choked down two cups of gunpowder while maundering on in the Peebles's parlor. He had no wish for more damned tea. Why did the ladies never contribute anything of substance to a conversation? They smiled and nodded and yes-my-lorded but never *said* anything?

"Order a tray with all the trimmings," Ramsdale said. "If I'm to interview starving scholars, I'd best feed the poor devils."

Then too, Pinckney would help himself to a biscuit and a sandwich or two, and nothing on the tray would go to waste. The footman and groom would see to that when supper was hours away.

The scholars, alas, proved a shabby lot. Two reeked of mildew, two could not fumble through a single sentence of Uncle's codicil, and the fifth wanted a sponsor for yet another expedition to plunder the Nile.

Time was running out, and defeat was unacceptable.

"Have any more responses come?" Ramsdale asked when the Nile explorer had been sent on his way.

"Not a response per se," Pinckney said, tidying tea cups and saucers onto a tray. "There is a gentleman below stairs who said he'd wait rather than make an appointment. Tidy young chap, relatively speaking."

"Tidy and skinny, I've no doubt."

The afternoon was gone and so was Ramsdale's patience. "Send him up, but don't bother with another tray. I doubt he'll be staying long."

Pinckney used a small brush to dust the crumbs from the table onto a linen serviette. "And will you be going out this evening, my lord?"

Ramsdale had been ruralizing in Berkshire for the past month, being a doting godfather to a friend's infant daughter. Had a fine set of lungs on her, did his goddaughter.

"I might renew acquaintances around the corner," he said. "If there's anything to miss about Town, it's the company of the ladies." Though the women who dwelled at the odd St. James address didn't consider themselves ladies.

Ramsdale had spent many a pleasant hour in their company, nonetheless. His favorite chess partner was a madam of no little repute, and he delighted in the linguistic variety her employees brought to an evening. French, Italian, and German were all to be heard in the main parlor, along with a smattering of more exotic languages.

Pinckney withdrew, and Ramsdale gathered up what passed for his patience as a slim young fellow was admitted by the footman.

"My lord." The scholar bowed. He had a scraping, raspy voice. He also wore blue-tinted spectacles that must have made navigating after dark difficult, and in the dim light of the sconces, his countenance was very smooth.

Too smooth. "Have you a card?" Ramsdale asked.

The scholar's clothes were loose—probably second- or third-hand castoffs—and his hair was queued back and tucked under his collar. He passed over a plain card.

Phillip Peebleshire. *Ah, well, then.*

"You look familiar," Ramsdale said.

"We are not acquainted, my lord, though I have tutored younger sons from time to time."

Probably true. "Well, have a seat, and lest you think to impress me with your vast qualifications, let's begin by having you transcribe a few lines from this document."

Of the two seats opposite Ramsdale's desk, Peebleshire took the one farther from the candles. Ramsdale passed over Uncle Hephaestus's first codicil—there were nine in total—and Mr. Peebleshire took out a quizzing glass.

"I have paper and pencil, or pen and ink if you prefer," Ramsdale said.

"This codicil," Peebleshire read slowly, "is made by me, the undersigned testator, Hephaestus George Louis Algernon Avery, being of sound mind and composed spirit, as witnessed in triplicate hereto, and does hereby revoke any previous codicils, but does not revoke my will, which document is dated—"

Ramsdale plucked the document from Peebleshire's pale hands. "You can translate at sight?"

"The legal documents all tend to follow certain forms, my lord. The vocabulary is limited, until you reach the specific bequests and conditions of inheritance. A modern holographic will written in such arcane language is unusual, though."

"My uncle was an unusual man." Generous, vindictive, devious, and merry. In life, Ramsdale hadn't known what to make of him. In death, Uncle had become purely vexatious.

Ramsdale repeated the exercise with the second codicil—the only one he himself had muddled through in full—and again, Peebleshire translated accurately at sight.

Bollocks. Ramsdale rose and took a candle from the branch on his desk. "What compensation do you seek for your services?"

Peebleshire named a sum per page—shrewd, that—as Ramsdale lit several more branches of candles around the room. The wages sought were substantial, but not exorbitant for a true scholar.

"How quickly can you complete the work?" Ramsdale asked.

"That depends on how much of it there is."

Uncle's will ran on for thirty pages, and the codicils for another sixty. As near as Ramsdale could fathom, seven of the codicils were rants against the established orders at Oxford and Cambridge, with much ink spilled on the reputation of one Professor Peebles.

"Nearly a hundred pages," Ramsdale said, "and I also have correspondence Uncle wrote to various scholar friends. Can you translate French?"

"Of course, my lord."

"German, Italian, Spanish?"

"German, and all of the romance languages, Greek, Aramaic, Hebrew, Latin. My Coptic is less reliable, and I am not confident of the Norse languages. I'm gaining proficiency in spoken Arabic, but the written language is a challenge."

If that recitation were true, Ramsdale would have to admit to surprise. "Then you are clearly qualified to meet my needs," he said, "but before we discuss the rest of the terms, I have one more question for you."

Because Ramsdale had lit every blessed candle in the room, he could see his guest well. Peebleshire sat forward, apparently eager for the work.

"What is your question, sir?"

"How will I explain to your dear papa, that his darling offspring has taken to parading about London after dark in men's clothing, Miss Peebles?"

◦∿◦

LINGUISTIC INSTRUCTION for young ladies seldom included curse words, but Philomena's father had educated her as if she'd been one of his university students, and thus she could wax profane in a dozen languages.

In Ramsdale's rented parlor, she remained outwardly composed, while mentally insulting his lordship's antecedents in Low German.

In very Low German.

"If I'm to parade about London with anything approaching freedom or safety, I dare not wear a lady's garb," she said, rising.

Ramsdale stood across the room, looking broody—which he did well—and amused, which made Philomena uneasy.

Uneasier. While waiting downstairs, she'd almost risen to leave a hundred times. A hundred and one times, she'd reminded herself that Papa's reputation hung in the balance, and if he was to have private students to keep his retirement comfortable, if his monographs were to receive a respectful reception, then finding the Duke—any part of the Duke—had become imperative.

"Come now, madam," Ramsdale said, sauntering closer. "All you need to assure your safety is a common fashion accessory."

"Firearms are noisy and unwieldy," Philomena said. "Knives are messy and can easily be turned against one."

Ramsdale peered down at her. "What a violent imagination you have. Merely drape an escort upon your arm and your troubles are solved. I will see you home, for example, and you'll find we traverse the streets entirely undisturbed."

His lordship smelled good, of leather and bayberry soap, and with his height and muscle, he'd doubtless scare off the footpads as easily as he attracted the ladies. Jane had intimated that Ramsdale had a reputation among the demimonde, suggesting his skills in the bedroom compensated for a lack of appeal in all other regards.

Thanks to the bawdy inclinations of the Greeks and Romans, Philomena's literary grasp of amatory pursuits was well informed to an unladylike degree.

"Thank you, no," Philomena said. "I will see myself home. Shall I take your uncle's will with me?"

Ramsdale stepped away and began blowing out the candles he'd just lit. "You recognized the signature?"

"Your uncle accounted himself my father's nemesis. I've seen that signature often enough. Every time Papa published an article regarding *The Duke's Book of Knowledge*, Hephaestus contradicted him, usually with no evidence whatsoever."

Ramsdale pinched out a flame with his bare fingers. "How does one prove a manuscript does not exist?"

Smoke wafted about him in the shadows, giving him a diabolical air—which he probably cultivated. His voice was a dark growl that carried even when he spoke softly.

"One cannot prove a book doesn't exist," Philomena said. "A brilliant scholar wouldn't attempt that logical conundrum, which is why Hephaestus Avery, otherwise accounted an intelligent—if eccentric—man, must have been motivated by something other than a passion for the truth."

Ramsdale's gaze followed the smoke trailing upward. "They collaborated, you know, once upon a time. Traveled the Continent together. Co-authored a review of Parisian restaurants."

Philomena sank back into her chair. "You're daft. They hated each other." And Papa would as soon eat shoe leather as he would breaded sole with truffle garnish.

"Which is why your father attended Uncle's funeral? Why he helped draft the eulogy?"

Papa hadn't told her that. He was often forgetful. "One can respect an opponent."

"One can, but as a gentleman, I am also bound to respect you, madam, and that means you should not be alone with me, in my rooms, at a staid and respected gentleman's club. Your presence risks my reputation and yours, so let's continue this delightful argument while I walk you home."

Philomena ought not to be alone with Ramsdale anywhere. He was an earl, and thus all but impervious to gossip, while she was the spinster daughter of an academic one step above obscurity.

"I've known you for ages," she said. "Seen you wolfing down jam and bread in my father's kitchen and watched him send you on your way with biscuits to hoard until your next tutoring session."

The earl had been a quiet boy—a large, quiet boy. Ramsdale was not academic in the usual sense, but he'd had an ear for languages that had deserved advanced instruction. He'd been among many students whom Papa had taught over the years. They'd all been hungrier for food than for knowledge, and most of them had been easy to forget.

"And here I thought you never even noticed the boys coming and going from your papa's study. I account myself flattered, Miss Peebles. Shall we be on our way?"

Not until Philomena had achieved her objective. "I can't stop you from wandering where you will, my lord, but I am well qualified for the translation work you need. Do we have an agreement regarding your uncle's will?"

Ramsdale leaned back against the desk, a mere two feet from where Philomena sat. She didn't want to look up at him, and she certainly didn't want to gaze at what was immediately in her line of sight.

"You want to see Uncle's will because you're afraid his testament discredits your father once and for all."

Well, yes. Now that Philomena knew the daft old man had left such a lengthy will, she did want to read it.

"Don't be ridiculous, my lord. I came here today not knowing who sought a translation of what document or for what purpose. You doubtless seek to support your uncle's criticisms of my father's work."

Ramsdale settled into the chair beside hers. The furniture was dark and sturdy, like the man occupying it, and yet, the impression he made was one of leisure and grace.

"Your father was the only instructor who saw any potential in me, Miss Peebles, and the main reason I didn't starve my first term. Why would I seek to impugn the reputation of a man I esteem? I'm more inclined to believe that you seek to discredit Hephaestus. He was a thorn in your papa's side, and you want posthumous revenge on him for demanding proof of a text no living soul has seen."

"We are back to the impossibility of proving something in the negative, my lord, for you ask me to establish what my motives are not. Your uncle has been gone these two years. I wish for him only the reward his Maker sees fit to bestow on him."

Philomena rose rather than admit that bickering with Ramsdale was invigorating—debating with him, rather.

Ramsdale rose, yanked a bell-pull, and met Philomena at the door. He prevented her immediate departure by virtue of leaning upon the jamb.

"My preference for the Albion is well known," he said. "You saw the advertisement I've been running in *The Times*, and in a flight of female intuition, the likes of which inspire sane men to tremble, considered that I, who have a known interest in languages, had placed the notice."

Philomena put a hand on the door latch. "As far as I know, the owner of Ramsdale House dwells at that location. Perhaps the Albion is closer to your preferred entertainments, my lord, but that is no concern of mine. If we're not to transact business, I'll be on my way."

He straightened as a servant brought in a greatcoat that could have made a tent for a family of six.

"Shall I wait up for you, my lord?"

"No need, Pinckney."

The older man bowed and withdrew, his gaze barely brushing over Philomena.

The earl shrugged into his coat, one long arm at a time. When he drew the second sleeve up, he got one side of the collar tucked under itself.

"Hold still," Philomena said. "You'll go out in public looking half dressed, and your poor valet will have an apoplexy, and the next thing you know, you'll be a caricature in shop windows with your breeches on backward and your watch fob dangling from your hat brim."

She sorted out his coat, passed him the hat sitting on the sideboard and then a walking stick that weighed more than her father's family Bible.

"I suppose you've had to develop managing tendencies," Ramsdale said. "You have no mama, and the professor grows easily distracted. Shall we be on our way?"

He gestured toward the door, and had Philomena not been so desperate for coin, she might have let his polite suggestion see her right out into the corridor.

"I want the work, your lordship. I can bring that will home with me and start on the translation this very evening."

"That is my only copy, Miss Peebles. Meaning no disrespect for your motives or your abilities, I'm not about to let it out of my sight."

This was merely prudent, also deuced inconvenient. "Then I'll simply wear my disguise, and nobody will be the—"

His lordship laughed, a booming, merry cascade of derision.

"Your disguise didn't fool me for two minutes, my dear. In broad daylight, it likely fooled no one."

Philomena wanted to smack him. "I sat downstairs in the foyer for *two hours*, my lord. Nobody gave me a second glance."

He tapped his hat onto his head, then paused before pulling on his gloves. "For two hours?"

"Perhaps longer, and may I say, the chairs are not as comfortable as they look."

Too late, Philomena realized that he was no longer having a laugh at her wardrobe. He stared past her shoulder for a moment, and she could feel him parsing evidence and testing hypotheses.

"You will tutor my sister in French," he said, "starting tomorrow at nine of the clock at Ramsdale House."

"No earl's daughter will be out of bed at that hour."

"Precisely, but my uncle's last will and testament will be available for your perusal in the library. My sister's French is in want of polish, and she intends a trip to Paris later this year."

"I see."

Philomena did not see. His lordship was making it possible for her to translate a long document without risking any harm to her person or her reputation. He must be desperate to know what was hidden in the details of his uncle's will.

The only other explanation—that he'd realized a woman who'd wait two hours for an appointment must be badly in need of coin—attributed to him both accurate intuition and a generous spirit.

Neither of which Lord Ramsdale possessed.

But he did make Philomena feel safer on London's dark streets. That much, even she could admit.

CHAPTER TWO

"I shall begin with the will," Miss Peebles said.

This morning, she was dressed as a female—barely. Her round gown had probably begun life as flour sacking, each finger of her gloves had been mended, and she wore not even a watch on her bodice for decoration.

But the intelligence snapping in her blue eyes sparkled like sapphires, and she moved about the library with radiant confidence. When faced with a linguistic challenge, she was not the drab Miss Peebles of Ramsdale's memory, but rather, some mythical creature who combined intellect, determination, and—confound it, when had this happened?—curves.

"There is no need for you to read the will," Ramsdale retorted. He'd ridden in the park before breaking his fast and should have felt more prepared for this encounter.

This argument. Everything with Miss Peebles had been an argument. She'd debated the best route to take homeward the previous evening, how long she would work per day, and whether her compensation should be paid at the end of the day or the end of each week.

Ramsdale didn't have weeks. He had days to find his assigned portion of *The Duke's Book of Knowledge*, only nine days now. His friends were looking for the other parts, and they'd all agreed that the professor's retirement dinner was the ideal occasion upon which to announce their findings.

If Ramsdale survived that long. His translator was as vexatious as she was skilled.

For every position Miss Peebles put forth, she had reasons by the dozen, in addition to corollaries, theses, supporting statements, and evidence. When on a flight of logic, she used her hands to punctuate her lectures, and twice while strolling down the street, Ramsdale had had to grab her arm lest she march across an intersection in the midst of traffic.

"If I'm reading the codicils," she said in patient tones, "then I must know the substance of the document they refer to."

"Chancery found the will quite valid," Ramsdale said. "The estate has been distributed, and the will itself holds nothing of any import." Except some specific bequests, that made Uncle seem more than half-daft.

Miss Peebles strode across his library, her heels beating a tattoo against the carpeted oak floor. "The settling of the estate was doubtless uncontested. Chancery waved this document under the nose of one elderly, overworked clerk and took a year to do that much. Let me see the will."

Chancery had taken a mere year and ten months, actually, which meant Ramsdale had seen the will in its entirety only a fortnight ago, when the document had been couriered to him in Berkshire.

And now he was wasting time arguing. "You will not write out a translation of the will," he said. "You will read it for your own reference."

Miss Peebles gave him the sort of look Ramsdale's friend, the Duke of Lavelle, gave his infant daughter. As if His Grace hoped that someday the little mite would speak in intelligible sentences, or at least refrain from bashing about the nursery heedless of her own well-being.

"You have changed your mind, my lord. Last night, you told me the translation effort included thirty pages of the will itself. You also look fatigued about the eyes, suggesting you might have spent the night studying the document yourself when I know your command of the law hand is indifferent at best."

Ramsdale had spent the night losing repeatedly to his friend the chess madam and refusing increasingly bold invitations to take the game up to her boudoir. Fatigue had doubtless dissuaded him. A remove to Town always taxed his energies, and one didn't acquit oneself less than enthusiastically in the bedroom.

Ever.

"I spent the night reacquainting myself with the blandishments London offers a peer of means, Miss Peebles. I am quite well rested, and a gentleman does not *change his mind.*"

Her gaze cooled, a fire dying out over a procession of instants. "Then logic compels me to conclude that you are not a gentleman, for yesterday you described the task before me as including a thirty-page will, and yet today—"

"I know what I said yesterday." When he'd been distracted by the degree to which the determined curve of a woman's jaw was revealed when she arranged her hair in a masculine queue.

"You do not trust my motives," Miss Peebles observed, stepping away. "And I do not trust yours. We must get past this, my lord, or your coin is wasted. I can claim the will translates into a recantation of Hephaestus's criticisms, while you could put anything before me and say it's a newly discovered codicil describing destruction of *The Duke's Book of Knowledge* thirty years ago. If Professor Peebles's own daughter translated those words, they'd be credible indeed. We are at *point non plus.*"

She wafted away on the faint fragrances of vanilla and cinnamon, rich scents at variance with her brisk words. Memories of warm biscuits and cold milk in the professor's kitchen stirred, along with the realization that the lady was right.

They either moved past this bickering, or Ramsdale was stuck, searching blindly for a document that had eluded discovery for centuries.

"What's wanted," Ramsdale said, "is a modicum of trust."

He was capable of trust. He trusted the Duke of Lavelle to gush tiresomely about his brilliant daughter and his lovely duchess, for example. He trusted English weather to be fickle. He trusted women to be bothersome, and poor relations to turn up at the worst times with the most pathetic fabrications of misfortune.

"Trust?" Miss Peebles took the seat behind the desk that had belonged to the Earls of Ramsdale for time out of mind. "Perhaps your lordship might explain himself."

She looked good in Ramsdale's armchair, self-possessed, ready for a challenge. Ready to tell a peer of the realm to *explain* himself.

"We will agree," Ramsdale said slowly, "that whatever is discovered or disclosed within these four walls will not be made public without the consent of the other party." Such a term should have been part of any contract for translation services, and yet, he'd not thought to draw up a contract, had he?

Hadn't wanted to involve the solicitors at all, and quite honestly did not have time.

Miss Peebles opened the left-hand drawer—not the right—and took out a penknife. "What do you fear I'll find in the will?"

She tested the blade against the pad of her thumb, then set to sharpening the quills in the pen tray. Her movements were quick and sure, and the parings accumulated on the blotter in a small heap.

"Your turn to offer some explanation, Miss Peebles. What do you fear the will might reveal?"

She swept the parings into her palm, rose, and dumped them into the dust bin on the hearth.

"I am afraid I will find proof that my father has been a fool, or—

worse—perpetrated a hoax the better to draw notice to himself. I am afraid that Papa's years of research have been for naught, that if he dies without finding proof of at least one volume of the Duke's wisdom, then nobody will take up the hunt in future generations, and a great literary treasure will be lost forever.

"I am afraid," she went on more softly, "that without the Duke, Papa will be unable to attract pupils to tutor, and his old age will be characterized by penury and despair."

She spoke of her father and of great literature, not of herself, and her concerns were valid.

Which would be worse, having a fool or a charlatan for a father?

Which would be worse, penury or despair?

"What of you?" she asked, remaining by the unlit hearth. "If you don't seek to vindicate your uncle's skepticism regarding the Duke, why go to the effort of translating a hundred pages of what appears to be rambling invective?"

She'd gleaned that much by glancing at one page of one codicil?

Ramsdale closed the door to the library, which was ungentlemanly but necessary if soul-baring had become the order of the day.

"Hephaestus left little to anybody," Ramsdale said. "His legacy was debts, a few books, and several obese felines. He was too poor to even house the tomes he'd collected. You see them here,"—he swept a hand toward the shelves—"but such was the enmity between my father and my uncle that having agreed to shelter Uncle's books, Papa in later years denied his brother access to the premises. Their quarrel was bitter and stupid. I would not want their disagreement to become public knowledge."

"Family linen," Miss Peebles said, packing a world of impatience into two words. "My mother's relations never stopped criticizing her choice of spouse. Mama married down, you see, which surely qualifies as the eighth deadly sin for a marquess's granddaughter."

"Any particular marquess?"

"My uncle is now the Marquess of Amesbury. He and Papa correspond annually at Yuletide."

The lofty title and its proximity to Miss Peebles herself was a surprise. An unwelcome surprise. An exceedingly unwelcome surprise.

For years, Miss Peebles had been one of the myriad figures on the periphery of Ramsdale's busy life. He liked and respected her father—he owed her father—and had continued both a correspondence and a social connection with the professor after leaving university.

As a decent female of humble station, Miss Peebles had occupied the status of nonentity to the young Ramsdale heir. He'd more or less forgotten about her as he'd taken up the reins of the earldom, and she'd doubtless forgotten about him.

To learn that he had something in common with her—family linen, of the wrinkled, stained variety—was oddly comforting. That she was brilliant, devoted to her father, and inconveniently logical made her interesting.

That she was a marquess's niece and had not been presented at court was wrong, and yet, polite society would not have been kind to one of her unique gifts.

"You probably don't like me," Ramsdale said, "which bothers me not at all. I like very few people myself. But can you consent to the terms I propose, Miss Peebles? We keep whatever we learn from the will to ourselves, unless we both agree otherwise?"

"You don't like me either," she replied, returning to the desk to put away the penknife. "That's a credit to your common sense, because I am difficult and overly educated. This has addled my female humors, and the damage is likely permanent in the opinion of Papa's physician."

She crossed the room at the brisk pace Ramsdale was coming to associate with her. Only when dressed as a man had she been capable of a leisurely stroll.

She stuck out her hand, a slim, pale appendage with a smear of ink at the base of her thumb. "We have a bargain, my lord. No disclosures unless we're both agreed in advance."

She expected him to shake hands with her, which was surely proof of her addled humors.

Perhaps Ramsdale's humors were a bit addled as well. He took her hand in his and bowed. When he straightened, Miss Peebles was smiling at him, a wonderful mischievous expression as surprising as it was heart-warming.

He did not like her—he barely knew her, and one could not like a woman whom one did not know—but he liked that smile.

He liked it rather a lot. Doubtless, Ramsdale would never see that smile again if she learned he was all but courting the Marquess of Amesbury's daughter.

"PHILOMENA MENTIONED nothing to me about tutoring Ramsdale's sister," the professor said.

"She told you last night at supper," Jane replied, taking a pinch of salt and sprinkling it over her soup. Cook had made a wonderful beef stew flavored with a hint of tarragon, but her efforts, as usual, had to compete with some tract or treatise at the professor's elbow.

"Is the Duke joining us at table again?" Jane asked.

The professor—without looking up—took a slice of bread from what happened to be Jane's plate and dipped it in his soup.

"You banished His Grace from supper five years ago. We're not eating supper."

That would be a yes. From some arcane manuscript unearthed by one of the professor's students at a bookstall in Prague, or at an estate sale in Italy, somebody had come across a fleeting reference to that dratted Duke.

"Professor, you are retiring," Jane said, gently moving the pamphlet away from his elbow. "Isn't it time the Duke retired as well, or that a younger generation of scholars debated his existence?"

Phineas Peebles had aged well, if not exactly happily. He still had snapping blue eyes, a thick thatch of white hair, and a posture many a military recruit would envy. He sat up very tall.

"Just because nobody has seen the manuscript for two hundred years doesn't mean it has ceased to exist. Britain has many documents that are much older, and Shakespeare folios and quartos seem to turn up every other year. Where's the butter?"

Jane passed him a dish sitting not eight inches from his pint of ale. "Why must you be the one to find him?"

"Jane, you wound me. When Lorenzo de' Medici commanded that the most significant knowledge of his day be set down in a single compendium, by God, you may trust that knowledge was set down. I am the Duke's champion in the present age, and every scholar and dilettante involved with ancient languages and philosophy knows it."

Mostly because they disagreed with the professor. A document of that size and significance would not simply disappear. Rumors abounded—perhaps the French had pilfered it from a Florentine villa, or the Spanish had married their way into possession of the Duke. Perhaps the four quires had been flung to the compass points in an effort to ensure at least one part of the treatise survived.

The professor had followed every hint, every shred of evidence, and they all confirmed—in his opinion—that the Duke of Buckingham had got hold of the entire work on behalf of James I.

"You won't find a document that has been missing for two hundred years in the next nine days," Jane said. "Will you devote the next thirty-five years of your life to the same fruitless cause as you have the last thirty-five?"

The professor buttered another slice of bread, tore it in two, and passed half to Jane. "My career has been distinguished by much scholarship, endless teaching responsibilities, and research into all manner of ancient documents and theories. Why attack the Duke now, Jane? In retirement, I will be more free than ever to track him down."

"Phineas, the Duke is not a person. We speak of him as if he's a distant relation who's wandered off after taking an excess of spirits. Your own daughter wanders off and you take no notice."

This criticism was pointless. Phineas loved his daughter if he loved anybody, but loving somebody and being able to show that love were not the same in his case.

"I noticed," the professor said. "You said she's teaching French to Ramsdale's sister, hardly a dangerous undertaking. Do you intend to eat that bread?"

Jane passed him the buttered half slice when she wanted to upend her soup in his lap. "Phin, you should be taking Philomena to visit her maternal relations. You will have time now. She's too old to be presented at court, but titled relations might help her meet an eligible man, might even see their way clear to—"

The professor held up a staying hand—and a half slice of buttered bread. "If you utter the word dowry, I will not answer for the consequences, Jane Dobbs. The exalted marquess well knows Philomena's circumstances and hasn't invited her to visit her cousins, much less to drag me into the countryside as her escort."

"Because you refuse to ask it of him."

"She doesn't want to go," the professor said, taking a bite of the bread. "She's smitten with the Duke too, though I defy you to explain how a woman can find what trained scholars have been unable to search out after two centuries' effort. Philomena's loyal, though, which is more than I can say for *some* people."

That was... that was the professor's version of a tantrum. For him to retire without finding any direct evidence that his precious Duke existed was turning his usually placid nature sour.

"You're right," Jane replied, pushing away her lukewarm soup. "Philomena is very loyal to her papa, while I am only her paid companion. She's approaching thirty, though, and nobody expects a confirmed spinster from a home of humble means to require a companion."

The professor put down his spoon. "What is that supposed to mean?"

"You are actually looking at somebody with whom you're sharing a meal. I will die secure in the knowledge that miracles occur."

He had the grace to look abashed. "Jane, I am much distracted of late, I know, and I do apologize, but the Duke... A man who unearths a treasure of that magnitude might aspire to a token of royal favor. He might attract the best tutoring prospects. He might be appointed a librarian or special lecturer, or curator to a significant collection. Without the Duke, I am merely another fading scholar, wearing my nightcap at odd hours and tucking scraps of paper where they do not belong."

Jane chose to be encouraged that Phineas was discussing his frustrations, but she could not afford to relent so much as one inch where Philomena's future was concerned.

"You have much to be proud of, not the least of which is your daughter. Can you not take a few months away from your obsession to see her settled?"

"Obsession is an ugly word, Jane."

"So is pride, Phineas. The Duke has waited two hundred years, wherever he's lurking. He can wait another few months."

Jane was angry, but she'd been angry with the professor for years. She'd hoped retirement would inspire him to finally act like a father to his only child, finally make room in his life for something other than scholarship. In Jane's opinion, that scholarship was merely a desperate quest for recognition from a lot of prosy old windbags who dropped Latin phrases into their conversations like debutantes showing off their French.

"The Duke cannot wait, Jane. You recall Mr. Handley."

"I have never met anybody named Handley."

"He's an apothecary with a shop in Bloomsbury. Makes excellent tisanes for aching joints."

Aching joints, such as one acquired when one spent long hours gripping a quill pen.

"What of him?"

"He attends monthly dinners with others of his profession, and he heard Mr. Eagan, of Eagan Brothers Emporium in Knightsbridge, bragging about a new source of recipes for love potions, one written in an ancient hand and stolen from an Italian monastery by the plundering French. That could only be the Duke, or a partial copy of the Duke, for our duke devoted an entire volume to the emotional workings of the human heart."

While the professor lately appeared to have no heart. "Magic potions are nonsense, particularly where amatory matters are concerned. What's wanted in that case is for two people to have mutual respect and compatibility."

The professor finished Jane's ale. "Such a romantic, Jane. In any case, rumors are based on facts, and while Philomena is off pretending to tutor Ramsdale's sister in French, I will be making a jaunt down to Knightsbridge."

Jane helped herself to the professor's ale. "Shall I hold supper for you?"

"Please. I expect Philomena will be back before I am."

He rose and collected his half slice of buttered bread, though he hadn't finished his soup. "My compliments to Cook. The soup was a bit bland."

Delicate. The soup had been delicate. Jane's nerves were growing delicate. "Philomena said she might not be back until after supper."

"Of course she'll be back," the professor said, picking up his treatise. "Ramsdale's sister spent two years at a French finishing school, and the earl is fluent in French. Her ladyship has no need of a French tutor, much less one underfoot the livelong day."

He resumed reading as he left the dining room, muttering under his breath and leaving a trail of crumbs on the carpet.

Jane drank the last of his ale and clung stubbornly to the notion that the conversation had been encouraging, for it had been a *conversation*. With the professor, that was an accomplishment in itself. He'd also set aside his reading for a good five minutes and noticed the peculiarity of Philomena's scheduled activities.

He had not, alas, noticed the woman who'd taken over looking after his daughter well over a decade ago.

Not yet.

~

THE WILL WAS A PUZZLE, just barely comprehensible in places, ridiculously satirical in others, and touchingly genuine in still others. Philomena had plowed through eight pages of cramped, slashing prose rife with idiosyncratic abbreviations and odd phrases before Ramsdale interrupted.

"That is enough for the present, Miss Peebles."

"You've taken notes?" His lordship had sat at the reading table, paper, pen, and ink before him, while Philomena had stumbled and lurched through the text from the comfortable chair behind the desk.

Once or twice, Ramsdale had snorted or guffawed, but he'd mostly remained silent.

"I have taken three pages of notes," he said, capping the silver ink bottle and laying his pen in a matching tray, "but mostly, I have enjoyed hearing my uncle's voice in your words. Luncheon should be ready, if you'd accompany me to the dining room?"

He rose and approached the desk. Philomena had the thought that he was about to toss her from the library bodily, then realized he expected to hold her chair.

"I hadn't planned on a midday meal, your lordship, though a tea tray with a few biscuits wouldn't go amiss. I promise not to get crumbs on your blotter."

She offered him a smile, lest he think to lecture her into acceding to his wishes. A day offered only so much sunlight, and Philomena needed to make use of every instant. Thus far, Hephaestus had made several references to "that misguided fool, Peebles," but had said nothing about the Duke.

Philomena hoped Hephaestus would wax eloquent about the volume of the Duke's manuscript that dealt with the secrets of the human heart— *de Motibus Humanis*—a topic Hephaestus had publicly declared Lorenzo the Magnificent would never have troubled over.

Why particularly discredit that one aspect of the ducal manuscript, unless—?

The earl braced his hands on the desk and leaned across. "Please join me for lunch, Miss Peebles. The mind grows dull without periodic rest, and I daresay if you're to make progress this afternoon with Uncle's specific bequests, then you will need more than a few biscuits to fortify you."

What magnificent eyes he had. Very... compelling.

"I am a trifle peckish," Philomena said, which was something of a surprise. "Perhaps you'd send a sandwich along with my tea?"

The earl leaned closer. "Perhaps you'd for once let somebody show you a bit of consideration and take a meal with me?"

How many times had Philomena and Jane made small talk over a beef roast, pretending that Papa hadn't once again forgotten to join them for his favorite meal?

"I'll bring this short passage," she said, picking up the first page of specific bequests. "We can work through it while—"

Ramsdale came closer, so he was nearly nose to nose with Philomena. "How can that brilliant and busy mind of yours fail to grasp the concept of respite, Miss Peebles? Allow me to explicate: respite, from the Latin *respicere*, to have concern for, to cast one's thoughts back to; and the Middle French, *respetier*, to save, show clemency to, or delay. In modern English, to rest from one's burdens."

Rather than raise his voice, he'd pitched his little lecture just above a whisper and come closer and closer, until Philomena could see that his eyes were not black, but rather, a sable brown.

He tugged on the page of vellum she held, and Philomena was abruptly aware that she was within breath-mingling distance of an adult male to whom she was not related. She had spent four hours alone with the earl in the library and not given *him* a thought, so absorbed had she been in her task.

"I'll join you for luncheon," she said, surrendering the specific bequests. "But we'll not linger over the meal, sir. Not when my progress this morning has been slower than I'd anticipated."

He came around the desk and held her chair. "We'll not linger over the meal, but we won't rush either, Miss Peebles."

He offered his arm, another small surprise. Philomena accepted that courtesy, and wondered why her own father never bothered with such a small gesture of consideration.

CHAPTER THREE

Ramsdale silently scolded himself for being high-handed—his sister Melissa often called him naughty—but Miss Peebles would have sat at that desk translating at sight until the opening of grouse season, left to her own devices.

Of course, she'd be done with Uncle's will long before that.

"Will Lady Melissa be joining us?" Miss Peebles asked.

The dining parlor table held only two place settings, one at the head, the other at the foot. The silver epergne in the middle of the table was piled two feet high with oranges, limes, and strawberries, and thus neither diner need acknowledge the other.

"Her ladyship will doubtless take a tray above stairs. This time of year, she's abroad at night more than in the daytime."

Miss Peebles wandered to the sideboard. "Who would sip gunpowder in solitude when she could enjoy such bounty instead?"

Better an aromatic gunpowder than the dubious sustenance of a musty document. "We will serve ourselves, and you must not worry about the leftover food going to waste. My staff eats prodigiously well."

Ramsdale gathered up the place setting at the foot of the table and moved it to the right of the head, then carried both plates to the sideboard.

"Have whatever you please and take as much as you please. My late father believed the natural appetites were meant to be indulged joyously."

Miss Peebles was busy inhaling the steam rising from a cloved ham and appeared not to notice any improper innuendo—though, of course, none had been intended.

She took one of the plates from Ramsdale. "I love a creative use of spices, and cloved ham has long been a favorite. Our cook does try, but Papa seldom notices her efforts."

Miss Peebles heaped her plate as if preparing to march for a forced march, and started for the foot of the table, then seemed to realize the cutlery had been moved.

"Do you and your sister typically dine twelve feet apart, my lord?"

"No, we do not," Ramsdale said, serving himself portions of ham, potatoes, and beans. "We typically dine thirty feet apart, on those rare occasions when we share a table."

The lady took her seat without benefit of his assistance. Ramsdale joined her at the table and poured them both glasses of the Riesling. He was about to sip his wine when he recalled that company manners were appropriate, despite the informality of the meal.

"Perhaps you'd say the blessing?"

Miss Peebles looked pleased with that small honor and launched into a French grace of admirable brevity.

"This ham has a marvelous glaze," she said. "Might I prevail upon your cook for the recipe?"

"Of course. We make our own honey on the home farm in Sussex, and in all humility, I must admit it's a superior product."

"Jane loves to collect recipes, though, of course, her treasures are lost on Papa. I do fancy a hearty German wine."

The disciplined, focused Miss Peebles became like a girl in a sweetshop when presented with a decent meal. As she waxed appreciative about everything from the buttered potatoes, to the apple tart, to the cheese, Ramsdale gained a picture of a household awash in intellectual sophistication—Miss Dobbs was learning Russian for the novelty alone—but starving for simple pleasures.

Miss Peebles's chatter between bites revealed a side to Ramsdale's mentor that flattered no one. The professor apparently ate without tasting his food and ignored his womenfolk at table the better to remain engrossed in his treatises. Birthdays and holidays caught him by surprise, and he tolerated their observation with an absent-minded impatience that never shaded into irritability, but had still made an impression on his only child.

"My upbringing emphasized different priorities from yours," Ramsdale remarked as he chose some strawberries and an orange from the abundance on the epergne. "We had diversions and recreations, one after the other."

"One envisions the aristocracy living thus," Miss Peebles said. "I'd go mad in a week."

Ramsdale passed her an orange. "I nearly did. Your father grasped my difficulty. I was a bright lad without adequate academic stimulation. I needed a challenge, and he provided it. Perhaps you'd peel that orange, so we can share it."

She sniffed the fruit and ran her fingers over the rind. "You don't want a whole one for yourself?"

Did she want the entire orange? Would she admit it if she did?

"I would rather share," he said, mostly because her brilliant father would never have said that to her. "A few bites will be enough for me. What do you make of the first eight pages of the will?"

As soon as he asked the question, he regretted it. The animation in Miss Peebles's eyes sharpened with an analytical edge where sheer enjoyment had been previously. She tore into the orange.

"Your uncle knew that document would receive significant scrutiny. My impression thus far is that we're wading through obfuscation, our senses dulled by arcane prose in prodigious quantity. The

specific bequests should be interesting, given that you claim he died
in penury."

Ramsdale missed the other Miss Peebles, the one who marveled
over a ham glaze and delighted in a brie flavored with basil. She was
interesting, or rather, that she existed in the same person with the
dedicated scholar interested him.

"Not penury—my father would not have allowed that, and
neither would I—but obscurity. Uncle was brilliant, never forgot
anything, and corresponded with acquaintances in half the royal
courts of Europe. Papa got the title, though, and the lands and
commercial ventures. Uncle envied Papa his status, Papa envied
Uncle his brilliance."

Miss Peebles passed over half of the orange. "Where did the heir
to the title fall?"

Through the cracks. "I could not be disloyal to my father, and yet,
I had far more in common with Hephaestus. They compromised by
sending me off to school as early as possible."

Though, of course, neither man would have called that decision a
compromise, and Ramsdale wouldn't have either, until that moment.

"Girls are lucky," Miss Peebles said. "We're not tossed out into
the world at the age of six and expected to become little adults by
virtue of overexposure to Latin and sums, and underexposure to fresh
air and good food."

Her father had likely told her that taradiddle, while being unable
to afford a good finishing school for her.

"Speaking of fresh air, let's enjoy a few minutes on the terrace
before we return to our labors." Ramsdale put his half of the orange
and the strawberries on a plate and rose.

Miss Peebles cast the sideboard one longing glance and allowed
Ramsdale to hold her chair for her.

He led the way to the back terrace, which was awash in roses.

"How beautiful," Miss Peebles said. "I don't believe I've ever seen
so many blooming roses."

"You've never been to the botanical gardens?" Ramsdale asked, setting the plate of fruit on the balustrade overlooking the garden.

"Jane says we should go, but Papa is busy."

Papa was a fool. Phineas Peebles had loomed like a god in Ramsdale's youth, a brilliant scholar who could make entire worlds come alive through languages and literature.

With maturity had come a more realistic view of Peebles: brilliant, but also burdened with ambition, and the narrow focus ambition required. The professor meant nobody any harm, but he'd taught in part because he loved to show off his knowledge, not because he'd loved to teach.

The disappointment Ramsdale felt in his former teacher should not have been so keen.

"I'll take you to see the gardens," he said, "once we find whatever Hephaestus was hiding. Have a strawberry."

He held up the plate, and Miss Peebles inspected all eight choices before selecting the most perfectly ripe berry.

"You have been unforthcoming about your motives, my lord. I am seeking the Duke, or any part of the ducal treatise, in order to safeguard my father's reputation, add to his security in old age, and delight the scholarly world. What of you?"

She bit off half the strawberry and held the other half in her fingers. The sight was deucedly distracting.

"Your father showed me how to navigate the path between my papa's demands and my uncle's expectations. I could have a lively interest in learning and be an earl's heir. That was a far better solution than turning into the sort of scapegrace lordling I'd have become otherwise. Have another berry."

"You owe my father?"

"I do, and I always pay my debts."

She chose a second berry. "You have no interest in the actual information that *The Duke's Book of Knowledge* contains?"

Ramsdale took the least-ripe fruit for himself. "Tisanes for easing grief? Elixirs to stir the animal spirits? Medieval love potions? I am a peer of the realm, Miss Peebles. I do not want for companionship from the gentler sex and hardly need alchemical aids to inspire the ladies to notice me."

She dusted her hands and marched off toward the house. "We'd best be getting back to work, my lord. For you, finding the Duke might be a matter of settling a debt, but for me, finding that manuscript looms as a quest, and I cannot achieve my objective while admiring your roses."

They were Melissa's roses. Ramsdale left the plate of fruit behind and followed Miss Peebles to the door.

"There's another reason why the Duke's tisanes and potions have no interest for me in and of themselves."

Miss Peebles acquired that testy-governess expression again. "You don't believe in the tenderness of emotion that characterizes the human heart? Don't believe in love?"

"I believe in many varieties of love," Ramsdale replied, "but if the challenge at hand is stirring a young lady's passion, I prefer to attend to the business myself, using the old-fashioned persuasive powers available to any man of sound mind and willing body."

She regarded him as if he'd switched to a language she could not easily follow.

A demonstration was in order. Ramsdale reached past Miss Peebles's elbow and plucked a pink rosebud from the nearest bush. He treated himself to a whiff of its fragrance, offered it to her, then held the door and followed her back to the library.

WORDS HAD MEANINGS, and those meanings might be varied and subtle, but they remained mostly constant in a given age. Philomena's definition of the Earl of Ramsdale was shifting by the hour, and that bothered her.

He was self-absorbed, arrogant, inconsiderate, and enamored of the privileges of his station—that's how earls went on. They did not trouble over boyhood loyalties, did not insist on small courtesies, and did not engage in whimsical gestures involving spinsters and roses.

And yet... Ramsdale had and he did.

He also showed relentless focus when it came to the task of translating Hephaestus's will. By the time the afternoon sun was slanting toward evening, they'd muddled through the entire will.

The specific bequests had been interesting.

To my niece, Melissa, I bequeath five years to enjoy her widowhood before she allows some handsome nitwit with an enormous glass house to coerce her back into the bonds of matrimony.

To my long-suffering housekeeper, Mrs. Bland, I bequeath the privilege of tossing all of the rubbish that had such sentimental value to me—my old slippers, my nightcap, a lock of fur from my Muffin, may he rest in feline peace.

Ramsdale had sat at the reading table, scratching down a note here and there or sitting for long periods in silence as Philomena did her best to render Hephaestus's commentary into English.

"He paid attention," Ramsdale said when Philomena had finished. "He was not the distracted curmudgeon he wanted people to think he was."

A King James Bible sat on the table on a raised reading stand. The book was enormous and had probably been in the family since the Duke had last been seen. The earl idly swiped at the dust that had collected on the leather cover.

"What do you make of his bequest to you?" Philomena asked.

"Read it again."

The list of specific bequests went on for pages. She had to hunt to find the lines tucked between the life of ease and comfort left to a beloved cat—Muffin's granddaughter, Crumpet—courtesy of that responsibility passing to a neighbor, and a case of piles bequeathed to a retired professor of theology who'd since died of an apoplexy.

"'To my nephew, dear Seton, a bright boy whose potential has been cut short by the dubious burden of an earldom, which will do the lad no good, but some things cannot be helped, I leave the honor of recording my demise in the family Bible, which tome yet rests among good friends I have not visited nearly enough, thanks to the parsimony and stubbornness of the late earl. Seton, you have your father's ability to overlook the treasures immediately beneath your nose, and please do not blame the dimensions of that proboscis on my side of the family, because your Danforth relations must clearly take the blame. In this particular, I wish your resemblance to the late earl were not so marked.'"

Whatever did that mean? Antecedents and pronouns in both the original and the translation were garbled, and Hephaestus had used abbreviations to ensure they remained so. Was it Ramsdale's nose that Hephaestus found regrettable, or a tendency to miss what was to be found immediately beneath that nose?

"I cannot fathom what he was about," Ramsdale said, rising and stretching. "Nor do I think further effort today will be productive. I'll study my notes tonight, and we can resume in the morning."

He moved to the sideboard and regarded his reflection in the mirror above it.

Philomena abandoned the desk to stand at Ramsdale's elbow. "I like your nose."

In the mirror, his gaze shifted from his reflection to Philomena's, who was turning pink before her own eyes.

"I'm rather fond of my nose," Ramsdale said. "At least when the roses are in bloom. Might you elaborate on your observation?"

Was he teasing her? Fishing for flattery? Philomena lacked the social sophistication to decide which, but she could be honest.

"Your nose has character," she said. "It's not a genteel feature. Somebody broke it at least once. Here." She traced her finger over the slight bump on the slope that divided the planes of his face. "I expect that hurt."

"The wound to my pride was severe. I walked into a door while reading Catullus. I was fourteen years old, and the concept of a thousand kisses was both intimidating and fascinating. How long would it take to bestow a thousand kisses?"

"Years, I should think, if the kissing were done properly." Oh, she had not said that. Had not, had not, had not.

Had too. As a slow smile took possession of the earl's expression, Philomena wasn't sorry.

His lordship's smile was merry and conspiratorial and shifted his mien from stern to piratical. He became not merely handsome—most men were handsome at some point in their lives—but attractive. Hard to look away from. Hard to move away from.

Philomena didn't even try. She remained beside him, smiling back at him stupidly in the mirror.

"I knew you had hidden depths," Ramsdale said, the smile acquiring a tinge of puzzlement.

"Perhaps we all do. I'll see myself out." The sun would be up for some time, and Philomena was not Lady Melissa, to be escorted at all hours when setting foot outside her own doorstep.

There went the last of Ramsdale's smile. "You will do no such thing."

"You said we were through for the day, my lord."

"So we are, but you will not travel the streets alone when I am available to remedy that sorry plan. Shall you take your rose with you?"

He plucked the pink blossom from the porcelain bud vase in which it had sat for the afternoon. The rose was only half-open, and the spicy fragrance had come to Philomena on every breeze teasing its way past the windows.

"The blossom is better off here," Philomena said. "That rose belongs in a Sèvres vase, surrounded by learned treatises, velvet upholstery, and Mr. Gainsborough's talent."

Ramsdale sniffed the rose and took out a monogrammed handkerchief.

"Mr. Gainsborough was to my father's taste more than mine, though I do like his equine portraits." He took the vase over to the dust bin and dumped the water over his handkerchief, then wrapped the wet handkerchief around Philomena's rose.

"The blossom should travel well enough if we don't stand about here, arguing over a simple courtesy," he said.

And thus Philomena walked home in the lovely summer sunset on the arm of an earl, who carried for her the single lovely rose. She realized as her own garden gate came into view that Ramsdale was being gallant, as men of his ilk were supposed to be—when it suited them. The title of earl, by definition, did include a certain mannerliness toward the ladies, even a lady of humble station.

Which meant the definition that no longer functioned must be the definition of Philomena herself, for she was most assuredly not the sort of woman to stroll along on the arm of a titled lord, conversing easily about bequests, Latin abbreviations, and the joys of translating a language that had no definite articles.

JACK AND HARRY EAGAN had learned the apothecary's trade from their father, in whose memory they raised a glass of brandy every Saturday evening as they counted the week's earnings.

Mama had been the family's commercial genius, though, and they recalled her in their prayers each day at supper. She'd been the one to insist her grandson Jack Junior be sent off to Cambridge and her other grandson Harry Junior to Oxford. The expenses had nigh bankrupted their papas, but the lads had acquired polish, connections, and a smattering of natural science that gilded advertisements and product descriptions with credibility.

Mama had also pointed out that ladies preferred the counsel of other ladies when purchasing a tisane for Certain Ailments, and thus the Eagan wives were usually on hand to help customers of the female persuasion.

In her later years, Mama had noticed that each social Season resulted in a crop of young ladies eager to employ any means to secure a good match. She'd watched as those young ladies had become increasingly desperate with the passing weeks, until—by early summer—they would have burned their best bonnets and sworn allegiance to the Fiend's housecat if the result was a titled husband.

The Eagans were all red-haired, slight, and energetic, which Mama attributed to having fiery humors, as evidenced by their coloring. Jack Eagan thought the red hair was indicative of quick wits, and Jack's hair was the reddest of them all.

"Poor dears," Harry said, closing the door after another lady's maid had been sent on her way clutching a bag of fragrant dried weeds. "As badly as they want to speak their vows, you'd think the young men of England would oblige them."

"Young men are fools," Jack replied, for that was the expected response and what dear Mama would have called an eternal verity.

"You were a fool," Harry said, twisting the lock on the shop door. "You should not have mentioned that *King's Encyclopedia* business at dinner the other night."

"*Duke's Book of Knowledge,* and it were Hal Junior who suggested we find it."

Hal Junior had gone to Oxford, which he tried without success to lord over his cousin. Jack Junior had grasped the potential to turn the language of science into coin, while Hal had learned to hold his drink.

"Nobody finds what's been lost for two hundred years," Harry said. "That's not a believable tale. We're more likely to find the king's common sense hiding under a toadstool."

"A good tale is only half believable," Jack retorted, "like a rumor on 'Change." He took a rag from beneath the counter and began polishing the shop's wooden surfaces. Harry would do the glass jars and windows, and thus the shop would be neat and tidy for tomorrow's customers.

"But you shouldn't have told that tale to the other chemists and apothecaries," Harry said, starting on the jars of teas and tisanes. The patent remedies were dusted once a week, on Mondays. Fewer people drank to excess on the Sabbath, hence demand for relief slackened early in the week.

"The other fellows will come up with their own schemes," Jack said, "and old manuscripts will be all the rage before the king's birthday. I do so love the smell of this shop, Brother."

Harry paused in his polishing to survey shelves of jars and bottles, treatises, sachets, soaps, elixirs, teas, pomades, fragrances, and recipe collections. Every product was guaranteed to enhance health or well-being in some regard.

"The smell of a successful family enterprise," Harry said, inhaling audibly. "But if all the other chemists have their old manuscripts, then ours won't be special."

Harry was a hard worker, and he took the welfare of the customers to heart. Jack was thus left to deal with more practical matters, such as parting those customers from as much of their coin as possible.

"You are worried about *The Duke's Book of Knowledge* because of that rumpled old fellow who came in here earlier asking about it," Jack said. "That fellow was none other than Professor Phineas Peebles himself."

Harry used his elbow to shine up the glass lid of a large jar labeled Fine English Lavender, though a small quantity of grass clippings might have strayed among those contents.

"What's a professor to me, Jack Eagan?"

"He's our pot of gold. Your own son studied under Peebles at university, and it's from Peebles that Hal Junior learned of *The Duke's Book of Knowledge*. The manuscript is famous, among them as studies manuscripts. Peebles has got wind of our tale, and he'll spread the word, and our shop will soon be the most popular apothecary in London."

Popular being a genteel version of profitable.

Harry repositioned a series of jars sitting on a table in the center of the shop, so they were lined up in exact rows.

"How does one old gent make our shop popular? He didn't buy anything, best as I recall, but took up a good twenty minutes poking about and asking questions."

The next part of the discussion had to be handled delicately, for Harry had inherited Papa's logical mind—logical, Mama had said, as if logic ever moved any faster than a funeral procession.

"Our Elixir of Aphrodite's Joy will be the one everybody buys," Jack said, "because it was discovered by a woman."

"Have you been nipping from the Godfrey's Cordial, Jackie, my lad?"

Lovely stuff, the cordial. It had doubtless soothed the nerves of many a frustrated wife.

"Peebles has a daughter—Hal Junior noticed her, said she's her father's right hand. She reads over everything the professor has published, lives for all that Greek-ish nonsense."

"Galen was Greek. Don't you be insulting our Galen."

Galen's Goodbody Elixir was a perennial favorite with the house-maids and stable boys.

"And the duke fellow," Jack went on, "who had this manuscript writ down was from Florence. The Florentines were powerful clever people, and the professor's daughter is clever too, says Hal Junior."

"He was probably sweet on her."

Hal Junior was sweet on anything in skirts, bless the boy. "So we put it about that the professor's own daughter dreamed that she'd find the recipe beneath the tallest tree on the Lover's Walk at Vauxhall, put there for her by the goddess Aphrodite, to be shared with every unmarried woman of good name in the most important city in the civilized world."

Harry started on the shop window, though most of the smudges and dirt would be on the outside. He cleaned the outside in the morning, the better to greet everybody who happened by and the better to show off the merchandise throughout the day.

In winter, a window cleaned at sunset would be dingy by dawn.

All of these small touches of genius Mama had devised, and Jack abruptly missed his dame. She would have seen the potential in *The Duke's Book of Knowledge*, and she would have concocted a better story than some goddess cavorting among the soiled doves of a London night.

Harry spit on his rag and went after a long streak. "You say Hal Junior studied under this Peebles fellow?"

"Your own dear boy, and Peebles is obsessed with this manuscript. Nobody has seen so much as a page of it since Good King James took the throne long, long ago."

Harry finished with the long streak, and the window sparkled in the evening sunshine.

"Seems to me that Cupid might have left something beneath that tree for the gents," Harry said. "Nothing sorrier than a young man's pangs of unrequited love."

Never underestimate the power of a logical mind. Mama had been right about that too.

"Just so," Jack said, fraternal affection warming his heart. "Gifts from the deities of old to the lovelorn of today, bequeathed to a scholar's plain-faced spinster daughter."

Harry tossed the rag in the air and caught it. "Is she plain-faced? Not like Hal Junior to pay a plain-faced girl much mind."

"She's a scholar's daughter," Jack said, taking a pencil and paper from beneath the counter. "They are always plain-faced. We need product descriptions, Brother. Even the gods benefit from effective advertising."

Harry got out the brandy—stored in a bottle labeled Hungarian Nerve Tonic—and poured two full glasses. Advertising was thirsty work.

Which great wisdom had not come from Mama, but from Jack's own modest perceptions.

CHAPTER FOUR

"But we know that what we imbibe, what we eat, even what we touch and smell, has an effect on our mood," Miss Peebles said. "Why is it outlandish to think that in former times, when folk were more attentive to their natural surroundings, some perspicacious monk noticed that a particular concoction resulted in a greater sense of affection for members of the opposite sex?"

Ramsdale and his translator strolled along in the lengthening shadows as clerks made their way home and shopkeepers closed up for the night. The earl was seldom abroad at this time of day, but he liked the sense of tasks completed, rest earned.

No chess for him tonight. He was too fatigued by his hours in the library with Miss Peebles and her relentless intellect. Then too, Lord Amesbury was a sharp fellow. Ramsdale would allow himself a nap before dressing to join the marquess for dinner.

"You know little of monks, Miss Peebles, if you think they needed a magic potion to increase their awareness of the ladies. The average monk wasn't supposed to be anywhere near the fairer sex, and thus he'd remark each woman he met with great... fondness."

Especially if he was a young fellow and the lady was comely.

Miss Peebles's brow knit, as if the habits of celibate males were one topic beyond the grasp of her brilliance.

"An apothecary, then," she said. "A man happily married, children frolicking at his knee of an evening. He notices that the ginger tea with rose hips he's made to combat sore joints or a bilious stomach also results in a mood that ladies find attractive."

She was passionate about her science, passionate about her languages, passionate about finding the Duke, of whom they'd seen neither word nor phrase. Would she be passionate otherwise?

By virtue of their linked arms, Ramsdale prevented Miss Peebles from charging headlong into the street as a fishmonger's empty wagon clattered by.

"I cannot imagine that ginger and rose hip tea would predispose me to anything other than profanity," Ramsdale said.

"And yet that ungracious observation might be the effect of the rotten-fish stink that came to you as yonder wagon passed us. Admit that the theory of a love potion is sound."

"The theory is not sound," Ramsdale countered, flipping a coin to the crossing sweeper. "You leap, my dear, from a potion having an effect on the person who imbibes it, to that same potion having an effect on the persons in the vicinity of the imbiber. Where is your supporting evidence?"

He cared little for her supporting evidence. He simply enjoyed watching her mind work, watching her free hand gesture for histrionic emphasis, watching the looks of passersby who were amused by a young lady discoursing at volume about Florentine monks and alchemical theories.

"Consider," she said as they turned down the side street that led to her back garden, "the intoxicating effects of spirits."

"My very point," Ramsdale replied. "One drinks to excess, one becomes intoxicated. One's companions do not, unless they too are drinking."

"Is this truly the case, my lord? Is it not more a matter of one man drinks, and his good spirits and bonhomie, his humor and garrulousness, inspire others around him to join him? He's drinking, and soon they are too?"

How could she know—? But of course, she'd know how university boys gathered round a barrel of ale or hard cider.

"That proves nothing. One man's sociability will result in others joining him. That doesn't prove the sociability was the result of..."

"Yes?"

The happy drunk was a fixture in any pub or gentleman's club, and few responded to him with anything other than good will, or at least, tolerance.

"You spout nonsense, Miss Peebles. The spirits work upon the one drinking them. Have you ever become inebriated by association with one consuming spirits?"

Her steps slowed. "No, but I am in company with only my father and Jane when spirits are on hand, and they never consume to excess. Papa would as soon drink ginger tea as wassail or sip flat ale as wine. You must, though, concede that when a lady wears perfume, that does have an effect on the gentlemen in her ambit."

Damn, she was relentless. "You're suggesting the *Motibus Humanis* is more about perfumery than intoxicants or tisanes?"

"You enjoy the scent of that rose, my lord. Most women and men of your strata would not dream of going out of an evening without first splashing on their fragrance of choice. They do so with the express intent of creating a more favorable impression. Who's to say that the impression created isn't..."

They'd reached the little alley running behind her father's modest dwelling. Venerable oaks arched above, and the racket and clatter of the street faded.

"You were saying, Miss Peebles?"

She looked around as if surprised to find herself a half-dozen streets away from where the conversation had started.

"*The Duke's Book of Knowledge* is of interest on a scientific basis, my lord. The ancients grasped the movement of the heavens more clearly than did our nearer ancestors. The same might well be true regarding scents and potions that stir the emotions or plants that aid the cause of medicine."

In the quiet of the alley, Ramsdale realized that the damned manuscript had inspired foolish hopes in an otherwise sensible young woman. Miss Peebles expected wisdom to flow from *The Duke's Book of Knowledge*, valuable insights, genuine science.

"You are daft," he muttered, setting the rose on the nearest stone wall. "Men and women have no need of magic elixirs or exotic scents when it comes to taking notice of each other."

"Beautiful women," she retorted. "Handsome, wealthy men, perhaps. What of the rest of us? What of the plain, the soft-spoken, the shy, the obscure? Do you begrudge them the benefit of science when their loneliness overwhelms them?"

Good God Almighty. She sought the Duke for *herself*.

"Miss Peebles, it is often the case that a woman attracts a man's notice, and because that man is a decent fellow and would not press his attentions uninvited, she remains unaware of his interest. She doesn't need the dratted, perishing Duke, she needs only a small demonstration of the fellow's interest."

Another demonstration. Miss Peebles regarded the rose resting on the stone wall a few feet away, the stem wrapped in Ramsdale's damp white handkerchief. She seemed puzzled, as if she'd forgotten the flower, and possibly the man who'd carried it halfway across London for her.

"Miss Peebles—Philomena—you will attend me, please."

Ramsdale took her by the shoulders. Her expression was wary and bewildered, and thus he schooled himself to subtlety. No one would see them in this quiet, shadowed alley, but by the throne of heaven and in the name of every imponderable, Miss Peebles would take notice of *him*.

He framed her face in his hands and kissed her.

～

RAMSDALE'S PALMS and fingertips were callused, while his kiss was the essence of tenderness. Philomena was so stunned by the earl's attentions, so utterly unprepared for such intimacy, that she wasted precious seconds searching for words to describe sensations.

Gentle, teasing, delicate, daring... oh, the adjectives flew past in a jumble as Ramsdale shifted, and a debate ensued between Philomena's mind and her body. Her intellect sought desperately to catalog experiences—his thumb brushing over her cheek, his body so tall and solid next to hers, the imprint of his pocket watch against her ribs— while her body railed against words and labels.

And her body was right: This experience was beyond her ability to describe. Rejoicing sang in her blood, while a great emptiness welled too—the unfulfilled longings of a woman invisible for too long, invisible even to herself.

She startled as Ramsdale's tongue flirted with her upper lip. So soft, so intimate that single touch.

He eased his mouth from hers, and Philomena sank her hand into his hair.

Don't go. Not yet. Not so soon. This experiment isn't over.

He wrapped an arm around her, and Philomena leaned into him, breathing with him and gathering her courage.

All day, she'd remained steadfastly loyal to her missing Duke, droning on and on about cats, nightcaps, megrims, and mulligrubs. She'd puzzled out abbreviations, resurrected forgotten vocabulary, and deconstructed sentences that were the grammatical equivalent of London's Roman wall.

Her mind was tired, her soul was lonely, and her body was clamoring for more of Ramsdale's kisses.

He apparently considered that little taste of intimacy enough, a mere pressing of mouths and bodies, a single flirtation of the tongue, and this half embrace in twilight shadows. Indignation organized itself from among the welter of emotions silently racking Philomena.

Indignation that her only experience of a pleasurable kiss should be so brief, so quickly over. Years ago, a few of the university boys had tried to steal kisses from her. Their larceny had been hasty, inept, and so very disappointing.

Philomena's history of kisses had nothing in common with the raptures Catullus had written of, and Ramsdale's kiss hinted of greater joys than she'd glimpsed. He ran his hand down her back, a slow caress that spoke of competence and confidence.

He drew a breath and slowly let it out, her cheek riding the rise and fall of his chest. "Philomena, I did not intend—"

No. No, Ramsdale would not apologize, reason away, or explain his kiss, not when he'd shared such a fleeting, paltry hint of what Philomena suspected a kiss—with him—could be. She took a firm grip of his hair, gave him one instant to stare at her in surprise, then joined her mouth to his.

He remained passive, drat him to the bowels of the British Museum, did not repeat that caress to her back, did not sigh against her mouth, but remained stoically enduring her kiss, as if some other man had shown her the cherishing tenderness he'd lavished on her moments ago.

Philomena did not know what to do, did not have a vocabulary of caresses or love words, so she resorted to imitation, to dancing her tongue across his lips, once, twice... To running her hand over his chest in a slow exploration of masculine contours. She pressed closer, until she could feel the mechanism of his watch moving in a tiny, mechanical march beneath her heart.

Do not leave me to wonder for another ten years what a kiss might be. Do not abandon me to uncertainty and ignorance. Do not set me aside, ignore me, or assume that you may determine all the parameters of our dealings.

All of this she put into her kiss. She conveyed to Ramsdale the longing and loneliness, the outrage and frustration, on a soft groan. He lashed his arms about her and lifted her bodily, bracing her back against the wall.

He plundered, she invaded. He lectured, she rebutted. He took her captive, and she declared victory, until they were both panting.

Ramsdale braced a hand above her head against the wall, and Philomena let him support her.

Her mind would not work, her body would not calm. Not in any language did she have words for what she'd just experienced.

With Ramsdale before her and the wall at her back, Philomena occupied a small world filled with the scent and heat of him, and with her own sense of vindication. There was more to life than Latin and mending. She had both hoped and feared it was so, and silently thanked Ramsdale for confirming her suspicions.

"I hear Catullus laughing," he said, straightening enough to trace a finger down the side of Philomena's cheek.

The earl was all self-possession and wry amusement, while Philomena felt as if she'd walked into a door. What mortal could survive a thousand such kisses, much less write poetry about them?

"Laughing at me?" Philomena asked.

The amusement in his eyes faded, replaced by what might have been sadness. "No, love." He straightened and ran a hand through his hair. "Should I apologize?"

"I will kick you if you apologize, my lord. Kick you in a notoriously vulnerable location."

He stepped back. Moment by moment, he was assembling his earl-lishness. Sardonic half smile, proud bearing, distant gaze, subtly unwelcoming expression... Philomena wanted to weep, to take his hand and place it against her cheek, to prove by touch that a man, not merely an aristocrat, shared the alley with her.

"Do you agree," he said, taking her rose from the top of the wall, "that one need not resort to potions or magic formulas to engage the attentions of a member of the opposite sex?"

Philomena took the rose from his grasp and brought it to her nose. He'd tried for lordly amusement and failed. His question had been flung too carelessly in her direction, his gaze remained too steadfastly on the cobblestone path they'd trod.

Philomena unlatched the gate to her father's back garden. "No, I do not agree. A wound might heal without medical attention, but heal faster if properly treated. You might attract a lady through your appearance, wealth, or skills, but capturing her heart could happen more easily if you had the Duke's secrets. We can discuss this at greater length when I resume translating tomorrow."

She was grateful for the deepening shadows and steeled herself for a witticism that would cut, for all it amused. Ramsdale apparently hadn't meant for that kiss to become so passionate, and that clearly bothered him. Philomena liked that he was bothered on her account, and that was foolish.

He bowed. "I'll bid you good evening."

A curtsey was in order. Philomena instead kissed the earl's cheek, then latched the garden gate behind her. She sat in solitude long after the earl's steps had faded, until darkness had fallen and the air had grown chilly.

And still, she had no words for what that kiss meant to her.

"IF YOU GENTLEMEN WILL EXCUSE ME," Lady Maude said, "I'll bid you good evening. Do enjoy the port." She curtseyed and aimed a demure smile at Ramsdale. The angle of her curtsey was such that a view of her décolletage was also aimed his direction.

"You're fond of chess," the Marquess of Amesbury said as his daughter quit the dining room. "Let's repair to the game room, shall we?"

"A fine notion."

Was Ramsdale fond of Lady Maude? Of all the young ladies on offer this year, he'd thought her the most appealing. She was sensible, of an appropriate station to become his countess, played the pianoforte well but not too well, and enjoyed apparent good health.

"How did you find His Grace of Lavelle?" Amesbury asked, taking a seat on the black side of the chessboard.

The game room was the most masculine domain in the entire town house, with fowling pieces, dress swords, and hunting portraits sharing equal space on the walls. A billiards table dominated the room, and the card table would seat eight comfortably.

The chess table had been set up by the fireplace, with screens positioned to reflect both light and warmth.

So why did the chess set feel like a metaphor for an elegant ambush?

"I found Their Graces well," Ramsdale said. "Their daughter thrives too. Berkshire is pretty at any time of year, and Lavelle's ancestral pile has benefited from having a duchess in residence."

Amesbury tidied up his forces, putting each piece at the exact center of the square. The marquess was a spare, dapper fellow with thinning sandy hair and an avuncular air that masked a keen interest in politics.

Ramsdale was not interested in politics, any more than most schoolboys were interested in sums. One endured, one did what was necessary. One did not pretend to a propensity one lacked.

"Lavelle's choice of duchess was unusual," Amesbury said. "But then, His Grace is without parents or elders to guide him on such a matter. Perhaps the duchess, being of gentry stock, will be a good breeder."

The comment was distasteful. Lavelle had married a neighbor of long-standing from a respectable family. More to the point, he'd married a woman with whom he was wildly in love.

Ramsdale moved a queen's pawn.

"Their Graces were well acquainted before the marriage," he said, "and the duchess comes from respectable family on both sides. Lavelle chose deliberately and well. Your move, sir."

Actually, Ramsdale was the one who should have been making a move. The purpose of this gathering, despite the meal served and the chess in progress, was for him to ask permission to court Lady Maude.

He'd made that decision in June, as the Season had ended. An earl needed heirs, and Ramsdale had no interest in entangling himself in that great drama known as the love match.

The marquess moved his king's knight, which usually presaged a slow march across the field.

"Lavelle chose expediently," Amesbury said. "His duchess, being of common stock, won't expect lavish entertainments or London extravagance. She'll be content to manage her nursery, but she'll hardly be a political asset."

While Lady Maude would be the perfect political hostess.

Ramsdale moved his bishop. Bishops covered a lot of ground in a single move and tended to be overlooked as weapons.

"I hope every mother would take an interest in the denizens of her nursery," Ramsdale said. "My own mama certainly did."

Amesbury sat back, as if the game had progressed past opening moves, which—where Lady Maude was concerned—it should have.

"Times were different," Amesbury said. "My own late marchioness knew better than to meddle where the boys were concerned, but she lavished the best governesses and tutors on our Lady Maude. My daughter had a different instructor for watercolors and pastels, a voice teacher, and a teacher for the pianoforte. She's quite accomplished."

Could she insult a man in Low German? Work at the same document for four straight hours? Make a feast of a simple luncheon and kiss as if she were promising her whole soul to the one who kissed her back?

Ramsdale pretended to study the board, though in his mind's eye, he was seeing Philomena seated at his desk, twiddling a goose quill while she sorted various possibilities for an obscure abbreviation.

Philomena gesturing enthusiastically as she explained the intricacies of the vocative case to Ramsdale along the length of Oxford Street.

Philomena grabbing him by the hair and kissing him so passionately he'd nearly started unbuttoning his falls.

"Your move, Ramsdale."

He advanced another pawn, a random, dilatory maneuver that fit into no larger strategy.

"How fares your bill?" Ramsdale asked. Amesbury always had bills churning about in the House of Lords.

"Which one? My bill for the establishment of a board to oversee the turnpike trusts is meeting with significant opposition, but then, we knew it would. I'll not be worn down by a bunch of pinchpenny barons who can't see that roads are the key to the realm's commercial success. Yes, we can ship a great deal by sea or canal, but how do the goods get to and from port, I ask you?"

As the game wandered along, Ramsdale lured Amesbury from one political diatribe to the next, though the marquess occasionally tossed in references to Lady Maude's attributes as a hostess, waltzing partner, and musician.

Before his lordship started mentioning how many teeth the lady possessed, Ramsdale brought the chess game to a close. The marquess played without guile, simply moving pieces about in reaction to Ramsdale's initiatives.

Such a man was easy to manage, and thus Ramsdale made the game look much closer than it was. Ramsdale did not, however, allow the marquess an unearned victory.

"Will you be attending Professor Peebles's retirement banquet?" Ramsdale asked, returning his pieces to their starting positions.

The marquess put the black queen on her square. "Phineas Peebles? Why do you ask?"

"I was under the impression he was a family connection. Am I mistaken?"

Amesbury considered the queen. "You are not mistaken, though Peebles disdains to recollect that notion. Academics can be eccentric."

The marquess, who'd waxed loquacious about turnpikes, excise taxes, and the economic implications of imported French soaps, said nothing more.

"Peebles has a daughter," Ramsdale said, setting the white king on his square. Ramsdale had looked for a resemblance between

Philomena and her cousin Lady Maude and found little. Lady Maude was dainty, blond, and graceful.

Philomena was substantial, plain, and ferociously passionate.

"Peebles has a daughter, as do I," Amesbury said. "A pity Maude could not play us a few airs while we enjoyed our chess. She's very skilled."

Skilled, not passionate. A proper lady had no use for passion, and if asked a week ago, Ramsdale would have approved of that view.

Then Philomena had shown up at the Albion, wearing those ridiculous blue glasses, waiting two hours for a chance to earn some coin.

When all the pieces had been positioned, Amesbury turned the board so he had the white pieces. "Shall we play again? I'll not be distracted this time by your parliamentary questions. You can fool me once, Ramsdale, but I'm wise to your tricks now."

Amesbury shook an admonitory finger at Ramsdale, the gesture intended to be playful.

Ramsdale was not charmed. The moment had come to raise the topic of paying addresses to Lady Maude, and Ramsdale wasn't charmed by that prospect either.

"The hour grows late," he said, the most trite of clichés, "and I'm not entirely recovered from ruralizing in Berkshire. I'll thank you for a fine meal and a good game, my lord."

Amesbury was too much the parliamentarian to show his dismay at this abrupt departure. He rose and accompanied Ramsdale to the stairs.

"You were hoping to spend more of the evening with Lady Maude, I venture. How can the chessboard compare to a young woman's accomplishments? Perhaps next week you'll share another meal with us. I'm free on Wednesday, and I know Lady Maude will rearrange her schedule at her papa's request."

Such an obedient female, was Lady Maude. Obedient, and... dull, bless her soul. Ramsdale would not have to exert himself to win her or woo her, wouldn't have to compete with Catullus or the mysteries of medieval law Latin to gain her notice.

"My schedule is as yet unsettled," Ramsdale said, making his way to the front door. "Perhaps I'll see you at Peebles's retirement banquet?"

This question was the equivalent of moving a pawn to distract from a larger strategy, a random exploratory gesture that amounted to nothing.

"Not likely. Why don't we plan on Thursday if Wednesday doesn't suit?"

"Perhaps the following week," Ramsdale said as the butler handed him his greatcoat. "I'll send 'round an invitation when I've sorted out my current obligations."

"And gained the permission of your cook," Amesbury said. "I know how the bachelor household is run. The right countess could spare you all that."

Hunt season had begun in the shires and apparently here in London as well.

"I'll bid you good night, my lord, and thanks again for a lovely evening."

Ramsdale did not run down the steps, though he set a brisk pace —a very brisk pace.

CHAPTER FIVE

"This is the worst codicil so far," Philomena said. "I'll need to start a list of terms I can't translate and have Jane help me with them."

Ramsdale had taken to wandering the library rather than making notes. That's how convoluted and hopeless the sixth codicil was. Philomena had been able to translate the first three at sight, the fourth by consulting a few references, and the fifth by consulting every reference Ramsdale's library boasted.

Five days remained before Papa's banquet, with three codicils to go and not a Duke or *de Motibus Humanis*—the portion of the work Hephaestus referenced most often—in sight.

Ramsdale peered into the lens of a telescope that was aimed at the leafy canopy of the square across the street. "You'd consult Jane rather than your father?"

"Papa thinks I'm teaching your sister French." That scheme had been Ramsdale's own invention, though for the past few days, the earl had been distracted—taking very few notes, mostly staring into space, while Philomena stumbled and thrashed her way through Hephaestus's verbal puzzles.

"Teaching Melissa her French, right." The orrery gained his

notice next. He gave Venus a gentle nudge with one finger and set the planets in motion. The solar system had been crafted mostly of copper, and midday sunshine pouring through the window turned the heavenly bodies to fire as they traveled in their orbits.

"My lord, if you're bored, I can struggle on here without you. I'm sure you have better things to do."

Better things to do than distract Philomena from her Latin, which Ramsdale did without even saying a word. The pull and stretch of his breeches over his thighs as he paced the library was a declension Philomena had never noticed before: need, want, desire, yearning, longing.

Ramsdale's mouth had become a conjugation of possibilities: I kiss, you kiss, he kisses, we kiss...

He halted the sun, moon, and planets. "I shall be going out. I can have your luncheon served here or in the breakfast parlor."

Philomena was certain that "going out" had not been on his lord-ship's agenda two minutes ago, but getting rid of him would be a relief.

Mostly. "In here will suffice. We are running out of time, and so far, I can't see a single clue among all of Hephaestus's rantings."

He'd gone Old Testament on them with the fourth codicil, pearls before swine, a dog returning to its vomit, all quite graphic and unpleasant, and much of it an exhortation in Ramsdale's direction.

"I'd rather you not consult with Jane, if you can avoid it."

"I can avoid it."

He crossed to the door, then paused and scowled at Philomena. "You are working too hard. You are tired, and I'll not have it said I was inconsiderate of your welfare."

Sleepless nights spent alternately regretting and reliving certain kisses and long evenings consulting Papa's reference books had cost Philomena much rest.

"While you have grown snappish, my lord. Be about your busi-ness. It's not as if I'll make off with your uncle's will."

Philomena had offered, daily, to take the will home with her, where those references would be closer at hand and the distractions fewer. She'd have to hide her work from Papa, and that didn't sit well, but her concern was moot.

Ramsdale was adamant that she work in his town house. He had latched on to the notion that further clues to the Duke's whereabouts lurked among his uncle's small collection of rare tomes, all of which were housed in the earl's library.

"You've tried to make off with the will," Ramsdale said. "You pester me daily to make off with that document, when you expressly agreed to do the work here."

Philomena rose, her back protesting even as other parts rejoiced to be free of the chair.

"I had no idea how complicated your uncle's prose would become. I had no idea you would be perching at the reading table like a mother cat at a mousehole. I had no idea..." Philomena stood before Ramsdale, truly looking at him for the first time that day. "*You* are tired, and you see your own fatigue when you look at me."

"Too much waltzing, one of the hazards of my station." Still, he didn't march off to his appointment, if any appointment he had.

"Do you want to kiss me again?" Philomena hadn't planned to ask the question, though it had filled every corner of her mind not already crammed with Latin.

Ramsdale's expression became very stern. "What I want doesn't matter, Miss Peebles. I should not have taken liberties with a young woman who has enjoyed a sheltered existence and, in a temporary sense, could be said to be under my protect—"

Philomena kissed him, mostly to stop him from spouting a lecture about propriety, deportment, and the temptations of the flesh.

Also, because she'd thought of little else but kissing him for days.

The experiment was a failure. Kissing Ramsdale in his library, Philomena found none of the surprise, none of the tenderness and wonder that she'd experienced in the shadowy alley. She might as well have been kissing the planet Saturn, warmed by the sun but inert metal for all its fiery—

Ramsdale's arms stole around her and pulled her close. "Drat you —" He drew the pencil from Philomena's chignon and tossed it over his shoulder. "All week, I have tried..."

That was encouragement enough. Philomena resumed kissing him, her pace more leisurely. Ramsdale was apparently not indifferent, but he was held hostage by gentlemanly scruples, for which Philomena had to like him.

"All week, my patience has been tried," Philomena said against his mouth. "Are you truly indifferent to a woman whom you've embraced so passionately?"

Jane said men were like that. Their pleasures did not involve their finer feelings, but Jane was a spinster, as best Philomena knew.

Ramsdale twisted the lock above the door latch. "Are you truly more interested in a lot of damned Latin than you are in my kisses?"

Philomena answered him without words, until tongues tangled, the world fell away, and she had the earl pressed up against the door. Delving into great books was a fine pastime for a lively mind, but as the mind gorged, the heart could starve.

Ramsdale had shown Philomena that with a single kiss.

"You are interested." Philomena glossed a hand over Ramsdale's falls. "I grew up in a house full of biological treatises and rude university boys. You are interested, my lord."

Ramsdale captured her hand and kissed her knuckles. "Ladies aren't supposed to *be* interested, and regardless of your father's reduced circumstances, you are a lady who enjoyed a sheltered upbringing."

Amid the joy and desire coursing through Philomena, confusion blossomed. Papa's circumstances weren't reduced, though compared to an earl's, they were humble. Comfortably humble.

Too humble for Philomena to have designs on a peer of the realm. "I am a spinster, my lord, and you spoke in error. I did not *enjoy* a sheltered upbringing, I *endured* one. My situation was all the more frustrating because I had access to the best literature penned here or on the Continent. The French have a far more enlightened view of women than we English do, and their women are doubtless happier as a result."

Ramsdale sidled away from the door and picked up the pencil he'd tossed aside earlier. "The French women you call happy I call left to fend for themselves, unprotected, even disrespected."

Nothing killed a tender moment as quickly as a philosophical disagreement.

"I'm sure the ladies of France would rather we'd killed fewer of their menfolk in the recent hostilities, instead of quibbling about the respect the women are owed now."

Ramsdale slid the pencil back into Philomena's coiffure. "I concede that point. I will also admit that, on the one hand, my knowledge of Hephaestus and his life will prove invaluable if we're to identify clues to the location of any part of the Duke. On the other hand, if I sit here any longer staring at your mouth, or your hands, or your other attributes, I shall go daft. We are at another impasse, Miss Peebles. As a gentleman, I apologize for my blunt speech. As a man, I owe you honesty. This arrangement is not working."

Philomena took the pencil from her hair—it was pulling at her scalp—and set it on the blotter.

"This arrangement is working well to get the will translated. Not another scholar in all of London, save Jane or my father, could undertake this exercise half so expediently as I have, and they'd charge you—"

Ramsdale put a finger to her lips. "Miss Peebles—Philomena—I am trying to be a gentleman. You agreed to translate the will in exchange for coin. I would be the basest scoundrel imaginable if I parlayed that agreement into an exchange of favors no gentleman would ask of a lady."

That finger slid across her lips, down her cheek, down her neck, to trace along the décolletage of Philomena's day dress. One touch, and she was muddled beyond speech.

Ramsdale was propositioning her.

No. He was trying *not* to proposition her.

"You don't even like me," he said. "I know well that kissing a man out of curiosity or boredom isn't at all the same thing as liking him. We have an animal attraction. I've been attracted before, doubtless so have you. It doesn't have to mean anything."

Had he spouted off in some obscure eastern dialect, Philomena could not have been more befuddled.

"I do like you," she said. "You are honorable, you are considerate, you are patient and determined. You are... I like your voice. When all I knew of you was the strutting earl, I did not care for your company. Now I know the man who keeps the fire built up, who insists on escorting me, who makes sure I eat and refuses to let me toil until all hours. You gave me a rose."

He studied the floor, a complicated parquet of blond oak. "Nobody gives you roses?"

"Nobody gives me roses, violets, or even daisies. Nobody fixes my tea just how I like it. Nobody demands that I put my books aside to take a pleasant stroll in the early evening sunshine. Nobody listens to me spout off about the lesser-used Latin cases."

"You are passionate about the vocative."

Also the locative, which everybody forgot. "I like you, my lord. I like you."

Happy surprise accompanied Philomena's words, because they were utterly true. The last, grumpy, lonely part of her still didn't entirely trust Ramsdale—he'd had years to hunt for the Duke, so why take on that challenge now?—but she did like him.

And his kisses.

"HE'S no longer interested in offering for me." Lady Maude sounded about eight years old, while her papa felt closer to eighty-seven. Late nights arguing politics took a toll, and young people these days were given to needless drama.

"Ramsdale will certainly not offer for you if your mouth becomes set in that unattractive pout, my dear. He's been back in Town but a fortnight, and he was most attentive to you when he took a meal with us."

"I am a marquess's daughter," Maude said, opening the cover over the pianoforte's keys. "He can't think to do better."

Amesbury set aside his morning newspaper, for he'd get no reading done once Maude started on her finger exercises.

"Don't put on airs, my dear. Ramsdale could well marry the daughter or sister of a duke. The earl has ever been close to the Duke of Lavelle, for example." Ramsdale and Lavelle had met under Phineas Peebles's roof, of all places.

Maude placed a sheaf of music on the rack, though after all these years of diligent study, she ought to have every drill and scale memorized.

"Lavelle's sister is married. Why must men be so fickle, Papa? Ramsdale showed me marked attention last Season. Everybody said so. Then he disappears to Berkshire, and it's as if he forgot all about me."

In all likelihood, given the blandishments available in the countryside, he had. A man of Ramsdale's robust nature didn't hare off to Berkshire just to watch birds.

"If it's any comfort, Ramsdale could barely give me his attention for the duration of a single chess game. Once you left us, he was incapable of focusing."

Or he'd been bored.

"I adore a rousing game of chess."

Rousing game of chess was an oxymoron, even with Ramsdale, who enjoyed deep stratagems and wily ploys. A pity the earl wasn't much inclined toward politics.

"One of your many fine accomplishments," Amesbury said, wishing for the thousandth time his marchioness had not abandoned him for the celestial realm. Her ladyship would have known what to *do* with Maude, who seemed one Season away from becoming shrewish and demanding.

And the poor lady was barely twenty years old.

"A countess must be accomplished," Maude said, beginning on an infernally gloomy minor scale at an interval of a sixth. This was one of her favorite exercises, one she could execute in every key.

"My dear, might you start off with a graceful air? I'll repair to the library, and the happy strains of your pianoforte will lighten my mood as I deal with the day's correspondence."

Amesbury started for the parlor door, while Maude brought her scale to a close in the bass register.

"Papa, I can't lose Ramsdale. He's not charming, he's not friendly, he barely makes conversation when he stands up with a lady, but he's an earl and well-to-do."

"So you've mentioned." Several dozen times a day for the past six months.

"He also singled me out last Season. I can't allow him to go strutting on his way, or I shall become an object of pity. You must make him offer for me."

Never had a stack of correspondence beckoned with such a sense of succor. "His lordship won't be marrying me, Maude Hermione. He'll propose to you. If you've set your cap for him, then you must be the one to inspire his addresses. He said he'd invite us to dinner when he was settled here in Town, but nothing is stopping you from enjoying the carriage parade at the fashionable hour or enjoying a quiet hack first thing in the day."

Ramsdale would never subject himself to the carriage parade. Maude would never leave her bed in time to ride at dawn.

"Everybody takes the air in the park," she said, embarking on the same lugubrious scale at an interval of a tenth. "I must be more bold."

"No, you must not. In my day, if a couple was thought to suit, their mamas would have a friendly chat, their papas would nod agreeably, and the young fellow and the lady would be given a few opportunities to get to know each other. Nobody grew desperate, nobody engaged in unseemly fits of pique. If Ramsdale senses that you have become so lost to dignity as to pursue him, then I assure you, he'll decamp for the shires without a glance in your direction."

Amesbury wanted to decamp for the shires, and Maude was his only begotten daughter.

She increased the tempo of her scales, and her fingers stumbled. "Mama was eighteen when she married you. I'm twenty, Papa. Twenty years old, and everybody knows it. Marilee Newcomb is plain, common, and only modestly dowered, and she's engaged to a marquess."

Maude's litany of indignities could go on for hours.

"The press of business does not allow me to discuss this topic at greater length, my dear, but lamenting and comparing gain you nothing. If you are interested in Ramsdale, then you must be where he will notice you in a favorable light. Show off your new bonnet, show off your French. He's known to be a fine amateur linguist, and I'll warrant Marilee Nobody can barely wish her marquess good day in any language but English."

Maude always had a new bonnet, also new shoes, new reticules, new gloves. She was nothing if not well attired.

"That's it," she said, leaving off in the middle of a scale. "My French. I'm quite clever at it. All of my tutors said so. Tomorrow, I'll pay a call on Lady Melissa, and we'll chatter away in French until Ramsdale is quite besotted. Thank you, Papa. It's a fine strategy, and when next we dine at the earl's home, he'll be smitten."

That was no sort of strategy at all. Ramsdale wasn't even likely to be home, much less at his sister's elbow when she entertained callers.

"Very clever, my dear. I'm off to tend to my parliamentary business. A keyboard serenade wouldn't go amiss, if you're in the mood to indulge me."

Maude set aside the book of finger exercises and laid her hands on the keyboard. A sinking sensation accompanied the pretty picture she made, for if she wasn't using music, that meant Amesbury was about to endure one of her party pieces.

He withdrew, leaving the door open, because Maude would

notice if he closed it. As he sat down to work at his desk across the corridor, strains of some sonata or other reverberated through the house, the tempo too fast, the dynamic too loud.

As usual.

NOBODY GAVE PHILOMENA PEEBLES ROSES—OR violets or daisies. This struck Ramsdale as a great wrong, beyond an injustice. Of all ladies, a woman whose imagination dwelled in ancient Rome, while her nose was in a book and her person stuck behind walls of treatises and tomes, deserved posies.

He held out a hand. "Come with me, Miss Peebles."

She crossed her arms. "I have work to do."

He dropped his hand. "And if you are to do that work efficiently, you must rest your eyes and your mind, take sustenance, and permit an occasional change of scene."

Her gaze went to the desk, where the dratted sixth codicil lay in its crabbed, arcane glory. Hephaestus was waxing dire about Sodom and Solomon, admonishing his nephew at length about abuses of titled power, as best Ramsdale could figure.

Or possibly, Uncle had been going on about the House of Lords. For the first time in days, Ramsdale didn't care.

"Miss Peebles, those documents aren't going anywhere. You will work more efficiently for allowing me to divert your attention to a different topic."

She studied her hands, the right one bearing various ink stains. "You might try asking."

Ah. *Of course.* "May I show you something?"

"Yes, you may." The mischief in her eyes transformed a modestly pretty woman into a siren. Ramsdale's imagination galloped off in unruly—*unclothed*—directions while he held open the library door.

"Where are we going, my lord?"

"Up to my office," he said. "I keep some references there rather than here in the library, this being a public room."

"Latin references? Histories?"

He accompanied her up the stairs, pausing only to ask a footman to have luncheon served on the back terrace.

"I work up here," Ramsdale said, ushering her into his private office. "Meet with my factors, tend to correspondence, and hide from my sister. She would no more disturb me here than I'd intrude on her sitting room."

Miss Peebles stood peering about near the doorway. The library was on the ground floor, the windows looking out on the street. Propriety was nominally maintained when Ramsdale was alone with an unmarried woman there, particularly with Melissa in the house and the library door open.

Or mostly open.

The office, by contrast, was private and much smaller. When Ramsdale had invited—ordered, asked—Miss Peebles to join him here, he hadn't considered what the chamber said about him or how intimate the closer quarters might feel.

"You are tidy," Miss Peebles said, "and you like to have beauty around you."

Landscapes rather than portraits, a few roses in a Venetian glass vase. "Yes."

"And you are attached to your comforts."

Worn slippers sat by the reading chair near the hearth. An afghan had been folded over the hassock, and Uncle's youngest cat, an enormous gray specimen named Genesis—the only tangible bequest from uncle to nephew—lay curled atop the afghan, his chin on his paws.

"I'm not half so attached to my comforts as that dratted feline is."

"Oh, isn't he splendid?" Miss Peebles advanced into the room and knelt by the hassock. "Such a handsome fellow and so soft."

Genesis began to rumble—he claimed nothing so refined as a purr —and Miss Peebles stroked his head and back as if she'd never before had such a privilege.

Genesis squinted at Ramsdale. *This lady can visit any time.*

"I'd give him to you," Ramsdale said, "except he'll eat you out of house and hanging hams without catching a single mouse. Genesis enjoys a contemplative existence."

Miss Peebles cuddled the cat against her chest. "You'd give away such a fine, handsome beast? You'll hurt his feelings with such jests."

Genesis rubbed his cheek along Miss Peebles's décolletage, then squinted at Ramsdale again.

Some expressions needed no translation, not even between species.

"By virtue of Uncle's final arrangements, Genesis and I are stuck with each other. If you can tear yourself away from his abundant charms, there's a book I'd like to show you."

She carried the cat with her to stand beside Ramsdale as he took a volume bound in red leather down from the shelves.

"You are in want of flowers," he said. "This is an herbal of sorts, published by Professor Axel Belmont. The illustrations are exquisite because the professor's discourse is on the medicinal use of common ornamentals."

Miss Peebles set the cat on Ramsdale's desk and took the book. "He dedicated it to his wife. How lovely." She leafed through the pages, and lovely became a woman standing in Ramsdale's office, her bodice adorned with gray cat hairs, a pencil sticking out of her chignon.

"If the book appeals to you, I want you to have it." *I want you to have me.*

That thought was like the solution to a chess riddle. Ramsdale had spent the past few days pondering, considering, cogitating—and lusting—when he ought to have been attending to Miss Peebles's translations of various codicils.

He desired her. That sentiment—those sensations—had been easily categorized. He wanted to join his body to hers and bring her pleasure as no ancient poem or elegant translation could. He wanted to make her burn and laugh and forget every word of every language she'd ever learned save pure physical expression.

He'd desired other women. She'd probably desired other men. Nothing profound there, though the attraction he felt for Miss Peebles bordered on the ungovernable.

Desire, however, wasn't the entire definition of Ramsdale's sentiments where Miss Peebles was concerned, and thus he'd devoted his attention to that riddle while she'd devoted her attention to Uncle's will.

What, exactly, did he feel for her?

She looked up from the book. "You are giving me this herbal? The illustrations belong in an art collection."

"Nobody gives you flowers," Ramsdale said. "These are flowers that will never fade, with descriptions that include the Latin names as well as the practical uses of each blossom. The book suits you."

She clutched it to her chest. "Because I am practical?"

He took the herbal from her and set it on the desk. "Because you have an attractiveness that will not fade, a luminous spirit that's as much passion as intellect, as much of the soul as the body, and I must kiss you in the next instant, or I will descend into bad verse and maudlin quotations."

He did not kiss her, but rather, waited for her verdict.

Desire could be as impersonal as it was intimate. A randy fellow sought a willing wench, a lusty wench sought a willing fellow. Beyond a few details of physical preference, the particular party on the other side of the bed in such an encounter didn't matter. Fondness might play a role, but attachment need not.

Ramsdale wanted Philomena Peebles to desire *him*—not the earl, not a willing, randy fellow—but Seton Avery, a man better than some, by no means a saint, who very specifically valued her. He wanted her respect, not simply her desire. He wanted her to enjoy his company, of all the daft notions, to look forward to being with him as he looked forward to being with her.

In some language or other, these inclinations of the heart likely had a name, probably among the incurable ailments and afflictions.

"You look so serious," she said, smoothing an ink-stained finger between his brows. "And so kissable."

She pressed her lips to his, gently, as if he needed coaxing, and yet, she was right. This kiss was different—premeditated, prefaced with what amounted to a declaration, for him—and a headlong descent into passion wasn't all that he needed from her.

Ramsdale took Philomena in his arms and rejoiced.

And then he kissed her back.

CHAPTER SIX

"Where are you off to?" Jane asked.

"Knightsbridge," the professor replied. "I don't suppose you'd like to come with me?" He posed the question casually, without much hope of an affirmative response. Jane was a pragmatic soul, and toddling about London hardly amounted to a productive use of her time.

Jane straightened the folds of his cravat, which were forever getting wrinkled into the creases of his jacket and waistcoat.

She took down a bonnet from the hooks beside the porter's nook. "Hold still."

Next, she extracted a nacre hatpin from the bonnet, repositioned the trailing ends of Phineas's cravat—he could never tie the damned things correctly—and used her hatpin to put his linen in order.

"Thank you."

She remained where she was, a woman no longer young for all she was still handsome and had a fine figure. Phineas wasn't young either, and he hoped Jane regarded that as a point in his favor.

"One doesn't want to presume on Dora's memory," she said. "But I can't have you going out in public looking half dressed."

"Mrs. Peebles left me to dress myself," Phineas said. His late wife had left him very much to his own devices, particularly after Philomena had arrived. Theirs had been a mésalliance, an act of rebellion on Dora's part, a fit of lunacy on his.

He'd not been able to keep her in the style she deserved, and she'd not been able to hide her disappointment.

"What is your errand in Knightsbridge?" Jane asked.

"I am dissatisfied with my interrogation of the Eagan brothers. They professed to have no knowledge of the *Liber Ducis de Scientia*. I had occasion to press Mr. Handley for details regarding his confreres, the Eagans, and he reiterated his tale of old manuscripts and secret potions."

Jane passed Phineas his hat, which he'd been known to leave the house without. "You think a pair of scheming shopkeepers have found a manuscript that has eluded your lifelong search?"

"I don't know what to think. Why would they come up with this notion now, Jane? Why, when my retirement is imminent, should anybody profess to have found even a single page of the document?"

Jane tied her bonnet ribbons in a soft bow. "My cloak, if you please."

Phineas obliged by draping her cloak over her shoulders, though he would not have assumed such familiarity was welcome. Jane was a grown woman, capable of asking for assistance when she needed same. She turned and raised her chin, as if Phineas was to...

He fastened the frogs of her cloak and, for a moment was distracted trying to recall a Latin word for the color of Jane's eyes. Periwinkle-ish with a hint of gentian was as close as he could come in English.

"Your gloves," Jane said, passing Phineas a clean pair. "We can cut through the park and enjoy some greenery while we're out, but when we get there, you let me talk to these shopkeepers, Phineas. You'll lecture them straight into the arms of Morpheus."

Jane took Phineas by the arm and led him into the bright midday sunshine. He'd not invited her to walk out with him in all the years they'd shared a household, which was remiss of him.

The birds sang more sweetly, the breeze blew more benevolently, and the city was more cheerful with Jane by his side. Why was it he never appreciated the women in his life until it was too late?

PHILOMENA HAD SPENT TOO many hours—too many days— shut up in the confines of Hephaestus's will. Her mind buzzed with secondary meanings and literary allusions, while her head ached.

But her heart... her heart was caught up in the possibility of actually finding the Duke or at least a portion of that great manuscript. Reading through the will's cramped, complicated writing, she had a sense of negotiating a briar patch. If only she were careful, if only she paid relentless attention to every detail, she'd find the ripe fruit of a clue, a hint, a solution to the mystery the Duke had posed for ages.

And every morning, when she arrived to Ramsdale's library, another sort of fruit awaited her—a bright gold sovereign, reverse side up on the desk blotter, so that even her remuneration included a few words of translation.

Honi soit qui mal y pense. Shame upon him who sees wrong in it...

Philomena saw no wrong in parting Ramsdale from his coin, just the opposite. She gloried in knowing that her years of study were worth bright, shiny coins, that her skills were not only admirable but *valuable.*

She loved the idea that she need not entirely rely on her aging father for security. The possibilities were heady, a whole new dictionary's worth of meanings and opportunity.

Why shouldn't a woman's mind merit the same respect as a man's?

Why shouldn't a woman find the Duke?

Why shouldn't a woman kiss whom she pleased to kiss, rather than waiting for the fellow to take the notion to kiss her?

So in the privacy of Ramsdale's office, she kissed him the way she'd longed to, slowly, savoringly. As she had rendered Hephaestus's ramblings into coherent English, Ramsdale's steady regard had been working a similar transformation of *her*, from bluestocking spinster daughter to a woman of highly trained abilities, a lady both admirable and desirable.

And she desired him.

Ramsdale was sentimental about a cat. His mind was drawn to beautiful landscapes, the movements of the heavenly bodies, and Latin poetry.

His body *was* poetry. His arms stole about her, and Philomena relaxed into an embrace both secure and cherishing. She could shelter in his strength and glory in her own. Ramsdale was far above her touch, he was not above her passion.

Philomena pressed nearer and realized that Ramsdale was growing aroused.

"We should stop," he whispered, the words tickling her neck.

She put her lips to his ear. "We should lock the door."

Ramsdale drew back to rest his forehead against Philomena's. "If we lock that door, what follows will have consequences, Philomena. Serious consequences, and I do not take that step lightly."

He was so wrong, so innocent of Philomena's reality. If Professor Peebles's plain spinster daughter stole an interlude with a wealthy earl, nobody would know, nobody would care. Philomena was not like her cousin, one of polite society's pampered darlings, raised in a gilded cage of manners, gossip, and pretty frocks.

And Philomena would never again be simply a plain spinster daughter.

"I would take that step with you." Philomena had never been tempted by passion before, never had more than an idle curiosity about erotic intimacy. She would trade everything—trade even the Duke—for this chance to become Ramsdale's lover.

Ramsdale looped his arms around her shoulders and kissed her forehead. "So be it."

He remained entwined with her for a lovely moment, then he put the cat out and locked the door. The cat's expression had been indignant, while Ramsdale's smile was lovely—intimate and naughty, a lover's smile.

And Philomena smiled right back.

SO BE IT.

Ramsdale had plighted his troth, and like everything else about his relationship with Philomena Peebles—soon to be Lady Ramsdale —the proposal had been unconventional and the acceptance more unconventional still.

Perhaps he was his uncle's nephew more than his father's son—or he was both.

"We have options," he said, surveying his office with new eyes. "My desk, for one, upon which I will likely spend the next fifty years tending to correspondence. A memory made with you there would shine through that entire half century."

Philomena looked at him as if he'd spoken in the lost Etruscan tongue.

Not the desk, then. "Perhaps the reading chair," he said, "which —given your literary interests—has a certain appropriateness."

"The chair seats only one, my lord."

My lord was not good, though Ramsdale would soon show her how that chair could accommodate two very agreeably.

"The sofa is a bit worn, but I've dreamed many a dream there nonetheless." Perhaps they'd conceive their firstborn on that sofa, in which case, the battered old thing would become an heirloom.

"I bow to your choice in this," Philomena said, "and I would like to bow to it *soon*."

Her gaze drifted over his face, his shoulders, down, down, down, and then back up. He thought she might have lingered particularly on his hands, which were at his sides, or possibly...

"We'll improvise," he said, the notion striking him as appropriate for the couple they were about to become. He was not the typical earl, and she'd be a magnificently different countess.

He spread the afghan from the reading chair over the rug before the hearth and followed with the pair of quilts from the sofa. Next, he sent several pillows sailing to the makeshift nest on the carpet, while Philomena's expression became bemused.

"The floor?" she said.

"I'm told the chair seats only one. On the floor, we'll be comfortable with room to spread out. The carpets in this house are kept spotless, and I promise I'll do all the work."

"If there's work involved, we'll share it. Does one undress?"

She was *adorable.* "Two do, unless you'd rather not."

Philomena advanced on him as if he'd threatened to steal her favorite Latin dictionary. "If we're to be lovers, then I want to be *lovers*, Ramsdale. Deal with me as you would any other woman to whom you've taken a fancy. I'm not a schoolgirl, and I intend to be very demanding."

Which, of course, made her blush, stare at her hands, and settle herself on the hassock more regally than a queen.

Ramsdale wanted to assure her that this was no mere fancy. Instead, he stowed the pretty words and knelt at her feet.

"Boots off," he said, gesturing toward her hems.

Philomena inched her hems up to just above her ankle. "They're worn. Practical. Not elegant."

Her self-consciousness might have a little to do with her boots, which were indeed far from new, but Ramsdale knew what she wasn't saying.

He'd trysted with any number of perfumed and proper ladies who would allow him to roger them witless for the space of a quadrille, but who'd be horrified at the thought of him seeing them in a pair of old boots. In unlit parlors, such a lady would lift her skirts and pant in his ear like a winded hound, but heaven forbid that a cat hair should touch her bodice.

Ramsdale pitied those women, and he spared a bit of pity for himself, rutting and panting right along with them, then stuffing himself back into his satin knee breeches in time for the supper waltz.

What an ass he'd been. "My field boots are the most comfortable footwear I own," he said, undoing Philomena's shoelaces. "I'd wear them everywhere, except that would cause a scandal."

She brushed his hair back from his brow, and he knew why Genesis purred.

Ramsdale drew off her boots and set them aside, then reached under her skirts to untie her garters.

Philomena surprised him by drawing her skirts up to her knees— but then, he suspected she'd frequently surprise him. Still, he denied himself more than a glance. The feel of her ankles and calves clad in nothing but silk...

"Are you always so...?" She fell silent as Ramsdale undid the left garter.

"Behold, my lady is already at a loss for words. My confidence swells apace." His confidence—among other noteworthy articles.

He drew off her stockings and tossed them in the direction of her boots. To unhook her dress and unlace her stays, he moved to the reading chair.

The pencil protruded from her chignon, and Ramsdale knew himself to be a man in love. He silently slid the pencil free and tossed it to the desk—a memento to be treasured in years to come.

Philomena's nape required some kisses, as did the soft flesh where her neck and shoulder joined. Ramsdale rose from the chair, the better to indulge himself, and she turned, pressing her cheek to his thigh.

"I'm in a hurry," she said.

Ramsdale stroked her hair, which he'd soon free from its pins. "Afraid you'll lose your nerve? You'll have nothing but pleasure from me, Philomena, as much pleasure as I can give you."

She peered up at him, as inscrutable as the cat. "And if you lose your nerve?"

His falls were about to lose their buttons. Ramsdale pushed aside that pleasant urgency to consider her question, because Philomena's queries mattered.

They would always matter.

He knelt before her, so they were face-to-face. "If you shout erotic Latin poetry when at your pleasures, I will answer in Middle French. When you publish your first treatise on alternative transla-tions of the Magna Carta, I will buy a hundred copies to donate to universities the world over. Your brilliance doesn't intimidate me, your sense of focus sparks only my admiration. If your father's colleagues or students feel threatened by your capabilities, that's a reflection on their petty conceits, not on you. I can't wait to play chess with you."

He'd given her plain truths, and he'd upset her, for Philomena— who could glower at the same curmudgeonly document for hours— wiped a tear from her cheek.

"I like chess," she said.

Ramsdale enfolded her gently, cursing Peebles for a dunderhead, cursing all the learned men whose cowardice and bigotry had tried to crush a bright spirit. The lot of them were purely frightened of her, and someday, she'd see that.

"If you get me out of these clothes," he said, "we can play chess naked."

Philomena started on his cravat, and even that—a mundane, almost impersonal assistance—fueled his arousal. His sleeve buttons and watch went next, and from there, matters accelerated, until Philomena stood in her shift and Ramsdale in his breeches, their clothing strewn over the sofa in a merry heap.

"Now what?" She ran a hand over his bare shoulder. "You are quite fit."

He captured her hand in his own. "To the blankets."

She sat and drew her knees up, and Ramsdale came down beside her. He'd locked the door perhaps ten minutes ago, but they'd been a long and self-disciplined ten minutes. In fifteen seconds flat, he had Philomena on her back amid the blankets and himself arranged over her.

When they had their clothes back on, and he could again form a coherent sentence, he'd offer her a proper proposal—bended knee, pretty words, the promise of a ring.

Now, the time had come to make love with his intended.

PHINEAS WAS A SURPRISINGLY COMPANIONABLE ESCORT, once Jane got him away from his treatises and tomes. He set a sauntering pace through Hyde Park, which was reaching its full summer glory, and he'd spared Jane any exhortations regarding his infernal Duke.

Jane hated that Duke, which was very bad of her. "Does any part of you look forward to retirement, Phineas?"

He tipped his hat to a pair of schoolgirls out with their governess. "Yes and no. Being able to settle here in Town, rather than haring up to Oxford or Cambridge, will be welcome. The best collections are here. Many of my colleagues are here."

"But?"

They came to a divergence of the footpath, which ran parallel to Park Lane, though beneath the towering maples of the park itself.

"But Lord Amesbury is here."

"What has his lordship to do with...?"

Phineas had spoken literally. Amesbury was driving a high-perch phaeton down the nearest carriageway, his daughter at his side. His lordship either did not see or chose not to acknowledge his brother-in-law.

Lady Maude was chattering at a great rate, exuding the forced gaiety of a young woman who had only her papa to drive out with.

"Every time," Phineas said quietly, "I see that strutting dunderwhelp with his pretty little barmy-froth of a daughter, I grow angry. The marquess might have done something for Philomena, might have eased her way. Now she's to be a spinster, no household of her own, no children. All of the scholars and lecturers I've paraded before her haven't gained her notice, nor she theirs. Amesbury hasn't lifted so much as a gloved finger."

The words vibrated with indignation, also with veiled bewilderment.

"You have written countless letters of recommendation for your former students," Jane said. "You've invited younger professors to serve as guest lecturers. You will read a draft treatise for any colleague. Your nature is kind and generous. Amesbury wasn't given your charitable spirit or your intellect. I suspect he's been waiting for you to ask for his help, Phin."

The phaeton disappeared around a bend in the path.

"Waiting for me to *ask*? Waiting for me to ask Philomena's only titled, wealthy relation to toss her a crumb of recognition? To invite her to a family gathering at the holidays? A house party or a musicale?"

Jane drew him gently along the walkway. "Does Philomena have a wardrobe that would allow her to attend those entertainments in style, or would she be shamed by comparison to her cousin?"

"Philomena has frocks."

"So does that nursemaid," Jane said, nodding in the direction of a young woman in brown twill leading a small boy by the hand. "If you don't know the state of Philomena's wardrobe, how can her uncle know? If she was asked to play a tune on the pianoforte, could she oblige without stumbling over the keys when earls and baronets were in the room rather than schoolboys and scholars?"

Phineas remained silent as they crossed from the park into Kensington. That he was annoyed on his daughter's behalf was a pleasant surprise. That he hadn't done anything to address the problem was to be expected. Amesbury was a marquess, and his neglect of his niece shameful.

"The Eagan Brothers' Emporium makes a good impression," Phineas said as they approached a sparkling shop window. Dried bouquets, groupings of patent remedies in colorful bottles, and artfully displayed herbals and sachets all enticed passersby to drop in.

"And what on earth are they advertising?" Jane asked.

For in the middle of the window sat a placard lettered in an extravagant hand: Secrets of the Ages! Your Heart's Desire, from the Long Lost Duke's Book of Science! Found by Wisdom's Handmaiden Right Here in London!"

"The flat-catching, bat-fowling scandaroons," Phineas spluttered. "They lied to me!"

"They're lying to every customer they can fleece," Jane replied. "But if we're to learn anything beyond the obvious about their swindling, then you will wait right here until I come back."

Before Phineas could gainsay her, she marched up to the shop and swept through the door.

THE TIME HAD COME for Philomena to take her first lover—very likely her only lover, ever, for Ramsdale engaged not only her curiosity and her desire, but also her esteem. He'd said he did not embark on this interlude lightly, and neither did Philomena.

However much regard Ramsdale brought to this lovemaking, Philomena brought more.

Nonetheless, she had no applicable experience.

"Do we resume kissing?" she asked. "Or is there something more?"

Ramsdale was braced above her, the sight of him shirtless making her itch to touch his arms and chest.

"There's more of whatever brings you pleasure, Philomena."

Certainly, there was more of *him*. He'd fit himself against the juncture of her thighs, and his weight felt good—and frustrating.

"When will you remove your breeches?"

Ramsdale closed his eyes, as if taking a moment for prayer. "Would you like me to tend to that detail now?"

Getting him naked was not a detail. "Yes."

His weight was gone, and then his breeches were sailing across the office to join the pile of clothing on the sofa. He stood over Philomena, a dark version of the aroused masculine ideal viewed from an interesting perspective.

"*Boni di.*"

"You resort to Latin," he said, resuming his crouch over her. "Was that a happy 'good gods,' or a dismayed—?"

Philomena lashed her arms and legs around him, wanting to envelop him bodily. She hushed his prattling with an openmouthed kiss, because the sight of him—fit, strong, and aroused—sent a wild boldness singing through her.

She—boring bluestocking, entirely unremarkable—was to have a lover, and *such* a lover.

Ramsdale laughed against her mouth and tried to hold himself away, but Philomena had locked her ankles at the small of his back, so he took her with him.

"Now, Ramsdale," she said. "Immediately. You promised me pleasure, and I'm holding you to your word."

"This instant? Where is the woman who will spend an hour noting every possible meaning for an obscure term? The woman who becomes so absorbed in the possibilities of the genitive case that she forgets to eat?"

"She's here, and she's absorbed with you."

Ramsdale hitched delectably close—why did that feel so lovely?—then brushed Philomena's hair back from her brow. "This is too important to rush. Please trust me, Philomena."

Trust him. He was in complete earnest, almost grave, when he'd been laughing a moment ago.

And he was right. This moment was important, not in the sense of ridding Philomena of virginal ignorance, though she was happy to be free of it, but in the sense that the experience should be savored, and Ramsdale knew better than she how to go about that.

"In this, I trust you."

He shifted so he was more over her, all around her, a blanket of warmth and wonder. As he pressed soft kisses to her lips, brow, and throat, she closed her eyes and explored him with her hands.

She learned textures—smooth, bristly, crinkly, velvety, silky—and tastes. A touch of salt, a hint of lavender. His palms where callused— Ramsdale was a noted equestrian—and his hair was thick and soft.

And she learned a new vocabulary. Ramsdale let her know that he liked her fingertips gliding over the slope of his back, liked her teeth scraping his earlobe. He sighed, he growled, he laughed, and when she glossed her hand down his belly, he drew in a swift breath, but made no move to deter her.

So she learned him, *there*, where he was most masculine and most vulnerable.

He bore her exploration silently, his head bowed, his mouth open against her shoulder, until Philomena positioned him against her sex.

"There's more," she said. "I know there's more you would show me, but Ramsdale, I cannot be patient. Not in this. Not any longer."

He shifted to meet her gaze. "My name"—he pushed forward the first inch, and the union was begun—"is Seton."

Seton. My Seton. My lover Seton.

Philomena might have made up a whole glossary of singular possessive endearments, but sensations crowded her intellect into silence. The intimacy was strange and new, the pleasure compli-cated. To join this way was an exquisite relief. Ramsdale somehow knew the tempo, the touches, the *everything* to satisfy her bodily cravings.

When to slow down and kiss.

When to gather her close and sink deep.

When to go still for a moment, so Philomena could revel in the intimacy and swallow past the lump in her throat.

And then he turned his attention to her breasts, and simmering desire became a wildfire of need. His hands were diabolical, until Philomena began cursing in a low, steady stream of French—modern French, which was all she could manage.

He answered in the same language. "Hold on to me, Philomena. Stay with me."

To hear that silky, sinuous tongue rendered in Ramsdale's night-sky voice destroyed the last filament anchoring Philomena to reason. She became pleasure, an incandescent spirit where a quiet, bookish woman used to be.

The physical experience was beyond words and ebbed barely short of too much. Philomena sensed Ramsdale's consideration in that intimate mercy, for the emotions flowed on unchecked even as he withdrew and spent on her belly.

Joy and tenderness swamped her, as did an inexorable undertow of sadness. She would have these moments with Ramsdale, but that's all she could have—moments.

Precious, wild, unimaginably intimate moments. The inspiration for poetry that endured for millennia, but still, for her there could be only moments. She could give Ramsdale her whole heart, and likely already had. She could love him without limit, but eventually—he was a peer, he needed legitimate heirs—she would have to let him go.

"I can feel that great, elegant brain of yours pulling you back to the damned library," Ramsdale growled. "I account myself proud that for all of twenty minutes, I could tempt you away from your quest."

Twenty minutes that would change the rest of Philomena's life, and she was not sorry.

She ruffled his hair. "Our quest. I feel as if an idea lurks in the shadows of those codicils, an insight that refuses to come into the light."

He rested his cheek against her temple. "A pattern that won't emerge. I know what you mean. Hephaestus is laughing at us. Don't move."

He was on his feet and rifling the pile of clothing in the next instant. Philomena lay on her back amid pillows and blankets, her shift undone and bunched beneath her ribs.

"What a glorious picture you make," he said, using a handkerchief to swab at himself. He was matter-of-fact about the whole shockingly personal business, handling his own flesh with brisk familiarity.

While Philomena felt as if she'd been reborn in another woman's skin. *I know so many languages and so little that matters.*

Without putting on so much as a shirt, Ramsdale knelt beside her and used the handkerchief on her belly, then tugged the shift down over her thighs and gave her a pat between her legs.

"Lest the sight of you tempt me to excesses my conscience forbids. Take a soaking bath when you get home tonight, please. I was not as restrained as I'd hoped to be. Next time..."

His gaze traveled over her, and a world of passionate possibilities blossomed in the silence. Philomena stretched up and kissed him.

He kissed her back, gently cupping her right breast, and a few of those possibilities crept nearer.

A soft scraping sound at the door intruded.

"I will make the damned beast into a pair of gloves," Ramsdale said, going to the door and opening it an entire six inches.

Genesis strolled in, tail held high, nose wrinkling.

"'A righteous man regardeth the life of his beast,'" Philomena quoted, "'but the tender mercies of the wicked are cruel.' I doubt Proverbs contemplated such a creature as Genesis."

Ramsdale pulled a shirt over his head as the cat stropped itself against his bare legs. They'd clearly done this often—the man donning clothing with the cat in casual attendance—and Philomena was jealous of that cat.

"I'm sure my breeches are somewhere..."

Philomena rose and passed Ramsdale his breeches. "Why did Hephaestus name his cat Genesis?"

Ramsdale took the breeches, shook them once, and stepped into them. "Because that cat is the originator of all mischief, perhaps?

Perhaps he's the runt of a litter of seven, all of whom were named in alphabetical order. I don't suppose you could locate—"

She passed him his waistcoat, and with each piece of clothing, Philomena yielded a little more to the pull of the library. Her heart wanted to linger here, where she and Ramsdale had become lovers. Her mind sought the safety of the linguistic challenge Hephaestus had bequeathed her, because she needed a refuge from her emotions.

"Your hair," Ramsdale said when the pillows and blankets were all put to rights and he was dressed but for his coat. "Your coiffure has been disarranged."

Philomena looked over at him between lacing up her left boot and the right. "By the wind, perhaps?"

Ramsdale slung his cravat about his neck and blew her a kiss. "By a mighty tempest."

Hephaestus had prosed on in several places about tempests. *With the flame of a devouring fire, with scattering, and tempest, and hailstones,* was his favorite quote.

"Was Hephaestus particularly religious?" Philomena asked as she tied Ramsdale's cravat.

"Hardly. Uncle had contempt for what he called the pious hypocrites of proper society. I want you again already, Philomena. I thought if we indulged our passions, I might have a prayer of—"

She kissed him and ran her fingers through his hair, which the tempest had also left sticking up on one side. "We have work to do, your lordship. Why so many biblical references from a man who disdained religion?"

Ramsdale caught her hand and kissed her palm. "Am I already back to being a lordship, Philomena?"

That one small kiss caused inconvenient, lovely stirrings. "When we leave this office, you will most definitely be a lordship, and I will be a Miss Peebles, sir. On that topic, I will brook no discussion."

He kept hold of her hand, leaned back against the desk, and drew Philomena between his legs.

"'She is more precious than rubies,'" he said, kissing her knuckles this time, "'and all the things thou canst desire are not to be compared unto her.'"

Some of the most beautiful words in the Bible, and Ramsdale looked like he was about to offer her more lovely quotes.

Philomena wanted to hear them, but *later*, because her imagination chose then to leap upon a potential connection.

"That's *it*," Philomena said. "The biblical allusions. Hephaestus uses them frequently, more than any other reference, almost to the exclusion of any other reference. For a learned man to limit himself to a single source of literary comparisons makes no sense."

"Philomena, might we discuss dear Uncle and his daft—?"

"Come along, Ramsdale. We must list every biblical reference in the will, because if I'm right, this could be a clue to the Duke's whereabouts."

The cat resumed his place on the hassock, and Ramsdale pushed away from the desk. "To the library, then, but let me see to your hair first."

Her—Philomena put a hand to her head—*hair*. Her thoroughly mussed hair. "Of course. I'm as bad as my father."

A gallant lover would have argued with her. Ramsdale smiled, tidied up her braid, and escorted her to the library.

CHAPTER SEVEN

Three days remained until Peebles's retirement banquet, and little remained of Ramsdale's sanity.

Philomena had hastened through the remaining codicils for the sole purpose of listing biblical quotes or allusions, while Ramsdale had done his paltry best to aid her. The family Bible—an enormous tome of ancient pedigree—probably hadn't seen this much consultation in all its decades of gathering dust.

Nor had the library been the scene of so many kisses.

Only kisses, alas. Ramsdale had ordered a ring for his intended, though he'd yet to settle on an inscription.

The front door banged and Genesis, who'd taken to supervising his owner, was startled from his napping place to the left of the desk blotter.

"My sister is apparently going out," Ramsdale said. Meaning the person most likely to intrude had considerately left the premises.

Philomena sat at the desk, petting the cat and staring out the window. She stared out the window often, and looked lovely doing it too.

"Her ladyship isn't off to pay calls," she said. "She must have a visitor. A coach and four have pulled up out front, very fine. Matched grays in harness."

Ramsdale went to the window, which had been cracked to let in the fresh air. Amesbury's crest adorned the coach door, though Philomena likely hadn't noticed that. She went back to scrawling quotations from the will, intent as ever on finding any trace of her Duke.

Ramsdale had found his countess and wished finding the dratted Duke were not still such a matter of urgency for her.

"If Melissa is entertaining, I'd best put in an appearance," he said, because he was nothing if not a dutiful brother. "Will you manage without me?"

Philomena waved a hand, not even looking up. "There's a pattern here, Ramsdale. I know there's a pattern. I can feel it."

The pattern was he longed to visit the office with her again, and she longed to find the Duke. Gentlemanly scruples weighed in favor of offering the lady a formal proposal—or at least chatting up the professor—before another such interlude.

If Philomena had to choose between spending one of the next seventy-two hours in her intended's bed or pursuing her Duke, he suspected she'd choose the Duke.

Ramsdale paused, his hand on the door latch. "You want to find the *Liber Ducis* for yourself, don't you? Not only for the professor."

The pen stopped moving across the page. Philomena looked up slowly. "Would that be wrong, my lord?"

"You need not my-lord me when we are private." More than her polite address, the caution in her eyes annoyed him.

"Would it be wrong for me to want all my years of study and scholarship to result in accomplishing what my father could not? Would it be wrong for me to claim a small portion of the respect and deference he's been shown his whole life?"

Ramsdale's every instinct told him to answer carefully. Philomena was tired, frustrated, anxious, and facing significant changes to a future she'd thought well settled.

"I understand that ambition, Philomena, but some quests take more time than we can allot them. My regard for you does not depend on your achieving the impossible."

As far as Ramsdale knew, none of his fellow bibliophiles had located so much as a page of the missing manuscript.

She stroked the quill over the cat's nose. "Is that why you neglected to pay me today? Because you don't think we'll find the Duke?"

Her gaze was as inscrutable as the damned cat's, and Ramsdale was abruptly at sea. They were no longer employer and employee. They were a couple all but engaged. But then, a woman raised without wealth was likely incapable of treating money casually, and they were not *quite* engaged.

"An oversight on my part," Ramsdale said. "I'll correct my error tomorrow." He crossed the room to kiss Philomena's cheek, though the gesture was awkward when appended to a discussion of wages.

He left the library for the formal guest parlor. When a marquess came calling, only the formal parlor would do, of course. If Lady Maude had accompanied her dear papa, then Ramsdale was doomed to take a cup of tea.

To his relief, only the marquess graced the pink tufted sofa in Melissa's parlor.

Amesbury rose, a tea cake halfway to his mouth, when Ramsdale made his bow.

"Amesbury, a pleasure, though I'm afraid my schedule does not permit me to linger. I do hope you'll be able to join us for dinner on Wednesday next?"

Almack's held its assemblies on Wednesdays, and Lady Maude would be well motivated not to linger over dinner when she might instead be waltzing. Melissa's slight smile said she knew exactly why Ramsdale had chosen the date.

"Dinner would be lovely," Amesbury said, finishing his tea cake. "Just lovely, though Lady Maude and I will soon be removing to the family seat. Only a fool remains in London during summer's heat, eh?"

A fool or a man intent on avoiding matchmaking papas.

"More tea, my lord?" Melissa asked, sending Ramsdale a you-owe-me glance.

"Until Wednesday," Ramsdale said, sketching a bow and nearly running for the door.

Melissa was a widow, and the occasional gentleman did call upon her, though why Amesbury, who was old enough to be her godfather, would trouble himself to pay a—

"My lord!"

Ramsdale had been halfway down the stairs, rounding the first landing, and thus he hadn't seen Lady Maude coming up the steps—or lurking below the landing. She clung to his arms, her grip painful as she sagged against him.

"You gave me such a fright, sir! My heart's going at a gallop. To think I might have tumbled to my death!"

For pity's sake. "Hardly that. The stairs are carpeted, my lady. I'm sure you'll catch your breath in a moment."

She'd chosen her opportunity well, because this flight of stairs was in view of the front door. Callers came and went all afternoon, and somebody was bound to see her plastered to Ramsdale's chest, panting like a hind.

The first footman remained at his post by the porter's nook, earning himself a raise by keeping his eyes firmly to the front.

"You are uninjured," Ramsdale said, trying to set the lady at a distance on the landing. "We didn't even collide."

Though not for want of trying on her part.

"But I am feeling quite faint," she retorted, refusing to stand on her own two feet. "I vow and declare I might swoon."

A door clicked open below—not the front door, thank the benevolent cherubs—the library door. Philomena emerged and, of course, moved toward the stairs.

She stopped at the foot of the steps, staring at the tableau above her.

Ramsdale knew what she saw: her almost-betrothed with a sweet young thing vining herself around him like a vigorous strain of ivy, and not just any sweet young thing—Philomena's titled, unmarried, younger, wealthy cousin.

RAMSDALE WAS his usual attentive escort on the way home, and he made a few attempts at conversation, but Philomena could not oblige him.

How sweetly Lady Maude had nestled against his lordship's chest. How delicately she'd clung to him—and how tenaciously. Ramsdale had grumbled about presuming women and scheming misses, but to Philomena's eye, he hadn't been trying very hard to dislodge Lady Maude from his embrace.

Not very hard at all.

Thank heavens that Lady Maude had not seen Philomena gawking like a chambermaid at the foot of the steps.

"You're very quiet, Philomena," Ramsdale said as they turned down the alley.

"I'm tired, also pondering the Duke. Tomorrow I'll make a list of the objects Hephaestus is referring to when he makes his biblical comparisons."

"Hang the damned Duke. I know what you think you saw, Philomena."

What she *thought* she saw? "We are not private, my lord. I am Miss Peebles to you."

"You will never be Miss Peebles to me again, dammit. We have been gloriously intimate, need I remind you."

The alley was deserted, else Philomena would have delivered his lordship a severe upbraiding for his careless words.

"You need *not* remind me, nor do you need to tell me what I *did* see with my own eyes. A comely, eligible young lady in your embrace in a situation where you and she had every expectation of privacy."

"The footman was at his post in the foyer, and she was not in my embrace."

Philomena stopped walking long enough to spare the earl a cool perusal. For a marquess's daughter, footmen were no source of chaperonage whatsoever. Even she knew that much.

"Then Lady Maude wasn't in your embrace, but you were certainly in hers, and it's of no moment to me in any case. Polite society has its rules, and I grasp them well enough even if they don't apply to me. I'll bid you good evening, my lord."

Philomena had too little experience arguing to make a proper job of it. She never argued with her father, never argued with Jane. She accommodated them and then found some other way to accomplish her ends.

With Ramsdale, that meek course would not do, even if he was an earl.

Even if his uncle's will did hold the key to finding the Duke.

"Philomena, please don't bid me farewell when we're quarreling. Lady Maude ambushed me. I've stood up with her from time to time, and she's gone two Seasons without attaching a suitor. I consider her father a friend and would not avoidably hurt a lady's feelings."

Philomena did not want to have this stupid disagreement. Ramsdale owed her nothing, save for a few coins. He'd made her no promises, and even if he had, she wouldn't have believed them.

"I don't seek an apology, my lord, or an explanation. I'm tired, peckish, and cross. I'll see you tomorrow."

He put a hand on her arm. Just that, and tears threatened.

Philomena wanted to be the only woman nestling against his chest. She wanted to wear pretty frocks that would catch his eye. She wanted her hair styled in a graceful cascade of curls artfully arranged to show off her features, not a boring old bun that also served as a pencil holder.

"We'll find your dratted Duke," Ramsdale said. "The damned

manuscript has put you out of sorts, but if anybody can find him, it's you. Until tomorrow, Miss Peebles."

Philomena would have fallen sobbing into his arms, except he gave her cheek a lingering kiss, and that... helped. The *earl* had put her out of sorts, but so had the Duke. She'd never felt this close to success, or this assured of failure.

She'd also spoken honestly. She was exhausted from successive sleepless nights, hungry, and frustrated.

"Until tomorrow, my lord."

He bowed. She curtseyed and mustered a smile.

He touched his hat brim, and Philomena slipped through the garden gate, latching it closed behind her.

Jane sat on the bench near the sundial, her expression as thunderous as Philomena had ever seen it.

"Don't you *dare* remonstrate with me, Jane Dobbs. I'm eight-and-twenty years of age, my father stopped seeing me as anything but a free translation service fifteen years ago, and my dealings with Ramsdale are my business. If you'll excuse me, I haven't had any supper."

She would have swept past the bench, except Jane began to slowly applaud.

"If his lordship has finally put you on your mettle, he'll get no criticism from me, but a certain apothecary in Knightsbridge claims you've found a portion of *The Duke's Book of Knowledge*. They've put that story about to lure young ladies into buying love potions, which—I can assure you—are flying off the shelves at a great rate."

CHAPTER EIGHT

The coins on the blotter winked up at Ramsdale in a shaft of morning sunshine, while the cat silently mocked him.

"She isn't coming," he informed Genesis. "Miss Peebles—I am to call her Miss Peebles—says she has an urgent matter to see to involving the Eagan Brothers' Emporium in Knightsbridge this morning. She will resume her duties tomorrow."

Ramsdale set Philomena's note—he *thought* of her as Philomena —before the cat, who gave it a sniff.

Knightsbridge was a hodgepodge of shops, taverns, inns, the occasional newly built mansion, and lodging houses more famous for the highwaymen who'd bided among them than for hospitality. What would matter so much to Philomena that she'd use the next to last of the Duke's ten days *shopping* and in such surrounds?

Genesis rose from the desk, leaped down, strutted across the library, and affixed himself atop the family Bible, which was closed for once.

"Blasphemer. Philomena is about the least-mercantile female I've ever met." Unlike Lady Maude, who likely kept half the shops in Mayfair in business.

Genesis circled twice and curled down into a perfect oval on his cushion of Holy Scripture. Ramsdale had the peculiar sense the cat was telling him to have done citing Proverbs and quoting Isaiah and *go after the lady*.

"It's a fine morning for a jaunt about Town. Guard the castle, cat. I have a countess-errant to find."

Purring ensued. At least somebody was having a good day.

Ramsdale's morning deteriorated as he cut through the park. Everywhere, couples were taking the air—happy, devoted, new couples, who had sense enough to enjoy each other's company without the interfering presence of a chimerical Duke.

"I must court my countess," he muttered, crossing south into Knightsbridge proper. "I wouldn't mind if she were to court me a bit too."

He would have gone on in that vein, except a dog nearly tripped him—one of the many strays running about London—and thus he looked up in time to see Philomena striding along ten yards ahead of him.

No maid, no footman, no handy aunt. Because the next Countess of Ramsdale was once again dressed as a young man. She'd changed her walk, changed her posture, queued her hair back, and donned the blue glasses along with a fancy cravat, top hat, and walking stick.

Marriage to Philomena would be an adventure.

She marched into the Eagans' shop, and thus Ramsdale had no choice but to march in right after her.

One of the proprietors, a spare leprechaun of a fellow, totaled a ledger behind the shop counter, his fingers clicking away on his abacus. A book bound in red leather sat at his elbow, while his pencil trailed down a single page of foolscap. An older woman in a bonnet sporting four different stuffed birds inspected shelves of patent reme-dies, and a young lady all in pink—two pink birds amid her millinery —sniffed at the tisanes stored in large glass jars.

Philomena went on an inspection tour, studying the shop shelf by shelf. She was very likely waiting until the other patrons left, and when they did, her gaze met Ramsdale's.

By God, she was good. Her perusal of him was exactly what a young gent would spare an older fellow of means. Brief and neither disrespectful nor envious.

"May I help you gentlemen?" the proprietor asked. "Jack Eagan, at your service. I believe you were first, young sir."

"He was," Ramsdale said.

"These Tears of Aphrodite," Philomena said, taking a blue bottle down from an arrangement on the shelves. "They're quite expensive." She uncorked the bottle and held it under her nose. "Rose water, cheap brandy, perhaps a dash of cloves. I hope you don't expect the young ladies to drink this."

The shopkeeper took off his glasses, a man prepared to be patient with a difficult customer.

"Have you any idea, sir, how unhappy the young ladies become when you gents fail to show them proper attention? When you dismiss all of their efforts to please you, put up with your conceits, flatter you, and endure your indifference? If I could sell my fair customers strong spirits in the name of medicine, I would, but that bottle you hold contains nothing less than a miracle of mythical proportions."

Ramsdale was uncomfortably reminded of Lady Maude—of all the Lady Maudes—and of Philomena's question about respect.

"I'm well aware of those tribulations," Philomena replied. "Does your elixir claim to end the young ladies' suffering?"

The shopkeeper folded his page of foolscap. "It can, indeed. Sometimes, what we need to see us through a challenge is a drop of hope. That bottle can give a young lady hope. My sainted mother believed that half of an apothecary's inventory was hope and the persistence it yields. How many problems can be solved by application of those two intangibles?"

Philomena jammed the cork back in the bottle and brandished the label side at Eagan. "You imply the recipe for this potion was discovered by the daughter of Professor Phineas Peebles. How did she come by her discovery, and why would she share it with you?"

Unease crept into Eagan's eyes. "You know the good professor?"

"And his daughter." Philomena's tone brought the temperature in the shop down considerably.

Eagan grasped his lapels with both hands. "Then you know that she's exactly the sort of young lady—a plain spinster, overlooked for years, no hope of marriage—who would have sympathy for others similarly situated, though I daresay her circumstances are none of your affair."

Ramsdale strode forward, shamelessly using his height to glower down at the shopkeeper.

"Miss Peebles is neither plain nor overlooked. She is brilliant, tenacious, passionate about her scholarship, and honorable to her beautiful bones. You slander the next Countess of Ramsdale at your *everlasting* peril. My intended would live on crusts in the meanest garret before she'd take another's coin under false pretenses. You either erase all evidence of your vicious scheme from this shop in the next hour, or expect a call from my man of business."

Eagan scuttled back behind his counter. "And you would be?"

Ramsdale dropped his voice to the register that carried endlessly even when he whispered. "Your sainted mother's worst nightmare."

Philomena came up on Ramsdale's side. "You behold the Earl of Ramsdale in a *mild* temper, sir."

"Mild..." Eagan cleared his throat and slipped his sheet of foolscap into a slit in the ledger's binding. "Mild temper. I see. Well. Then."

He kept two sets of books, and he swindled young women. Probably swindled old women too, and anybody desperate enough to rely on his pharmaceutical products. He did not sell hope and persistence.

He sold lies.

Except for Eagan and Philomena, the shop was empty. Would she truly mind if Ramsdale indulged in a bit of pedagogic violence?

She was staring at the ledger, at the barely discernible slit in the red leather binding into which Eagan's foolscap had disappeared. Staring more fixedly than she stared out of windows, into fires, or at her tea.

Not more fixedly than she'd regarded Ramsdale in the office, though.

"What is it?" Ramsdale asked.

"I know where the Duke is. Ramsdale—or at least where the *Motibus Humanis* is, *I know.*"

"We've no need to involve a duke," Eagan sputtered. "I'll happily relabel—I mean, remove the offending bottles. Cupid's Tears would sell quite well, or Cupid's Revenge. I rather like—"

Ramsdale grabbed Eagan by his neckcloth. "No tears, no revenge, no more profiting from the false hopes of the lovelorn with your greed and dishonesty."

He gave Eagan a slight shake—a minor, almost gentle shake, truly —but didn't let him go until Philomena flicked Eagan's cravat.

"Every bottle," she said. "Gone, before the next customer sets foot in this shop of horrors. I have it on good authority that the professor is about to unveil the contents of the real manuscript, and your paltry scheme will be similarly unmasked."

Eagan changed colors, from pale to choleric. "No more love potions. I understand. I do understand, my lord. Sir. I mean—I understand."

"Come," Philomena said, taking Ramsdale by the arm. "We have a Duke to set free."

RAMSDALE HAILED THEM A HACKNEY. As a female in polite society, Philomena would have traveled with him in a closed conveyance at risk to her reputation. She had never occupied anything but the tolerated fringe of good society, and to all appearances, she was not a female.

"I wanted to hit him, Ramsdale. I wanted to ball up my fist and plant him a facer. Draw his cork, put up my fives. He lied. His whole shop is a lie."

Ramsdale kissed her cheek. "The soaps and sachets seemed genuine enough. I wanted to do more than hit him."

How Philomena loved the menace in Ramsdale's voice and the affection in his kiss. "The soaps and sachets are lures for the unwary, and when we're upset, we're all unwary."

Ramsdale took her hand. "I can bring a lawsuit for the way he maligned you, and that would be the end of his chicanery. I should have taken that execrable sign with us as evidence. To think that my future countess's scholarly research was bandied about as fodder for shop-window gawkers. Perhaps I'll threaten him a bit, give him a few sleepless years."

Frightening the little toad within an inch of his larcenous wits had probably already accomplished that aim.

"Ramsdale, be sensible. You lied too." All in good cause, but the nature of those fabrications dulled the golden lining from the morning's adventure.

Ramsdale turned a lordly scowl upon her. "I am not prone to dissembling, Philomena. Unlike some people, I present myself as I am in all particulars at all times."

How did he make the hackney's interior shrink? How did he fill the entire space with two indignant sentences?

"I've seen your particulars, Ramsdale, and I'd like to see them again soon, but you told that scoundrel I am your prospective countess. I doubt he'll be gossiping about your conversation, but you did mis-state matters."

Though Philomena had dreamed. Despite all common sense and logic to the contrary, she had dreamed. She knew where the Duke was, though, and thus her dreams, and even her time with Ramsdale, were over.

How ironic, that finding the Duke meant losing the earl.

"Shall I kneel in the dirty straw of a moving conveyance, Philomena? Shall I go down on bended knee now, when the ring I ordered has yet to be delivered and your infernal Duke has revealed his whereabouts to you?"

Two realities collided as Philomena searched Ramsdale's gaze.

At this moment, she didn't care one whit for the Duke. Let Papa's reputation rest on decades of sound scholarship and inspired teaching. He didn't need the Duke to polish his academic halo.

Philomena didn't need the Duke either. She needed the earl.

And apparently, *the earl needed her.* "You aren't jesting."

"When do I ever jest?"

"When you haven't any clothes on. You tickled me. That's a jest of sorts. You truly want a bluestocking spinster for your countess?"

He did not lie. He did not dissemble. He did not... well, he did embrace pretty young women on staircases, or they embraced him. Philomena had embraced him at the first opportunity, so she couldn't really blame Lady Maude for attempting to secure Ramsdale's notice.

"Spinsters are fine company," Ramsdale retorted. "They are fearless and direct, also given to independence and blunt opinions."

"You've just described yourself, my lord."

He kissed her on the mouth. "So I have, but it's not a spinster to whom I offer my hand in marriage. I plight my troth with a brilliant, dauntless, wily, unstoppable, beautiful, passionate woman, to whom I'd consider it the greatest privilege of my life to be married. What say you, Philomena?"

The hackney swayed around a corner, pushing Philomena away from Ramsdale, and yet, he held her hand. She mentally searched for words—any words, in any language—and found only one.

"*Yes.* I say yes, and yes, and yes. I will be your countess, your wife, your lover, your greatest privilege."

"And if I haven't any connection to His Perishing Literary Grace?" Ramsdale asked. "If all of Uncle's maunderings are only that and no part of the Duke lies in my possession?"

That this bothered him gave Philomena's conscience a pang.

"What matters the Duke when I can possess myself of the lover, the husband, the companion?"

The hackney slowed.

"You're not enamored of the earl?"

"Let's repair to your lordship's office," Philomena said. "I'll show you just how enamored of the earl I am."

THANK GOD FOR THE SERVANTS' half day and for a widowed sister with a sense of discretion. Ramsdale had taken "Mr. Peebleshire" not to the office and not to the library—*so there*, Your Grace—but to the earl's private sitting room.

Which adjoined the earl's bedroom, of course.

The midday sunshine turned the skin of Philomena's shoulder luminous as she slept on Ramsdale's chest. Her hair was a chestnut and cinnamon riot tumbling down her back and her breath a soft breeze against his throat.

They'd worn each other out, twice.

Ramsdale was determined that their next bout of passion would wait until after the vows had been spoken, so that his bride—and her groom—could fully enjoy the wedding night. Philomena would probably poke eight holes in that strategy before next week, and what pleasurable holes they'd be.

"You're awake," Philomena said, pushing up to straddle him.

"I'm engaged, also in love."

She blushed, which on a naked woman was a fascinating display. "As am I."

For a polyglot, she could be parsimonious with her declarations.

Ramsdale patted her bottom. "You're shy. No matter. I will earn your passionate devotion, and soon you'll be declaiming panegyrics in my honor from the—"

"Dining parlor," Philomena said. "I'm hungry. Your passionate devotions have put an appetite on me."

Also a rosy flush and a smile. Ramsdale's whole body was smiling in response. "I could order a tray."

"We'll go down to lunch. Do you suppose your sister might lend me a dress? We're of a size."

Melissa made that loan without a question, though it would likely come at a high rate of sororal interest. Ramsdale played lady's maid, Philomena served as valet, and a composed and proper couple descended to the dining parlor.

"You wouldn't rather stop by the library first?" Ramsdale asked.

"The Duke has waited two hundred years," Philomena said. "He can wait another hour."

"A fine notion."

Philomena did justice to the food, Ramsdale did justice to the wine, and the afternoon was half gone before they joined the cat in the library.

"I should put him out," Ramsdale said, lifting feline dead weight off the Bible. "He's overdue for a trip to the garden."

"Let him stay," Philomena said. "We can all admire the roses together once we've found what we came for."

She was eyeing the Bible, and chess pieces rearranged themselves in Ramsdale's head. "All those biblical references and allusions."

"But only when your uncle was discussing you or your father. For everybody else, Dante, Chaucer, Voltaire... but for you, always the Bible. For the cat, a book of the Bible. Your uncle would have been in this room, probably alone, on those few occasions when he was allowed to visit his books."

Philomena carried the Bible over to the desk and sat.

"I'd examine the front first," Ramsdale advised. "He named the cat—my first bequest—Genesis."

Said cat began to purr.

Philomena took up Ramsdale's quizzing glass, peering at each edge of the front cover. "Here, right along the edge. The stitches are so fine, I can barely see them even with your glass. It's here, Ramsdale, but I'd best not wield a knife when my hand is shaking."

Something lay beneath the binding covering the front of the family Bible. When Ramsdale joined Philomena at the desk, he could feel the slight bump beneath the leather and feel the lack of a corresponding bump under the back cover.

The cat sat on the blotter, as if having called the meeting to order himself.

"It might be a map or a letter," Ramsdale said, "or another codicil."

"We can give it to Papa to translate, then, something to occupy him in retirement." She sent Ramsdale a look that promised he'd be too busy to aid the professor—and so would she.

Ramsdale tested the edge of a penknife against his thumb. Sharp, not too sharp. Stitch by stitch, with Philomena holding the quizzing glass for him, he worked his way down the binding.

"Do you suppose Uncle enjoyed taking a knife to an heirloom?"

"Not at all. He knew that of all your possessions, the one you'd likely carry from your home in case of fire or flood, the one you'd safeguard against mobs or invading armies, was this Bible."

Philomena's confidence was comforting, also convincing. Uncle had been eccentric, not unhinged.

"Something has been secreted in here," Ramsdale said when the last tiny stitch had been cut.

"You do it," Philomena said. "Do it carefully."

Little care was needed. The old leather was supple, and a document about a half-inch thick and maybe seven by ten inches otherwise, slid easily from behind the Bible's binding.

"That's it," Philomena said softly. "Don't open it. Give it a chance to adjust to the air and light, but that's it."

The weight of the volume suggested vellum rather than paper pages. No glue had been used to fasten the pages to the leather protecting them. A Latin title had been scripted onto the leather in a handsome hand: *Liber Ducis de Scientia — de Motibus Humanis.* Below the title was an ornate numeral 4 and golden shield bearing three fleurs-de-lis on a blue circle with six red balls beneath.

THE WILL TO LOVE

229

"That's the Medici coat of arms," Philomena said. "The number of red balls tells us this cover is dated from..." She fell silent, a tear meandering down her cheek.

Ramsdale set the manuscript aside, out of reach of the cat, and took Philomena in his arms. "You found your love potions. You put together the clues, you did the translations, you had the combination of knowledge, dogged persistence, and inspiration to find the treasure, Philomena. The world is in your debt, and I am *obnoxiously* proud of you."

Tears intended to manipulate could not move him, but honest tears—of relief, joy, gratitude, and exhaustion—earned his respect. Philomena shuddered in his embrace for a time, the cat stropping himself against her hip all the while.

"You helped," Philomena said at last, stroking the cat's head. "You perched on the Bible, you kept us company. I want to be married in this room, Ramsdale."

"And shall we travel to Florence on our wedding journey?"

If he'd given her the other three volumes of the *Liber Ducis*, Ramsdale could not have earned a more brilliant smile from his countess.

They were married in the library, and they did travel to Florence —also Rome, Siena, Paris, Budapest, Berlin, Vienna (the professor and Jane, also on a wedding trip, met them there), Copenhagen, St. Petersburg, and Amsterdam.

And Philomena eventually had an opportunity to study the entire compendium of *The Duke's Book of Knowledge*—tales for another time—and what did Ramsdale inscribe on his beloved's engagement ring?

Amor omnia vincit—of course!

TO MY DEAR READERS

To my dear readers,

I hope you enjoyed these two stories of women who were doing *just fine* without a titled man making their lives complicated. When I met Ramsdale in ***His Grace for the Win***, I thought, "That guy is not going to be content with sidekick/shoulder angel honors for long. Mark me on this, oh ye pussycats. There's another novella on the way..." At the first opportunity he involved himself in, of all things, a bookish adventure.

And my pen has been busy with novels, too!

April 2020 will see the release of my fourth **Rogues to Riches story**, *A Duke by Any Other Name*. Lady Althea Wentworth has retreated to the wilds of Yorkshire after failing miserably in one London Season after another. She's determined to fit in with rural society, but realizes she will need the *entrée* that only her neighbor, Nathaniel, the reclusive Duke of Rothhaven, can provide. His Grace is sympathetic to her situation, but family secrets have rendered him more prisoner than recluse. She longs for acceptance and social cachet, he needs to be left alone... or so he claims. Silly duke. Excerpt below.

And June (May in the **web store**) will see the publication of my next **True Gentlemen**, *A Lady's Dream Come True*. Oak Dorning is off to the bright lights of London, where he will finally, finally begin establishing himself as a professional portraitist. A temporary job in the wilds of Hampshire restoring some paintings for the widowed Mrs. Verity Channing is simply a means to earn the blunt that a London lifestyle requires. Verity was married to a successful artist, and she has no interest whatsoever in the small minds and endless gossip she endured in Town.

And then... well, you can read the excerpt below. Here there be smoochies!

I am also nibbling away at organizing my backlist and re-releasing some other novellas that have been de-published for various reasons. *A Duke Walked Into a House Party* was the first of those projects. The *Windham Ducal Duet* (The Courtship/The Duke and His Duchess) will follow shortly.

If you'd like to stay up to date with all of these illustrious doin's, the easiest way to do that is to follow me on **Bookbub**. They never spam you, and only send alerts when there's a new release, discount, or pre-order on the horizon. You might also keep an eye on my **Deals** page, because every month, I have either an early release or a discount happening somewhere. Then there's always my **news-letter**, if you'd like more of the details and kitten pictures.

Happy reading!
Grace Burrowes

EXCERPT—A DUKE BY ANY OTHER NAME

The usual polite means of gaining an introduction to Nathaniel, Duke of Rothmere, have failed Lady Althea Wentworth utterly. Being a resourceful woman, she's turned to unusual measures to achieve her goal...

Althea heard her guest before she saw him. Rothhaven's arrival was presaged by a rapid beat of hooves coming not up her drive, but rather, directly across the park that surrounded Lynley Vale manor.

A large horse created that kind of thunder, one disdaining the genteel canter for a hellbent gallop. From her parlor window Althea could see the beast approaching, and her first thought was that only a terrified animal traveled at such speed.

But no. Horse and rider cleared the wall beside the drive in perfect rhythm, swerved onto the verge, and continued right up— good God, they aimed straight for the fountain. Althea could not look away as the black horse drew closer and closer to unforgiving marble and splashing water.

"Mary, Mother of God."

Another smooth leap—the fountain was five feet high if it was an inch—and a foot-perfect landing, followed by an immediate check of the horse's speed. The gelding came down to a frisking, capering trot, clearly proud of himself and ready for even greater challenges.

The rider stroked the horse's neck, and the beast calmed and hung his head, sides heaving. A treat was offered and another pat, before one of Althea's grooms bestirred himself to take the horse. Rothhaven—for that could only be the dread duke himself—paused on the front steps long enough to remove his spurs, whip off his hat, and run a black-gloved hand through hair as dark as hell's tarpit.

"The rumors are true," Althea murmured. Rothhaven was built on the proportions of the Vikings of old, but their fair coloring and blue eyes had been denied him. He glanced up, as if he knew Althea would be spying, and she drew back.

His gaze was colder than a Yorkshire night in January, which fit exactly with what Althea had heard of him.

She moved from the window and took the wingchair by the hearth, opening a book chosen for this singular occasion. She had dressed carefully—elegantly but without too much fuss—and styled her hair with similar consideration. Rothhaven gave very few people the chance to make even a first impression on him, a feat Althea admired.

Voices drifted up from the foyer, followed by the tread of boots on the stair. Rothhaven moved lightly for such a grand specimen, and his voice rumbled like distant cannon. A soft tap on the door, then Strensall was announcing Nathaniel, His Grace of Rothhaven. The duke did not have to duck to come through the doorway, but it was a near thing.

Althea set aside her book, rose, and curtsied to a precisely deferential depth and not one inch lower.

"Welcome to Lynley Vale, Your Grace. A pleasure to meet you. Strensall, the tea, and don't spare the trimmings."

Strensall bolted for the door.

"I do not break bread with mine enemy." Rothhaven stalked over to Althea and swept her with a glower. "No damned tea."

His eyes were a startling green, set against swooping dark brows and features as angular as the crags and tors of Yorkshire's moors. He brought with him the scents of heather and horse, a lovely combination. His cravat remained neatly pinned with a single bar of gleaming gold despite his mad dash across the countryside.

"I will attribute Your Grace's lack of manners to the peckishness that can follow exertion. A tray, Strensall."

The duke leaned nearer. "Shall I threaten to curse poor Strensall with nightmares, should he bring a tray?"

"That would be unsporting." Althea sent her goggling butler a glance, and he scampered off. "You are reputed to have a temper, but then, if folk claimed that my mere passing caused milk to curdle and babies to colic, I'd be a tad testy myself. No one has ever accused you of dishonorable behavior."

"Nor will they, while you, my lady, have stooped so low as to unleash the hogs of war upon my hapless estate." He backed away not one inch, and this close Althea caught a more subtle fragrance. Lily of the valley or jasmine. Very faint, elegant, and unexpected, like the moss-green of his eyes.

"You cannot read, perhaps," he went on, "else you'd grasp that 'we will not be entertaining for the foreseeable future' means neither you nor your livestock are welcome at Rothhaven Hall."

"Hosting a short call from your nearest neighbor would hardly be entertaining," Althea countered. "Shall we be seated?"

"I will not be seated," he retorted. "Retrieve your damned pigs from my orchard, madam, or I will send them to slaughter before the week is out."

"Is that where my naughty ladies got off to?" Althea took her wing chair. "They haven't been on an outing in ages. I suppose the spring air inspired them to seeing the sights. Last autumn they took a notion to inspect the market, and in summer they decided to attend Sunday services. Most of our neighbors find my herd's social inclinations amusing."

"I might be amused, were your herd not at the moment rooting through my orchard uninvited. To allow stock of those dimensions to wander is irresponsible, and why a duke's sister is raising hogs entirely defeats my powers of imagination."

Because Rothhaven had never been poor and never would be. "Do have a seat, Your Grace. I'm told only the ill-mannered pace the parlor like a house tabby who needs to visit the garden."

He turned his back to Althea—very rude of him—though he appeared to require a moment to marshal his composure. She counted that a small victory, for she had needed many such moments since acquiring a title, and her composure yet remained as unruly as her sows on a pretty spring day.

Though truth be told, the lady swine had had some *encouragement* regarding the direction of their latest outing.

Rothhaven turned to face Althea, the fire in his gaze banked to burning disdain. "Will you or will you not retrieve your wayward pigs from my land?"

"I refuse to discuss this with a man who cannot observe the simplest conversational courtesy." She waved a hand at the opposite wingchair, and when that provoked a drawing up of the magnificent ducal height, she feared His Grace would stalk from the room.

Instead he took the chair, whipping out the tails of his riding jacket like Lucifer arranging his coronation robes.

"Thank you," Althea said. "When you march about like that, you give a lady a crick in her neck. Your orchard is at least a mile from my home farm."

"And downwind, more's the pity. Perhaps you raise pigs to perfume the neighborhood with their scent?"

"No more than you keep horses, sheep, or cows for the same purpose, Your Grace. Or maybe your livestock hides the pervasive odor of brimstone hanging about Rothhaven Hall?"

A muscle twitched in the duke's jaw.

The tea tray arrived before Althea could further provoke her guest, and in keeping with standing instructions, the kitchen had exerted its skills to the utmost. Strensall placed an enormous silver tray before Althea—the good silver, not the fancy silver—bowed, and withdrew.

"How do you take your tea, Your Grace?"

"Plain, except I won't be staying for tea. Assure me that you'll send your swineherd over to collect your sows in the next twenty-four hours and I will take my leave of you."

Not so fast. Having coaxed Rothhaven into making a call, Althea wasn't about to let him win free so easily.

"I cannot give you those assurances, Your Grace, much as I'd like to. I'm very fond of those ladies and they are quite valuable. They are also particular."

Rothhaven straightened a crease in his breeches. They fit him exquisitely, though Althea had never before seen black riding attire.

"The whims of your livestock are no affair of mine, Lady Althea." His tone said that Althea's whims were a matter of equal indifference to him. "You either retrieve them or the entire shire will be redolent of smoking bacon."

He was bluffing, albeit convincingly. "Do you know what my sows are worth?"

He quoted a price per pound for pork on the hoof that was accurate to the penny.

"Wrong," Althea said, pouring him a cup of tea and holding it out to him. "Those are my best breeders. I chose their grandmamas and mamas for hardiness and the ability to produce sizable, healthy litters. A pig in the garden can be the difference between a family surviving through a hard winter or starving, if that pig can also produce large, thriving litters. She can live on scraps, she needs very little care, and she will see a dozen piglets raised to weaning twice a year without putting any additional strain on the family budget."

The duke looked at the steaming cup of tea, then at Althea, then back at the cup. This was the best China black she could offer, served on the good porcelain in her personal parlor. If he disdained her hospitality now, she might...cry?

He would not be swayed by tears, but he apparently could be tempted by a perfect cup of tea.

"You raise hogs as a charitable undertaking?" he asked.

"I raise them for all sorts of reasons, and I donate many to the poor of the parish."

"Why not donate money?" He took a cautious sip of his tea. "One can spend coin on what's most necessary, and many of the poor have no gardens."

"If they lack a garden, they can send the children into the countryside to gather rocks and build drystone walls, can't they? After a season or two, the pig will have rendered the soil of its enclosure very fertile indeed, and the enclosure can be moved. Coin, by contrast, can be stolen."

Another sip. "From the poor box?"

"Of course from the poor box. Or that money can be wasted on Bibles while children go hungry."

This was the wrong conversational direction, too close to Althea's heart, too far from her dreams.

"My neighbor is a radical," Rothhaven mused. "And she conquers poverty and ducal privacy alike with an army of sows. Nonetheless, those hogs are where they don't belong, and possession is nine-tenths of the law. Move them or I will do as I see fit with them."

"If you harm my pigs or disperse that herd for sale, I will sue you for conversion. You gained control of my property legally—pigs will wander—but if you waste those pigs or convert my herd for your own gain, I will take you to court."

Althea put three sandwiches on a plate and offered it to him. She'd lose her suit for conversion, not because she was wrong on the law—she was correct—but because he was a duke, and not just any duke. He was the much-treasured dread duke of Rothhaven Hall, a local fixture of pride. The squires in the area were more protective of Rothhaven's consequence than they were of their own.

Lawsuits were scandalous, however, especially between neighbors or family members. They were also messy, involving appearances in court and meetings with solicitors and barristers. A man who seldom left his property and refused to receive callers would avoid those tribulations at all costs.

Rothhaven set down the plate. "What must I do to inspire you to retrieve your *valuable* sows? I have my own swineherd, you know. A capable old fellow who has been wrangling hogs for more than half a century. He can move your livestock to the king's highway."

Althea hadn't considered this possibility, but she dared not blow retreat. "My sows are partial to their own swineherd. They'll follow him anywhere, though after rioting about the neighborhood on their own, they will require time to recover. They've been out dancing all night, so to speak, and must have a lie-in."

Althea could not fathom why any sensible female would comport herself thus, but every spring she dragged herself south, and subjected herself to the same inanity for the duration of the London Season.

This year would be different.

"So send your swineherd to fetch them tomorrow," Rothhaven said, taking a bite of a beef sandwich. "My swineherd will assist, and I need never darken your door again—nor you, mine." He sent her a pointed look, one that scolded without saying a word.

"I cannot oblige you, Your Grace," Althea said. "My swineherd is visiting his sister in York and won't be back until week's end. I do apologize for the delay, though if turning my pigs loose in your orchard has occasioned this introduction, then I'm glad for it. I value my privacy too, but I am at my wit's end and must consult you on a matter of some delicacy."

He gestured with half a sandwich. "All the way at your wit's end? What has caused you to travel that long and arduous trail?"

Polite Society. Wealth. Standing. All the great boons Althea had once envied and had so little ability to manage.

"I want a baby," she said, not at all how she'd planned to state her situation.

Rothhaven put down his plate slowly, as if a wild creature had come snorting and snapping into the parlor. "Are you utterly demented? One doesn't announce such a thing, and I am in no position to..." He stood, his height once again creating an impression of towering disdain. "I will see myself out."

Althea rose as well, and though Rothhaven could toss her behind the sofa one-handed, she made her words count.

"Do not flatter yourself, Your Grace. Only a fool would seek to procreate with a petulant, moody, withdrawn, arrogant specimen such as you. I want a family, exactly the goal every girl is raised to treasure. There's nothing shameful or inappropriate about that. Until I learn to comport myself as the sister of a duke ought, I have no hope of making an acceptable match. You are a duke. If anybody understands the challenge I face, you do. You have five hundred years of breeding and family history to call upon, while I..."

Oh, this was not the eloquent explanation she'd rehearsed, and Rothhaven's expression had become unreadable.

He gestured with a large hand. "While you...?"

Althea had tried inviting him to tea, then to dinner. She'd tried calling upon him. She'd ridden the bridle paths for hours in hopes of meeting him by chance, only to see him galloping over the moors, heedless of anything so tame as a bridle path.

She'd called on him twice, only to be turned away at the door and chided by letter twice for presuming even that much. Althea had only a single weapon left in her arsenal, a lone arrow in her quiver of strategies, the one least likely to yield the desired result.

She had the truth. "I need your help," she said, subsiding into her chair. "I haven't anywhere else to turn. If I'm not to spend the rest of my life as a laughingstock, if I'm to have a prayer of finding a suitable match, I very much need your help."

Order your copy of *A Duke by Any Other Name,* and read on for an excerpt from *A Lady's Dream Come True*!

EXCERPT—A LADY'S DREAM COME TRUE

Oak Dorning and his temporary employer are having an interesting discussion…

Mrs. Channing swept past Oak into the gloom of the attic, her faint floral fragrance blending with the scents of dust and old wood.

"I don't go around kissing strange men, Mr. Dorning," she said, facing away from him. "You were kind to Catherine, and that touched me, and I still should not have… I should not have kissed you. Not even on the cheek."

So they were to have a *discussion*. Very well. "Why not?" Oak asked. "Kissing is enjoyable, provided all parties to the activity are consenting adults."

"Because…" She turned slowly. "One shouldn't kiss strangers, in the first place."

"One should not *be caught* kissing strangers, perhaps. What's in the second place?"

She drew a finger across the shelf of a sconce that held an empty oil lamp. "I haven't wanted to. Kiss any strangers, that is. Kiss anybody."

Oak pushed the door closed. "You have been in mourning." He took out a handkerchief, dusted off the top of a sea trunk, and gestured for the lady to take a seat, which she did. "Might I have the place beside you?"

"We're discussing kisses, Mr. Dorning. You need not stand on ceremony."

"And yet, you call me Mr. Dorning." Vera Channing was pretty, and she was more than pretty. She was sensible, devoted to her children, no stranger to grief, and she had a fine sense of humor. Oak wanted to capture the *more* on canvas, not simply the lovely face and gracefully curved figure.

He also wanted to kiss her, and not only on the cheek.

"Who do you think did that landscape?" she said, frowning at a canvas resting against the far wall.

Oak rose from the trunk and forced himself to consider the sheep, the clouds, and the little stream running diagonally through the scene.

"This might be the work of Hanscomb Detwiler. He's quick, accurate, and a good mimic, but he lacks a sense of adventure when it comes to brush work." The painting held other clues to the artist's identity—the specific blue of the sky, the manner in which sunlight was flatly reflected from the cottage windows—but Oak wasn't particularly interested in the painting.

He was interested in the woman wearing the old dress as she sat on the dusty trunk. "Will you kiss me again?" he asked.

"I want to, but I'm trying to determine my motivations. Behaving impulsively is the province of artists, not their widows."

Oak resumed the place beside her. "I cannot afford to behave impulsively. I know what I want: a career as a respected painter. That has been my ambition from earliest youth and remains the objective I will pursue when I've restored your paintings."

"Honest," she said. "I appreciate honesty."

"I thought you might. I certainly hope to be dealt with honestly." And that seemed to settle the matter. Neither of them was looking for a permanent attachment, and neither of them wanted a mindless indulgence.

"Would you like to kiss me?" Vera asked.

"Very much." More than kiss her too. She had to know that.

She rose and twisted the lock on the doorlatch. "Why don't we give it a try and see how it goes?"

Oak remained seated, the better to ignore the evidence of arousal this conversation was inspiring. "Will you regret this?"

"Will you?"

Oak considered that question, or tried to, as Vera stood before him. He would leave Merlin Hall in the autumn, and whether he painted her portrait or not, he'd have canvases for Sycamore to hang in his club. He would travel to London to deliver those paintings in person, and to embark on his activities as a professional portraitist. Nothing on that schedule precluded a few friendly interludes with a willing widow.

"No regrets," Oak said. "No expectations and no regrets."

Vera stepped between his legs and looped her arms around his shoulders. "This is an experiment, Mr. Dorning. You will in some ways be my first. Moderate your expectations accordingly."

"Oak." He took her by the hips and drew her closer. "An experiment then."

She pressed a luscious, lingering kiss on his mouth, and desire reverberated through Oak like a thunderclap. Her hands winnowed through his hair and he rose, the better to gather her in his arms and lose himself in her embrace.

Coherent thoughts tried to swim against the tide of pleasurable sensation. Some notions were irrational. *I've missed you*, for example, made no sense at all, though missing the voluptuous joy of an erotic kiss made all the sense in the world.

And other thoughts were howlingly inconvenient: Oak would be Vera's first, as she'd said. Her first affair, her first intimacy as a widow, her first foray into non-marital overtures. She'd waited several years to take this step and chosen him from among many options.

Oak was mindful of the honor she did him and he offered her respect, liking, and desire in return. Even so, he could not ignore the plaintive, *foolish* voice in his head that admitted to envying the man who could take a permanent place at her side.

Vera made a soft, yearning noise in her throat, and a final conclusion managed to coalesce in Oak's mind: The experiment was a success. If the hypothesis had been that he and Vera could enjoy a shared kiss, the hypothesis had been proved gloriously true.

Order your copy of ***A Lady's Dream Come True!***